"You really love it here, don't you?"

"Oh yes." Alex sighed happily.

Jon was silent long enough that she paused and looked up at him. He was studying her intently. Treat it lightly, she cautioned herself. "What?" she asked.

"You look beautiful. Very beautiful."

His words had been a caress, and her heart had responded to them. He wasn't flirting; his words had held a note of deep sincerity. *No,* she thought. He was too dangerous.

"Don't close up on me," he said softly. "Every time I start to break through that shell of yours, you don a new one. I've never been too crazy about enigmas, but something about you makes me want to keep trying."

She looked away quickly, lest he see the longing in her eyes.

"I'm going to kiss you, Alex."

Her heart skipped a beat. She felt as if her senses were at war as she both leaned forward and tried stepping back at the same time. "Soviets never kiss in public."

"I'm not a Soviet. And neither are you."

Dear Reader,

The holidays are almost here, and with snow whipping through the air and cold winds blowing—at least in my part of the country!—I can't think of anything I'd like more than to escape to a warm climate. Let Barbara Faith help you to do just that in *Lord of the Desert*. Meet an American woman and share her adventures as she is swept into a world of robed sheikhs and sheltering desert dunes. You may not want to come home!

This month's other destinations are equally enticing. The Soviet Union is the setting of Marilyn Tracy's *Blue Ice*, and intrigue and danger are waiting there, despite the current spirit of *glasnost*. Paula Detmer Riggs returns to New Mexico's Santa Ysabel pueblo in *Forgotten Dream*, the story of a man who has forgotten much of his past and no longer has any memory of the woman he once loved—and is destined to love again. Finally, reach *Safe Haven* with Marilyn Pappano. When Tess Marlowe witnesses a murder, her only refuge is a secluded house in the Blue Ridge Mountains —and the embrace of Deputy U.S. Marshal Deke Ramsey.

In coming months, look for new books by such favorite authors as Nora Roberts, Heather Graham Pozzessere and Lee Magner, as well as a special treat in February: four brand-new authors whose debut books will leave you breathless.

Until then, happy holidays and may all your books be good ones.

Leslie J. Wainger
Senior Editor and Editorial Coordinator

MARILYN TRACY

Blue Ice

SILHOUETTE·INTIMATE·MOMENTS®

Published by Silhouette Books New York

America's Publisher of Contemporary Romance

SILHOUETTE BOOKS
300 East 42nd St., New York, N.Y. 10017

ISBN: 0-373-07362-3

First Silhouette Books printing December 1990

Printed in the U.S.A.

Books by Marilyn Tracy

Silhouette Intimate Moments

Magic in the Air #311
Blue Ice #362

MARILYN TRACY

writes romances during the day, and in the evenings she rewrites them into songs on the piano or guitar. She feels that country-western music lends itself most readily to a real romantic storyline. Each story she's written has its own soundtrack.

Marilyn didn't always have a quiet place to write romances and music. After several years of working in television-news broadcasting and for the State Department in Tel Aviv and Moscow, she jumped off the fast lane and into what she calls a life of paradise in her home state, New Mexico, where she lives with her son. From traveler to homebody, from rover to writer of her own romance novels, Marilyn's sure her life is a dream come true!

Chapter 1

"*Gospoda*, please fasten your safety belts in preparation for landing in Sherymetyeva Airport," the stewardess's low-pitched voice advised. She had spoken in Russian, using the plural and formal word *people* to address them, and now repeated the instruction in German for the benefit of the passengers who had joined the Aeroflot jetliner in Frankfurt. She didn't repeat the phrase in English.

Aleksandra Shashkevich checked her already-buckled belt, no stranger to either the Russian language or the bucking Aeroflot ride.

"It is necessary to be of completing the declaration of money forms at this time," the stewardess cautioned. The heavyset woman—a direct contrast to the common image of airline stewardesses—stepped from behind the curtain, nodded to Aleksandra and passed through the first-class cabin, deemed *myaki,* or soft, and began collecting the small slips of paper from those passengers in "hard-class."

Alex reached into her shoulder bag and withdrew both her passport with the coveted permanent business visa and the monetary declaration form. She was entering the Soviet

Union with more than ten thousand dollars in American currency. If luck ran with her, that amount of money could just cover the down payment for a remarkable collection of items she was winging her way toward purchasing. But what she would really be buying was a secure future for an entire family.

She withdrew a thick manila envelope and emptied twenty photographs and a single newspaper clipping into her lap. She ignored the clipping for the moment and raised one of the color photos to the small light.

Despite the clutter of objects in the background, the photograph displayed the center-most object remarkably well. The overhead light caught and reflected off a single gold chalice with heavy embossed symbols around the rim and base. A man's dark and hairy-knuckled hand held a metric ruler beside the chalice, showing the size to be fourteen centimeters in height.

Looking at the pictures now, tension coiled in Alex's stomach.

When Hans Saalard, longtime friend and, lately, a strong business contact, had spread these photographs out on her desk in Washington, she had been stunned. Collections like this didn't drop into private hands very often. She had met Hans's eyes with barely suppressed excitement. He had smiled broadly and lifted his shoulders as if to say, Would I give you less than perfect? Alex had smiled back; Hans knew her too well. She had shared meals with his large family around their small trestle table in the kitchen, Norwegian slippers on her feet, his children shyly leaning against her.

And now he was dead. She still couldn't think of his death without pain, couldn't think of his passing without that wrenching ache of loss. He had played such an important role in her life, such an understanding one. And now he was gone.

Her mind kept replaying his last visit to her gallery office over and over, wishing she could have another chance to call him back. It almost seemed as if he could suddenly drop into the seat beside her in the airplane, a smile on his craggy face, a tale about one of his children on his lips, that easy, non-judgmental assessment in his blue eyes. And, Lord knew, he'd had enough to judge her for.

But with no sense of foreboding on his square face, he had leaned back in his chair that day, his eyes lit with amusement. "I am told they are currently undergoing authentication. They should look very good in your gallery, Alex."

She had nodded, almost too excited to speak.

"Even if they should prove to be reproductions," he said, "they are still unique. I knew you'd want them the second I saw the photographs. I flew straight over with the pictures." He scratched idly at his right hand. A smile curved his lips. "I didn't imagine you'd want them housed anywhere but Dupont Circle, no?"

Alex hadn't gained her reputation, both for being an honest businesswoman and an expert on foreign art, by ignoring the signs of the quick deal, which were stamped all over this offer. But Hans was as honest as she was, and her friend a dozen times over. If he had stretched his tight budget for a transatlantic flight all on a collection he'd never seen, he must really believe in its worth. Of course, just as Hans was one of the few people on earth who knew about her past, she was one of the few who knew how dangerously close to poverty the charming older man really was. It was part of the reason she'd convinced him to serve as her agent in locating rare art.

It was a debt she owed him. A debt he had never allowed her to pay. It was a debt not of money, but of love.

She had asked the collection's price and withheld a blink at the staggering rejoinder as she looked at the photographs again; for that price, they would have to be utterly and wholly unique. A quiver of excitement ran through her. This was more than just an interesting collection. It seemed perfect. Mentally, she had started a list of potential buyers.

While the collection was primarily secular, a few religious items had been included—a fairly rare occurrence. The artifacts, ranging from the gold chalice to several ornate crosses, a couple of candlesticks and a prerevolutionary samovar or two, were all of seemingly excellent quality and workmanship. There were some forty pieces in all.

"Where did you say they were from?"

"Armenia," Hans had answered.

Alex had frowned slightly, certain that the Baroque touches on the chalice and one of the samovars showed another heritage. So did the scroll work at the base of the candlesticks.

"Funny, they have a distinctly Ukrainian influence."

Hans had smiled again, unperturbed, scratching his right hand as he spoke. "So do you. I thought he said Armenia—I thought they might be relics from the earthquake. I could have misunderstood him."

The filigreed touches intrigued Alex. The collection was not quite Ukrainian, not quite Armenian. The possibility of such a melding of two distinctly different cultures, especially a prerevolutionary melding, was an entire world beyond exciting. It was completely and utterly unique.

"How is it that the Soviet government is allowing them to be exported?"

"Something to do with raising funds for some new exchange program the U.S.S.R. is launching."

Alex had nodded; such exchanges were becoming common for the Soviet Union, and the explanation made the sale of the artifacts a logical option.

"Who's your contact in the Soviet Union?"

"That's the best part," Hans had said. "An American at the embassy in Moscow. Roger Copple. He called me about two weeks ago, said he'd been contracted by the Soviet government to export these items. Seems Frank Hedrickson— you remember him? He isn't with the embassy anymore— recommended me to this Copple."

"Is Copple also in the economic-commercial section?" Alex had asked. Hans had shrugged, to Alex's amusement. For all that Hans handled—*had* handled, she thought painfully—artifacts from around the world, he seldom worked directly with embassy personnel. That was Alex's forte. She was the one with the foreign-service contacts.

It was probably the only positive residue from her marriage to Tony Hamilton.

"Copple's single," Hans said with a grin.

Alex had waved that remark away. "Half the world's population is single," she answered.

"Most of them don't like it, though," he said. "What you need is a good man who—"

"What I need is this collection," Alex had interrupted firmly, smilingly steering Hans away from the subject of marriage. Of all people, Hans knew how fearful she was of reentering a marriage. Any marriage. After Tony...

"He's quite a dramatic fellow, this Copple. He said you could call him anytime, day or night."

Alex raised her eyebrows. "Sounds like he's hungry for the sale. What's in it for the U.S.? Or is he thinking there will be something in it for him personally?"

"The Soviets have been known to pay quite a healthy commission," Hans answered, scratching his right hand again.

"Speaking of which, who pays yours?" Alex had smiled to ease the awkwardness of the money question. It was always difficult to discuss money with friends, especially those she knew were not well-off financially. Hans had many children to support. She would, of course, offer to reimburse him for the travel he had undertaken on her behalf, but knew he would decline. She was, therefore, doubly relieved to hear it was the Soviets, through Copple, who would provide—and handsomely—the negotiator's fee for the collection.

She had nodded then, knowing she wanted these pieces. Wanted them badly. She was eager for Hans to reap the reward, as well. She would not have been able to afford the pieces *and* the commission.

"All right, then, Hans, tell your Roger Copple he's got a fish on the line."

Already mentally rearranging her gallery, Alex had smiled, and they had shaken hands, a binding contract among traders.

With a broad wave and a smile, the big Norwegian had left her office, ducking his head against the fine drizzle outside.

That was the last time she had seen Hans Saalard alive.

"May I see your papers, please?" the stewardess asked.

Alex looked at the woman blankly. "What?"

The stewardess repeated the request, raising her voice slightly and speaking a little slower. Alex handed up her passport and the declarations statement. While the stewardess read the statement and carefully surveyed Alex's picture, Alex replaced the photographs in the manila envelope but retained the newspaper clipping.

The headline was common enough in Washington's largest newspaper: International Businessman Found Slain in Motel Room. She had read it so many times that its impact should have been lessened. But on that morning three weeks ago when she found that the newspaper photo matched Hans Saalard's square, craggy face, Alex had gripped the newspaper until it tore in her hands.

The police, the article said, were unable to determine a motive in the slaying. It was possible that he had been killed in a random mugging, since his belongings had been rifled and the mattresses ripped in an apparent search attempt. He had been stabbed three times in the chest region and pronounced dead on arrival at the hospital.

Shocked, her mind melding this article and its headline with a long-ago story about her father, Alex had felt a wash of grief and loneliness sweep over her. She had felt as if part of her had died, as she had felt on the day a bullet claimed her father's life.

Hans was one of the few people on earth who knew her history, understood her. Their meeting had been as unusual as his death; he had been there for her when she had needed friends most, offering support. He was her friend and her adopted uncle.

And, as she had sat with the torn newspaper in her hands, she had felt guilt, an overwhelming, crippling guilt. She felt it now. Hans had been in Washington because of *her*.

Alex had helped make the arrangements, working with Hans's widow and the Norwegian embassy, all the while fighting the ghosts of her own past. No matter how high the protective walls she built around herself, she still let a few special people inside. Hans and his family had been among them. She hurt for them now, and ached over her own loss and the many losses of the past.

It wasn't until Hans's body was actually en route to Norway that Alex truly thought about the collection Hans had been representing. The photographs had made her feel more despondent than she had in years, in some undefinable sense making Hans's passing all the more painful.

It had been at that moment that Alex had decided to shift her buying trip forward by four months. She would go for the collection herself. She would make certain the commission and negotiator's fee would go to Hans's family. And any commission on the individual sales of the artifacts would also go to them.

Somehow, in some strange manner, retrieving the artifacts would give some meaning to his death. To allow the collection—and the money he would have made from it—to pass to other hands would be to reduce his death. To retrieve it, to put the artifacts on display as Hans had pictured them in her gallery, to establish a trust for his children, all of this would somewhat mitigate the guilt she felt over his death, his family's loss. It was all she could do for Hans Saalard, the man who saved her sanity, the man who had brought her back from the brink of total self-destruction, who had prevented her from committing the most heinous crime of all.

Prior to her departure, she had called the United States Embassy in Moscow and asked for Roger Copple. She had been advised that Mr. Copple was not in his office, nor was he at home, when she tried that number.

He was still unavailable the next morning. And the next afternoon. And the next evening.

Moments before boarding, Alex had called a last time, but instead of seeking Roger Copple, she asked for another of her old friends, James Bowden, a midcareer cultural attaché with the embassy. As always, she hesitated before asking for him. He was her friend, certainly, but he had been Tony's friend first. And possibly because of this, Alex had always maintained a strong reserve around James.

She'd been connected within seconds, and a very sleepy-voiced James answered. He only groaned at being asked to arrange an escort through customs for her and to book a room in the Hotel Rossiya for an indefinite period of time.

Yes, she had said, she was moving her buying trip up to mid-March. And no, she had continued, it wasn't all that unusual. Just a whim. She sidestepped James's oft-repeated invitation to change her mind regarding a warmer relationship between them. Like Hans, James had been a witness to the most serious blunder of her life, and he knew that was a door she had closed years ago and had no intention of opening... for any man.

Just before ringing off, Alex asked James if he knew anything about the collection Roger Copple was representing on behalf of the Soviet government. James hadn't answered for a long moment and when he did, he uttered the alarm phrase he had long ago arranged with Alex to mean, Can't talk now, listening devices.

"Have you heard from Dorothy?"

Because it had been so long since he had concocted the silly code, and because her question had been completely innocuous, Alex almost ignored the warning. But something in his voice sent a rash of goosebumps up her arms. "No," she had replied slowly. "Is she still up to her old tricks?"

"Oh, definitely," James had replied. Had it been relief in his voice? Relief that she had caught on so quickly? Or relief that she had let the subject drop?

"You are staying how long?" the stewardess asked.

Alex started. She'd been lost in recent memories. "Two weeks, maybe longer," Alex answered, taking her passport back, then shoved the clipping into the manila envelope and jammed it into the fold of her passport.

The stewardess leaned on the seat in front of Alex and smiled. "You are coming at the best time," she said.

Alex smiled back. "I don't usually come to the Soviet Union in the winter."

The stewardess looked shocked. "But this is March. You are arriving in spring! Spring snow is different." She narrowed her eyes in an appraising manner. "You are Russian?" she asked.

"My family is from there," Alex replied.

The stewardess nodded, and the narrow appraisal lifted. "You look as if you come from Latvia or Lithuania. Except for your dark hair. You sound as if you are from there, too."

Alex smiled. Her Russian was flawless, but her intonation carried an American cadence, rising where it should fall, turning her questions into statements, her commands into requests. As a result, she sounded as if she came from one of the Baltic countries.

Her shoulder-length black hair curled softly about her pale face, a frame for her dark blue eyes. *Sini,* her mother had called them, using a nontranslatable Russian word that loosely means that rare shade of evening-sky blue. She had the small nose inherent to Russians and the broad cheekbones of the Kazack. Though she stood taller than most Soviets, she was only of moderate height by American standards.

The stewardess smiled shyly. "I have a cousin who lives in Chicago. He emigrated many years ago." Her voice dropped and she she looked over her shoulder. "Maybe you know him?"

"I doubt it," Alex said. "I'm from Washington."

"His name is Pyotr Borolev."

Alex shook her head and shrugged with a smile. "Sorry."

"Chicago and Washington are both large cities."

"Not so large as Moscow," Alex said, knowing the proper response.

"Nothing is as great as Moscow." The stewardess began to move away, holding the declarations statements in her hand. She read Alex's and turned back. "You are carrying a large amount of money, *dyevushka*. You must be very careful of the *huligani*."

Alex smiled, both at the thoughtfulness behind the stewardess's warning and the Russian adaptation of the English word *hooligan*. In Russian, the word meant everything from thief to murderer, and it was always used in the plural. "I'll be careful," she said, thinking that had practically become her motto. She was always careful now. Her youth and her marriage had taught her that hard lesson.

The wing dipped suddenly, and Alex saw the winding Moskva Rica—the Moscow River. It shimmered white and frozen in the street lamps lining the walls along its banks. The afternoon light had already disappeared and the long winter evening had descended, though it wasn't yet four o'clock. Alex glanced in another direction and saw the red brick Kremlin with its spires, a glowing red star perched upon the highest tower, a beacon of red light against a dark, cloudy sky.

After the plane landed and taxied to a large snow-covered area some four hundred yards from the terminal, Alex disembarked alone as the only soft-class passenger. The courtesy was short-lived, however; she was detained at the shuttle bus.

A few minutes later, she moved with a group of noisy Germans and small, dark Soviets into the Sherymetyeva terminal, a massive, gray hangar. Her back was shoved and poked by elbows and shoulders and her slender hips brushed against others.

The hundreds of bare-bulb lights scarcely illuminated the large barnlike building, and the interior seemed as gray as the exterior. Groups of tired travelers were pushed into seemingly random lines by square-bodied uniformed women. Mumbling men and women, defeated looking, clung to each other, clutching their string bags of clothing, boots, oranges and books.

Everyone talked at once, softly complaining or crying or jeering. Music blared over the loudspeakers, and the odor of too many bodies in one place smelled of fear, anticipation and impatience.

And over the music, over the noise of a thousand people speaking at once, Alex heard the muted roar of thousands of baggage bindings opening and closing, popping like firecrackers.

She wasn't singled out and was soon pushed with the crowd toward a customs booth. She looked for James Bowden, but saw no sign of him. Normally his diplomatic card would have whisked her to the front of the line, and then through the crowd and outside. Instead, she shifted in the long line, pressed tightly between a Soviet woman loaded with a string bag and paper packages and a German with hard elbows. At last, her suitcases already thoroughly searched and deemed acceptable, she handed her passport to the man inside the booth. She smiled at the stony-faced customs official and was reaching for the manila envelope when she heard her name called.

James Bowden's voice cut through the noise in the cavernous room. Heads turned, Alex's with them. She spied a navy-blue, pin-striped arm waving above the heads of the crowd.

In poorly-accented Russian—he had the same inaccurate accent in German and Italian—she heard James proclaiming his status with the American Embassy. Soon, with a hug and an overenthusiastic kiss—which shocked many of the Soviets nearby and made most of the Germans smile—

James stood by her side, smiling one of his rare genuine smiles. Alex thought again, watching him, that it had been this smile that had sealed their friendship and made her continue to like James despite the little things he did that chafed at their relationship—the mean streak he displayed while drinking, the whining note that crept into his voice when he complained about his career status, the refusal to accept her reasons for never giving in to his proposals. His smile, the one he used so rarely, was the magic in James.

That, and the fact that he never chided her about the past.

"God, it's good to see you, Alex."

She read his unspoken question through the thick lenses of his glasses. She smiled and shook her head slightly. Still no, James, she thought.

James turned away from her to gaze at the customs official in some surprise. "She's with *me*," he said.

Alex frowned when she saw what had prompted James's sudden hard voice: the customs agent was holding tight to Alex's passport.

"A moment, please," the man said. "What is this document, please?" He held up the manila envelope.

"Oh, it's nothing," Alex said in Russian. "I just put it there so I wouldn't lose it."

"May I look inside it, please?" the official asked. The question was rhetorical. Alex waved her hand at the envelope, thinking that this display of authority was simply an example of petty power in action.

"What is this, *dyevushka?*" he asked, using the polite form for addressing a young woman. He withdrew the photographs.

"What difference does it make what it is?" James snapped. "It has nothing to do with her visa. Just stamp it and leave her alone."

"*Dyevushka?*" the customs official said, his eyes cold, his face alert. "What are these?" He held up the photographs, his thumbprint blurring the top image.

"Just pictures of some art I hope to purchase," Alex said truthfully. She summoned a smile. James wasn't the only one with a magic smile. But it didn't faze the dour official.

He studied the photographs solemnly, then looked sharply at Alex. Turning from her, he reached for a telephone and dialed a number, then he spoke softly and rapidly. Alex couldn't make out his words over the roar of the crowd. Outwardly calm, she nonetheless felt a cold knot form in her stomach. *What was wrong?*

As he spoke, the official sifted through the photographs. A new thought sparked fear in Alex: were the artifacts hot? She pressed closer, trying to hear what the man was saying.

"What's this all about...?" James began, but hushed at Alex's quick gesture. He took her hand, and she clung to it gratefully.

The customs official was telling someone that, yes, these certainly looked like the photographs he'd been alerted to look for. Then he asked if he should let the woman go or detain her.

The knot in Alex's stomach twisted uncomfortably. Though she was of Russian heritage, she was American enough that the thought of detention in the Soviet Union made her legs feel weak.

After listening for several heartstopping moments, the official replaced the receiver and looked pointedly at Alex. He ignored James, though Alex suspected he was fully aware of the other man. He cleared his throat finally, and spoke in English, his stilted phraseology underscoring the tension of the moment. "I hope you will be understanding that these photographs are much needed by the Ministry of Culture."

James sputtered in quick anger, but the official looked neither left nor right. His pale eyes bored into Alex's. She knew he was lying about something, the photographs, the Ministry of Culture...something. And she could see that he understood she knew it also. "You are requested to attend the minister tomorrow morning at ten o'clock. His name is

Gospodin Makarov. He will explain the matter to you at that time. It would be wise to be prompt, of course.''

"Of course," Alex echoed faintly, relief making her almost ill. She had nothing to fear, she told herself. She had done nothing wrong. She was an American citizen, and standing beside her was the long arm of the American Embassy. Yet despite her rationalizations, she felt the atavistic fear her ancestors must have felt during the centuries of tsarist rule, then the violent years of the revolution.

The customs official replaced the photographs in the envelope, stamped her passport and handed it back to her. Then he placed the envelope in a narrow drawer and kept his hand on the closed aperture.

"Enjoy your visit, *dyevushka,*" the customs man said with all the enthusiasm of a surly American clerk saying, "Have a nice day." He signaled the next person in line, dismissing Alex.

"What was that all about?" James said, pulling her a few steps away from the booth. "What did he take?"

"He confiscated some photographs of that collection I mentioned."

"What!" James turned as if to return to the booth. "We'll just see—"

Alex grabbed at his elbow. "Wait. Don't. He told me to be at the Ministry of Culture tomorrow morning. Andre Makarov will explain. It's okay. I know Makarov." James looked doubtful. "Let's just go."

"That guy can't just take something of yours!" James barked. "It's against—"

"He already has," Alex interrupted, trying to quell the tingle of fear along her spine.

"What is this? Why are you blocking the flow of traffic?" A uniformed woman stood beside them, her hands on her ample waist, her small eyes glaring at James.

"Let's get out of here," Alex said quickly, pulling at James.

"Not until—"

"James! Please, they almost detained *me,* as well. Tomorrow morning will be here soon enough." The knot of tension had tightened until she now felt physically ill. "I'll find out what this is all about then."

"All right, but I don't like it. We'll lodge a protest in the morning. First thing."

He led Alex down several steps to a quiet street behind the terminal and held open the door of a white Chevrolet van. It never failed to amuse Alex that the embassy used Chevy vans and compacts as their official vehicles. It seemed a far cry from the movie version of black limousines with flags flying.

Alex leaned against the high cushions, drawing a deep breath, willing the fear to ease. She was quiet, her mind locked on the small customs booth, scarcely seeing the dark, leafless birches and snow-covered fields whizzing past. It was mid-March, but it looked like early January.

"I've arranged a dinner party tonight," James said. "In your honor, of course."

Alex nodded, relaxing despite the unusual events at the airport. This was James's life; once it had been hers. Conversation would be pleasant, remote and soothing. Wine and vodka would flow, coffee would be strong and the dessert lousy. She might even find out something about this art collection. And about Roger Copple. "Your apartment?" she asked.

"Yes. There will be four other couples there tonight." He shot her an odd glance. "And the doctor."

Of all people she'd ever met at the embassy, the doctor was one man she didn't enjoy. She curled her lip. "Turner?"

"No, he's gone on to Nairobi. This is a new guy. He's only been in the country a couple of months. Jonathon Wyndham."

"Okay," Alex said, smiling, "I'll bite. Why the doctor?"

James looked pointedly at the back of the chauffeur's head. Alex knew he meant that the man could be listening. "He's an interesting man," James said. "I think you'll like him.'' He looked out the window for a moment, then said, ''We'll drop your things off at the hotel, then go round to my place for a drink first, shall we? Everyone will be there by seven.''

A few moments later, the van broke out of the countryside onto a wide, urban thoroughfare that would take them to the center of Moscow. Ivan, their driver, dodged around large, green, military trucks with canvas covers. Yellow-green taxis passed them, their passengers pinned against the seats. Snow mounds, some four feet in height, flanked broad, snow-covered sidewalks and, from the few antennas Alex saw, hid small cars beneath.

Women dressed in long, black coats and woolen scarves walked arm-in-arm with other women. Men in fur hats stopped to read open newspapers in display cases or to smoke the short smelly cigarettes known as *papirozi,* which were simply shredded paper. Everyone carried string bags or paper containers filled with bread or large heads of cabbage. Mothers pulled old-fashioned sleds, and the children riding behind them sported bright red cheeks.

Alex had often been to Moscow, but never in the cold season. She had never seen the Cyrillic signs over doorways coated with snow, dripping with icicles. She had often stopped to purchase ice cream from the narrow white booths on the street corners, but she had always assumed these were closed in the winter. Not so. Each stand was surrounded by a small crowd of people, handing over kopecks for the vanilla or chocolate treat.

The closer they came to the heart of the city—the Kremlin—the older and more ornate the buildings became. Telephone and electric wires spanned the streets, and the tired, unkempt buildings with their elegant lines and rococo trim looked forbidding in the falling snow.

Ivan carried Alex's bags to her room, and both he and James went back downstairs to wait for her in the car. After quickly showering and changing into a multilayered outfit—it was usually freezing outside and too warm inside—Alex rejoined them and they sped away to the old

American Embassy, now standing dwarfed by the new—and empty—building.

They took James's car from there and traveled the dark, quiet streets to an older apartment building some two miles from the embassy complex. When Alex attempted to bring up the topic of the confiscated photographs, James deflected the subject, circling his finger at the car, his eyebrows raised in significance. Instead they talked of trivialities and soon were passing the small booth manned by the militia guard watching over the parking lot of the embassy apartments.

James waved at the guard, who waved back and picked up a telephone receiver. He talked briefly into it and hung up.

"Telling someone you're home?" Alex asked. The thought chilled her as it had never done before. But she'd never come to Moscow and been threatened with detention before.

"That's right," James said absently, edging the car into a narrow space. "All set?" He cut the engine and told her not to lock the door.

"It'll freeze up," he said. "And alcohol doesn't take the chill off of locks like it does people."

Alex looked at James in speculation. His voice had been bitter. Was he, like so many of his fellow workers—and so many Soviets—succumbing to the Soviet cure for the cold, dark nights?

He escorted her up the pockmarked steps leading into his apartment building. Alex smiled. Winter or not, the inside of James's apartment building looked just the same as it had the last time she'd seen it. Broken black-and-white tile crunched under their boots, and a dirty, streaked wall heralded the diplomat's quarters.

They rode the wire-cage elevator that clanked and groaned and stopped six inches below James's floor. He yanked the door open, stepping out first and holding down a hand to her. Alex wondered if heaving a passenger up to the floor was included on the list of twenty-five how-to-ride-the-elevator rules posted inside the cage.

They left their coats, boots, hats, gloves and scarves in the guest bedroom, and James just managed to pour them both a Scotch and water when his guests began arriving.

They were the usual embassy group, attractive women in slightly outdated clothes and distinguished men in trousers giving out at the knees. Only one man stood apart from the rest, both literally and figuratively.

Of medium height, he had the posture of an athlete, sure and confident. That confidence extended to his clothing. Where the other men in the room sported three-piece suits or suit coats over sweater vests, he wore a bulky rag-wool sweater and a pair of khaki trousers. His hair was a dark golden brown and seemed to catch and hold the light from the candles in the room. His eyes had seemed black when he first walked in the door, but now, in the candlelight, they appeared a warm gold. Small laugh lines radiated from the corners of his eyes and crinkled as he watched her assessing him.

Alex stepped backward involuntarily, as if to escape his regard. But her movement only seemed to catch his attention further and he advanced, never taking his eyes from hers. She felt a momentary pique; she was too tired to foil attempts at flirtation. But as her eyes linked with his, she discovered a wholly new sensation: relief. While the frank appreciation remained, the overall message in his eyes was one of warmth, simple kindness. He projected it like a visible aura.

"You must be Alex Shashkevich," he said, and held out his hand. "James's friend."

Her hand was in his without her consciously thinking about it. Involuntarily. Warmed. Still his gaze held hers. The depths in his eyes stirred something in her. She could see a pain there, a hunger. And it reflected her own. Her heart beat uncomfortably in her chest; she knew her fingers trembled. A predatory look, a determined desire, she could deflect easily. This gentleness, this unaccustomed sense of kindness, wasn't so easily dismissed. His eyes, she thought a little wildly, it's his eyes.

"I'm Jon Wyndham," he said, squeezing her hand lightly, then releasing it. It was also his touch, she thought.

She imagined she could actually feel an electrical current running between them. She pulled away slightly, fighting with the unfamiliar sensation, and forced words through her constricted throat. "The doctor?"

He smiled and the curve of his full lips drew her, too. "James prepares his guests well," he said. His voice was like his hair and eyes: honeyed, burnished. "And you're the art expert."

"Well, gallery owner," she temporized, fighting the urge to relax in his company, to respond to the unexpected current between them. "I just have a small gallery."

He surprised her, however, by shaking his head. "I've been in your 'gallery.' You have a remarkable collection of art."

She was surprised. Her gallery was good, but not well-known. She smiled, less easily than he might have guessed. "It's a living."

"It's a lot more than that."

Something in his tone, a wistfulness, an almost unguarded yearning, sounded in his words. She felt an unaccustomed pang of kinship. "Yes," she said, "it is a lot more than a mere living."

"Found each other, have you?" James interrupted. Alex was relieved, for the first time grateful for the Foreign Service's unwritten rule governing conversations: two never, three ever, four break away and form a new group of three. "Have you met?"

"Yes," she and the doctor said simultaneously, and both smiled. A new friend? Alex wondered, and couldn't help but think of Hans. As one passes, another emerges?

His eyes met hers, brown to blue, fire to ice.

"Oh, yes," Jon said, his rich smile lighting his face. "We've met."

Chapter 2

On a cold winter's day when everything is the same, snow covered, obscured, and each moment is consumed with wondering if the long lines in bitter cold will reap a chunk of beef or an out-of-season fruit, an unexpected warm spring wind can seem like a miracle. It can seem like a lifeline to a drowning man.

And so Alex seemed to Jon Wyndham.

Her eyes were the blue of a desert sky; her laughter carried the husky cry of great-winged birds fleeing south for a more temperate clime. Her dark hair curled softly against creamy skin, inviting rearranging. And her hands, soft and warm, small and delicate, were like the first flowers in the park in spring.

But a man so inured to the winter's dark promise has difficulty in accepting the warm spring wind as anything but a false hope, an illusion of better times to come. And so, also, did Jon Wyndham look at Aleksandra Shashkevich.

He waited for the questioning look on her face to express itself in words, but it was James Bowden who spoke, not Alex.

"Good. I'm glad you've met," James said. "We should certainly find a great deal in common, we three. The recently-widowed doctor, the lonely career officer, and...how do we tag you, Alex? The forever-single world traveler?"

Jon noted Alex's quick look of surprise. The words were innocuous enough, but James's tone had been bitter. Jon watched Alex, but his mind was on James. James knew how Jon's wife, Margaret, had died, and Jon knew, from rumors here and there, that James ran from any form of marital commitment. He was in love with someone, somewhere, the rumors ran.

Jon looked at Alex. Was this the woman who kept James Bowden from giving in to the lure of hearth and home?

Then, as James took another long pull at his drink, Jon understood. The man's words had been slightly slurred. He was more than halfway to being blitzed. A not-so-hot cure for the common blues. If Alex was more than a friend, there was definitely trouble in paradise.

"Well, here's to marital bliss," James said, raising his drink to Alex in a brief salute before draining his glass. "What was it Nietzsche said? 'What doesn't destroy me makes me stronger'?"

Alex's eyes met Jon's briefly, her embarrassment obvious, and behind the embarrassment, something else. Jon smiled to reassure her and was oddly touched by the look of surprise on her face. What kind of men did she know, that a simple smile could create surprise?

He glanced back at James, and a frown creased his brow when he noted the man's pallor, heard the reedy breathing. He forced his features to an easy grin. He was a doctor, not the man's keeper. "Better go easy on that stuff, pal. You haven't been off the antibiotics for more than a couple of days. Your system's not up for abuse."

Jon was rewarded by the quick flash of Alex's grateful smile. It was a reward he hadn't been expecting, the kind of smile that made him think of firesides and soft caresses.

James chuckled. "I've got the cure, though," he said. "What I need is a wife. I've been trying to talk Alex into taking the position, but she's playing the ice queen."

Jon felt his eyebrows raise, but before he could say anything, James suddenly turned to an apparently stunned Alex. "My knees. Do you want me to get down on my knees? I'll beg if you want. All you hafta do is say the word."

When she didn't answer—Jon suspected she couldn't—James issued a bitter laugh and turned to him. "Love 'em and leave 'em. That's our Alex."

Where shock had held her still, anger made her move. Her slender hand shot out and took the drink from James's loose grasp. She set it down on a side table with an audible thump and walked away. She was no weakling, Jon thought, handing James a napkin, his eyes on Alex.

Alex knew her cheeks were flaming, though she felt cold. She could still hear his voice, but was far enough away that his words were indistinct. She wondered what he was saying to Jon Wyndham, wondered if he might be talking about her, and then wondered why the thought of him saying anything bothered her. If the gold-eyed doctor knew James at all, then he knew how alcohol affected the diplomat's view of life.

"Have you known James long?" a woman at the buffet table asked her.

Alex started and met a sympathetic gaze, then looked across the room at James. He seemed more in control now, talking with someone else, a cup of coffee in his hands instead of the drink. Dr. Jon Wyndham was nowhere to be seen.

"Yes," she said, forcing a smile to her lips. "We've been friends for about seven years."

"Are you married, my dear?" the woman asked, her voice neutral, her eyes speculative.

"No," Alex said.

"Never?" the woman persisted.

"Once," Alex replied. She knew the terse answer was rude, yet was unwilling to offer any details.

"Did James know your husband?"

Alex's stomach, already tense from the flight, from James's behavior, from that brief connection she'd experienced with Jon Wyndham, tightened even more. For the sake of being polite, she had answered this woman's questions, but the brevity of her answers should have made the woman realize it was a subject she would rather avoid.

"Yes, he knew my husband," Alex said wearily. Tony Hamilton, witty, dashing, altogether destructive. Oh, yes, James had known him well. He'd been best man at both of Tony's weddings. Hers and Marja's.

"Divorce?"

Alex turned slightly, meeting the woman's eyes. "Annulment," she answered clearly and coldly.

"Excuse me, Madge," the doctor said from right behind them, cutting into whatever shocked question the woman might have uttered. "I had promised to show our visitor the view from the balcony."

Without another word, his hand loosely clasping her elbow, Jon guided Alex to the French windows at the far side of the apartment.

"Thank you," she said as soon as they were outside and the door was closed behind them.

"Doctors always take two degrees," he said, knocking a six-inch stack of snow from the metal railing and leaning against it. "One in medicine, the other in knight errantry."

Alex drew in the cold air gratefully, both to ease the tension in her and as a relief from the overwarm room. She smiled. "You've been knight erranting quite a bit this evening."

To her surprise, he didn't dodge her meaning. "Oh, James," the doctor said. "He's been pretty down lately."

"He's been ill?"

"A flu bug. Common enough here," he answered, but looked significantly at the French doors. "But messy with alcohol." His eyes met hers, but there was a look there now

that hadn't been there before James's outburst. Wariness?
Speculation?

The night air was no longer soothing; it was dangerous,
fraught with a myriad of conflicting emotions. Alex shivered.

The door behind her opened and James poked his head
through the narrow opening. "I didn't mean to chase you
outside," he said, contrition evident in his voice. "Come
back in. I promise I'll be good." He smiled and held out his
hand.

Alex's eyes briefly met Jon's. He shrugged and smiled,
gesturing toward James's extended hand. Alex smiled stiffly
in return and placed her cold fingers against his slightly
damp palm.

"I really *am* sorry, Alex," he murmured as she passed
him. "I was out of line."

She relented, almost amused by the prim note in his voice.
His dark eyes were unreadable through the heavy lenses of
his glasses.

"I suppose it was just jealousy," he continued.

Alex hoped his voice was too low for the doctor's ears,
hoped the bustle of reentering the room would mask her
surprise at James's words.

She sighed and glanced over her shoulder. The doctor had
joined another couple and was smiling easily at something
the man was saying.

"James . . ." she began.

"I know, don't tell me. It was over for us before it ever
even began, wasn't it? You set the rules from day one—
don't get close." He glanced in Jon's direction. "I'm not
usually so obvious."

"It's okay," Alex said listlessly, suddenly too tired to
either continue idle cocktail chatter with the group or heavy
emotional scenes with James. There was only one person she
really wanted to talk to, and she didn't have the proper defenses in place to do that. She couldn't seem to put anything into perspective, least of all her reaction to Jon
Wyndham.

"I saw you talking to him, Alex, and I guess I just saw red. You know, it's the first time I've ever seen you flustered. Your eyes were soft, almost inviting. It made me a little crazy, I think."

"Oh, James . . ."

"He's had a bad time of it, too. His wife was killed by terrorists in Lebanon." James took a hold of Alex's arm and squeezed it lightly. "Don't make him fall in love with you, Alex. He doesn't need that kind of grief."

She pulled her arm away. "I don't deserve this, James," she said quietly and firmly. She looked across to where the doctor had been, but found him gone. A look to her left, however, told her that he'd been close enough to hear James's words. His eyebrows were raised, a curious expression on his face. She looked away quickly, lest he read too much.

"I wanted you to meet him for another reason altogether," James said. Alex waited, half expecting another outburst. James's voice lowered considerably. "You asked me about Roger Copple yesterday . . ."

"Yes?"

"And why would someone this pretty be asking about Roger Copple?" one of the older men at the party asked. Alex had seen him frequently on her visits to the Soviet Union but had never officially met him. Following the rule of three, he had joined them just in time for the last part of their conversation.

James started visibly, spilling his coffee. "Sternberg! I didn't hear you come up. Have you met Alex?" He performed the introductions. They murmured hellos at each other.

"What's this about Copple?" Ned Sternberg repeated.

"Alex asked about him before she left the States. I was just telling her that she should talk to the doctor about him."

"I see," Ned said, and though his voice was friendly, his eyes were cold. Alex wondered just what it was he saw.

"That reminds me," James said. "Alex had a bit of a problem at passport control when she arrived today."

"Such as?" Ned prompted, looking at Alex.

She looked first at James, who nodded slightly, then at her questioner. "I was carrying photographs of some art work I've been offered for purchase here in the Soviet Union. The customs official made a phone call to some superior and kept the photos."

"Do you speak Russian? Did you hear what he said?" Ned asked. His voice, though considerably lowered, had hardened somewhat. His blue eyes became steely as Alex nodded.

"He told the person on the other end of the line that he had the photographs, and then he asked if he should detain me, as well."

"Did you protest him keeping the photographs?"

"No," Alex replied.

"Why not, Ms. Shashkevich?"

Alex was surprised at the question. She wasn't a diplomat. "He scared me. I've never had anything held before, and I didn't want to be detained, as well." She nodded at James. "James was ready to protest, but I just wanted to get out of there."

The older man smiled again and took her hand. "I can certainly understand that. I would appreciate it if you could find time to stop by and see me tomorrow. We can have a chat about this matter. Anyone can direct you to my office. It's on the fourth floor."

"It really isn't much of a matter—" she began, but James cut her off.

"Let Sternberg be the judge of that, Alex," he said. "He's in charge of the—"

Sternberg coughed, and James flushed. "He's in charge of the econ-political section."

Alex tried looking unaware but suspected she had failed when she caught the doctor's eyes a few feet away and he lifted one expressive eyebrow in amusement. He hefted his glass in a slight salute. She wasn't sure if the gesture was to confirm Sternberg's supposed position or if he was saying something else altogether.

Jon listened with unabashed curiosity. Roger Copple? She'd asked about Roger? Alex Shashkevich was Roger's connection? He frowned, thinking about the implications. He stepped closer, the better to hear, but turned his back slightly so that he appeared to be in conversation with another couple.

"Where did these photographs come from?" the quiet interrogation continued.

Alex paused, then answered slowly. "Hans Saalard."

Jon heard a note of pain in her deep voice.

"Ah, yes. He deals in art, doesn't he?" Ned asked. "But didn't I just read something about him?"

"He was murdered a few days ago in Washington," Alex said, and Jon understood the pain he'd heard in her voice. They had been close. How close? He glanced at her. Very close, if her drawn features were any indication.

"That's tragic," Ned murmured, but Jon didn't see any sympathy in the intelligence officer's eyes. If anything, they hardened even more. "And you knew him well?"

"We were friends. I knew his family," Alex said. Jon could see that the lack of sympathy in the man's eyes angered her. "We had just agreed on a purchase when he was killed."

"And that purchase was in the Soviet Union?" Ned asked astutely.

Alex's smile looked forced. It was entirely different from the smile she'd given him, Jon thought. The notion pleased him.

"Yes," she answered simply.

Ned frowned slightly. "I was under the impression that the Soviets aren't too keen about selling their treasures."

"As a rule," she answered, "they're not. However, I understand they want to raise some funds for a new exchange program. The collection—at least, from what I've seen in the photographs—is fairly impressive. Armenian with a

Ukrainian influence, or vice versa. More like very old Ukrainian."

Jon heard the puzzled note in her voice and felt a tremor of fear creep down his spine. The room had grown almost silent. All ears were trained on Alex, though most eyes remained elsewhere. Ned looked up, as though irritated, and conversation broke out in multivoiced confusion.

"And where is this collection now?" Ned asked.

Alex smiled. "That's why I wanted to talk with Mr. Copple. He's the one who contacted Hans Saalard."

The tremor that had moved down Jon's spine settled in his stomach, a cold, tight lump. Dear God, he thought. Did she know? He turned, not caring who knew he was eavesdropping, and stepped forward.

Alex felt all eyes swivel to her. She saw the look of slack surprise on James's face and the shuttered expression on Ned Sternberg's. She met the doctor's gold eyes again. His expression carried a warning, and his lips were pressed together in a tight line.

Ned coughed slightly. "I gather you haven't heard that Roger isn't with us any longer."

Alex dragged her gaze from Jon Wyndham and refocused on the not-so-kindly face beside her. "What? Has he been sent to a hospital? Is he that ill?"

Ned's eyes bored into hers. "Ill?"

Alex looked at him in some confusion. "Did I misunderstand? I assumed that was why I should see the doctor about him. I had the impression he was sick."

"He was," Ned said.

"Then I don't understand..." Alex began, but suddenly she did. She stared at Ned, her eyes widening.

The older man nodded, his expression sadder than his eyes. "Yes. I'm afraid he's gone in a much more literal sense than I led you to believe, my dear. Roger Copple is dead."

Alex's eyes flew to Jon Wyndham's in time to see a spasm cross the doctor's face. It didn't look like sorrow; it looked like anger.

"What did he die of?" she asked.

"Appendicitis," James said.

"What?" Alex asked stupidly. Her eyes unconsciously sought Jon's for confirmation.

Slowly, his meaning made clearer by the deliberateness of his action, Jon shook his head.

Standing outside the Hotel Rossiya, huddled in a thick Finnish hunting jacket, looking up through the fine drifting snow at the many stories of the massive hotel, Jon Wyndham wondered who he was kidding, why he was manufacturing reasons to visit Aleksandra Shashkevich.

He didn't have any illusions about why he'd come. Oh, he had something to discuss, something to tell her, but it was more than that; he felt as if he *had* to talk to her, a compelling need that had nothing to do with words. He'd felt an affinity with her, an ease. And much more.

He'd watched her laughing eyes and smiling face across James Bowden's crowded living room. A drink in one hand, a laugh on her lips, a hint of tomorrow in her eyes, she seemed a vibrant, vital warm wind sweeping into his empty life.

Aleksandra. Even her name was unusual, different, as romantic as this dramatic country, as rich as the heritage behind it. This woman was something special. Everyone felt it, he thought. Ned Sternberg. His wife, Anna. Silly Madge Harrigan. Even James Bowden, the usually urbane example of America's attempt to subdue a teaming world, felt her difference.

Jon wanted to go inside the Rossiya. He'd come for that reason. He'd come to talk to her. To *tell* her. And yet he hesitated outside, snow collecting on his hair and coat, feeling that the time in his life meant for talking to beautiful, warm women had long since gone by.

The time, perhaps, had gone, but not, apparently, the urge. And she'd conveniently provided a perfect excuse. He had to talk with her—walk with her, see the glow from the streetlights touching her hair, her eyes—he had to tell her what he knew about Roger Copple. What he knew and what the official word was. He'd seen the shocked expression on her face when Ned Sternberg told her about Roger. And he'd seen the look of doubt immediately afterward. He'd seen the surprise on her face when he shook his head, denying the bureau chief's words. She'd been fairly quiet after that, but he'd felt her gaze on him several times.

He wanted to tell her. But the truth was, he also wanted to hold her in his arms, feel her warmth, the flowering of spring. He sensed something in her, a tension, a fear, at variance with James's ridiculous outburst. James had made Alex sound cold, heartless, but Jon suspected that James didn't really know Alex, not the inner Alex. But he found himself wishing James was right, that Alex would prove a woman of today only, a woman of the present, not the future, that she wouldn't want tomorrow.

Because Jon didn't believe he had any future left in him.

How long had it been since he'd felt the need, the desire, for a woman? Long before his wife succumbed to a terrorist's bomb. And yet it was his wife's shade, her ghost—and his guilt—that kept him from seeking what his heart, his body, desired.

And if James's words were true, then now, tonight, Jon could have Alex without fears for a tomorrow he couldn't give. He'd seen the tentative desire in her eyes, had felt the trembling in her fingers. She couldn't have known that when James spoke so harshly, the sheer vulnerability on her face had reached straight to Jon's heart. He'd stiffened, wanting to believe James's words, not the puzzled hurt in her eyes.

From the loudspeakers mounted on the street-corner lamp-post came the hourly bells chiming the first two bars of "Moscow Evenings." He glanced at his watch. It was late. Almost midnight. The unofficial curfew was already in effect; the metro would stop running in an hour. A trio of drunks wove in front of him singing "Kalinka" at the top of their vodka-tainted lungs.

"Sing with us," one of them called to him in Russian.

"I was," he replied. The trio all nodded sagely, inanely, accepting his lie. They saluted him with a nearly empty bottle of Stolichnaya, which, ironically, meant one-hundred-percent perfect, and continued their bleary singing, weaving down the broad sidewalk, clinging to each other to remain upright.

Perhaps it was their camaraderie, or perhaps it was the lonely wail of "Kalinka" on the cold air, that made him decide to go inside. Or maybe it was, prosaically, that his feet were growing cold.

He flashed his embassy ID card at the hotel guard and was soon going up the elevator to her floor. The floor hostess, calmly eating her midnight supper of soup, cheese and bread at the small central desk, carefully reviewed his ID card, then directed him down the hall to Alex's room. As he moved away, the hostess told him he must leave by 1:00 a.m.; it was against the rules for a unregistered guest to remain in the hotel after one.

Jon glanced over his shoulder at the bank of room keys hanging on the back of her desk. Unlike western hotels, the *dijournaya,* or floor hostess, controlled the keys, locking and unlocking the doors for the hotel guests. It was a practice most Americans found disconcerting. It took away a measure of control.

He loosened his hunting jacket and shook his head to rid it of the collected snow. After studying his hand for a moment as if it belonged to someone else, he rapped on the narrow door to Alex's room.

His loins tightened at her throaty invitation to enter. No, he thought, turning the knob, he wasn't kidding anyone, least of all himself. He would talk to her about Roger. But he was there for one reason only: Alex herself.

Thinking the person at the door to be the floor hostess, Alex issued an invitation without bothering to rise. She already had her hand inside her purse to tip the woman for her late-night tea when the silence from the doorway made her look up.

Standing on the other side of the threshold was the very man she'd been sitting there thinking about. It was as if her thoughts had conjured him from the cold night air to plant him solidly in her vision. She could even feel the cold emanating from his bulky jacket. The light caught and reflected off the snow melting in his hair.

She automatically clutched the folds of her dressing gown, keeping her hand tight against her throat. She could feel her suddenly rapid pulse beating against her knuckles. She couldn't have spoken. Why was he there? What did he want?

She rose unsteadily, her purse slipping to the floor with a dull thud.

"It's bad luck to talk over a threshold," he said, recounting an old Russian superstition. Alex knew the superstition well, was Russian enough to half believe it, but in this instance felt it would be safer if he remained in the doorway.

He didn't. He stepped inside her room and though he left the door ajar, it seemed as if they were in a wholly private world. The room was suddenly too small, her shabby dressing gown too flimsy and her heartbeat too loud.

"I needed to talk to you," he said. His voice was slightly hoarse, as if he hadn't spoken in some time. He shoved his hands deep into his pants pockets and rocked slightly on his heels, saying nothing.

She felt foolish, standing there prudishly, her heart thundering, her hands trembling, not speaking. "I didn't expect you," she said finally, a breathless note in her voice.

"I didn't expect you, either," he said, robbing what little self-possession she had. He didn't look away; his gaze remained locked with hers.

"I'm glad you're here," she said, then shocked at the ring of sheer honesty in her words, at her husky tone, she continued quickly. "I wanted to talk to you, too."

He smiled slightly, and though there should have been mischief in the look, Alex saw only sincerity. She fought against trusting her instincts and stiffened even more, wariness creeping through her.

He nodded, and his smile twisted. Alex thought she detected a strange hint of sorrow in that smile. He had the look of a man who'd had some bit of bad news confirmed; he knew he'd been right, but didn't particularly like it. He cleared his throat. "Shall we go for a walk?"

She threw him a half-panicked glance, then looked over her shoulder at the dark, steamy window. "Now?" she whispered, waving toward the window.

Jon drew in his breath with a harsh whisper of sound. She had released her dressing gown as she gestured toward the window, revealing a hint of her full curves. She wasn't a mere foreshadowing of spring, she was a scorching summer wind. He had to look away or be lost in the depths of her mysterious eyes.

He pointed to the wall and then to the ceiling, and almost laughed at the sudden comprehension on her face. Again she took hold of her dressing gown, this time as if hiding her body from the listening devices in the room. Slowly, she nodded. Jon felt a pang of conscience. To ask her to accompany him on a walk at midnight, with the temperature outside at something less than ten below, was nothing short of outrageous.

"I'll get dressed," she said.

"I'll wait," he said.

Alex watched him leave the room and for a moment, didn't move. He had sounded as if he meant something more than kicking his heels in the hall while she dressed. He had said the words as if he'd meant he would wait for *her,* period. She threw off the notion—and the wistful wrench it gave her—and quickly pulled on enough warm clothing to survive a late-night walk in Moscow in mid-March. She frowned, thinking about Jon Wyndham, about her reaction to him. He had looked at her as if she already meant something to him; his eyes had seemed to convey a message far beyond his words.

For a moment, Alex actually wondered what it would be like to be with Jon Wyndham. When he'd first walked into the room, she'd had the odd feeling that a connection between them was as inevitable as clouds in the sky or water in a riverbed. She shivered, seeing the sensual curve of his lips, the long fingers and broad hands. And she shivered again, knowing it was impossible; she would never allow herself to fall into that trap again. Out of sheer self-preservation, she had denied herself the kind of trust that would permit that kind of sharing.

It wasn't as James had implied earlier that night; she was neither heartless nor cold. And it wasn't because she was too independent, too conscious of what her freedom meant, to stay in one place very long, though she often allowed people to assume that *was* the reason. She would smile and give the excuse of having come from a long line of fiercely independent people, of having the inherited memory of rejecting oppression and running to freedom ingrained in her.

But it wasn't true.

And what was it about the way Jon looked at her that made her believe he knew it wasn't?

She joined Jon Wyndham in the fifth-floor lobby and retrieved her coat, fur hat and gloves from the hostess.

"I am of locking the doors at one," the hostess said.

"But you will let me in," Alex said with a smile, holding out a fifty-ruble note.

The *dijournaya* took the note, which represented at least one-quarter of her monthly salary, and laid it on the table beside the remains of her meal. "Of course," she said. "It will be a pleasure." Her eyes never left the money.

Jon pressed the elevator button and escorted Alex inside with a light touch. The door slid closed, and they slowly traveled to the ground floor.

"You're fairly adept with your bribes," he said.

She glanced up at him, considering his words, seeking another meaning behind them. "When in Moscow . . ." she said with a slight smile.

He smiled back, and Alex felt her breath catch in her throat. Standing this close to him, feeling the heat from his body, the sharp tang of his after-shave lotion in her nostrils, she was conscious of an odd desire to erase the worry lines from his forehead, of a sensation of rare empathy. When the elevator door opened, she stepped through quickly, her heart thudding with an irregular rhythm.

His answering smile had been a bribe all its own.

Chapter 3

The night air was even colder than she'd anticipated; it snatched at her breath and burned in her lungs. The glow of hundreds of street lamps lit the street to a near-daylight brightness, while obscuring the tops of buildings. Heavily-bundled women with brooms and snow shovels worked at clearing the sidewalks, and the alternating sounds of the brooms' swishing and the shovels' scraping lent an odd rhythmic melody to the late night walk.

They walked in silence for a few blocks, their footsteps matching the shovels' rhythm. Alex's thoughts were chaotic. It seemed she wasn't the only one who had felt that current of electricity pass between them. He'd felt it, too. The thought caused her breath to catch in her throat and her hands to clutch at the collar of her coat.

She didn't want, couldn't trust, these feelings he inspired in her. She risked a glance in his direction. He wasn't classically handsome; his face was too broad, his lips too full, his deep-set eyes fringed by eyelashes that were too long. Involuntarily her lips parted.

"Moscow's beautiful at night," Jon said, looking across at the dark, quiet, walled Kremlin. The single red star glowed in the cloud-heavy sky.

The street lamps lit his face, and Alex wanted to run from the gentleness she could see there. This was a man who could storm her defenses; everything about him cried out to her to trust him. She pulled ahead, stamping her feet to drive the chill away.

Her actions seemed the signal for him to speak.

"Roger Copple didn't die of appendicitis," he said abruptly. His tone carried the same lack of inflection it had when he had pointed out the zoology store—the reptile pet shop—on the corner of Prospect Marksa.

"So I gathered," Alex said dryly.

"That's the *official* line."

He could only be telling her this because Roger Copple's death had something to do with her; the obvious conclusion, the only meeting point, was the collection of artifacts. "I see," she said, keeping her tone neutral, hoping he would elaborate. "What did he die from?"

She had the uncomfortable sensation of being watched and looked over her shoulder. About a block away, a man had stopped to light his cigarette. Alex couldn't help but smile at her own sense of melodrama.

Jon took her arm and propelled her forward. "You'll freeze if we stand in one place." He didn't speak for several steps, then continued, "Copple died of radiation poisoning."

Alex looked at him sharply. "Radiation poisoning? As in—as in what? Nuclear war? Atomic bombs?"

Jon's mouth twisted in a wry smile. "Copple's white blood cell count was sky high. Do you know anything about white blood cells?"

"Antibodies?" she asked, culling from who knew what dim memory of her college biology classes.

She was rewarded with a broad smile. It made her heart do a slow somersault. She looked away quickly. Nervously.

"That's right. In an appendicitis attack, the victim's white-blood-cell count shoots up. Doctors can usually determine the need for an appendectomy from a simple blood test."

"Yes?" she said politely, shivering against the chill air, wondering where this was leading and fearing what it might have to do with her, fearing that if she spent any more time in his company her instincts would once again betray her.

"The white blood cell count is also affected when a victim is subjected to microwave poisoning."

She looked up at him, startled. "I thought the Soviets had stopped the bombardment of microwaves at the embassy."

"By and large, they have."

"But that still killed Copple?" Alex stepped on a slick patch and slid, swinging her hands to maintain her balance. If he hadn't been holding her arm, she would have fallen. He tightened his grip, reaching his free arm around her shoulders to steady her. Her breath caught at the reaction the simple gesture caused.

"I don't think so." He continued, unaware of the tension he was causing in her, "I don't think it was microwave poisoning at all."

"I'm sorry," she said, puzzled, wishing he would take his arm away. She couldn't think clearly. "I'm lost. What *did* Roger Copple die from?"

"I'm not sure. The classified word is microwave poisoning."

"But you said it wasn't that."

"I know. He had the classic signs of radiation poisoning, but I just can't believe there were sufficient quantities of microwave bombardment to kill him."

"Has anyone else been sick?" she asked.

He shook his head. "That's exactly what bothers me. I ran a routine blood test on everyone in the embassy, and the only other person who showed any signs of a white blood cell imbalance was Copple's girlfriend, Nancy Abernathy. And she recently had a bad bout of stomach flu. Her reading wasn't inconsistent with her illness—not to mention that she still has her appendix and could actually be suffering an attack. And none of her other symptoms were consistent with radiation poisoning." He shrugged. "Not another soul has shown any signs of imbalance. It doesn't make any sense."

"What does all this mean?" Alex asked. She wanted to ask why he was telling her, but she didn't, half afraid of his answer.

"I don't know. No one else has symptoms like Roger Copple's. We've had two miscarriages, one emergency appendectomy... but no skin sores, no loss of hair. No rashes on the extremities. Nothing like Copple."

Alex felt a shiver that had nothing to do with the cold, nothing to do with the man beside her. In a low, emotionless voice, she said, "Hans Saalard had a rash on his right hand."

Jon stopped walking and gripped her shoulders. "Blistered? Angry red?"

Alex shook her head. "N-no. It was rough, dry looking."

Jon expelled his breath in quick relief. His grip on her arms loosened, then dropped. He raised a hand to his face and rubbed his forehead. "Secondary contact, at the most. If that. Even if it is, it won't hurt him."

"He's dead," she said bleakly.

Jon looked astonished, almost panicked, then embarrassed. "I'm sorry. I forgot."

She stifled a desire to check her own hands, fought an imaginary itch. "Why are you telling me all this?" she asked. "Why did you come here tonight?"

His eyes met hers, then slid away. In the uncertain light, it was difficult to tell if his sudden color had come from the cold or from something he was thinking. "I think you might know something."

"Me? What could I possibly know about all this? I didn't even know Roger Copple was dead," she protested. She shook her head. "I don't know anything. I only heard of Copple for the first time when Hans mentioned his name."

"I know. But he was trying to sell you some artifacts he'd come across."

She had been right; this did have to do with the collection. Suddenly she was gripping his arm, not the reverse.

"And the man who was trying to sell them to you was murdered."

Alex stopped walking again, turning to him in shock. "Are you implying that their deaths are connected? That Copple was *murdered?*" At Jon's lack of response, at his closed expression, Alex shook her head vehemently. "That's ridiculous," He raised an eyebrow. "I'm sorry, but it is. Hans was killed by muggers. Senseless, tragic, but his killers were common thugs." Was her voice a shade less than confident? Her legs certainly felt that way.

"The photographs you carried were confiscated at customs."

Alex frowned heavily. He had offered the statement as if it were proof of his theory. "That's apples and oranges," she said. "One doesn't have anything to do with the other."

"I think it does," he said quietly, urging her to keep walking.

Her mind refusing to speculate on the implications of his words, she focused instead on how he'd known about the confiscated photographs. "You have excellent hearing, don't you?" she asked. The same thought made her glance behind them. The man with the cigarette was gone, though Alex still had the feeling that someone was watching them.

Jon didn't pretend to misunderstand the path her thoughts had traveled. "Occupational hazard," he replied with a smile. "The doctor of a post is allowed access to almost everything, but seldom is included in anything beyond a need-to-know basis, so I fell into the habit a long time ago of listening closely."

"So you heard everything there tonight?" she asked, thinking not of her conversation with Ned Sternberg, but the low words with James Bowden.

Again he didn't dodge her question, nor did he look embarrassed. "James had had too much to drink," he said quietly.

She fought and mastered an urge to defend both herself and James. "What is it you think I might know?"

"I'm not entirely certain. But Roger Copple is—was—one of the biggest black marketeers on the embassy circuit."

"What?" Alex stopped, staring at him, appalled.

"You didn't know?"

"Didn't know?" Alex gasped. A thousand implications of his words filtered through her mind—none of them generous. She stifled an urge to slap him. She did jerk her arm from his hand. "How dare you!"

"What?" he asked, blankly. "What did I say?"

"You just implied that I'm in the business of importing stolen goods." She glared up at him. "I don't appreciate it, doctor."

He had the grace to look thoroughly discomfited. "No, no. I didn't mean it that way. It's such common knowledge at the embassy that—"

"Well, it wasn't common knowledge to me!"

"I'm sorry," he said. He held out his gloved hand. She ignored it. "Look, I didn't mean anything. I apologize."

She scarcely glanced at his still-outstretched hand. "No? Just what did you mean when you said, 'You didn't know?' as if it were the most natural thing in the world that I would hustle artifacts on the black market?"

Jon did a full turn, raising a hand to his hair and sweeping the snow from his head. "I'm sorry, all right? I wasn't thinking. I didn't mean anything by it."

Only slightly mollified, Alex resumed walking, feeling somewhat foolish over not accepting his twice-offered apology. Being angry wouldn't answer her questions. "I didn't have a clue about Copple's dirty dealing. Anyway, it's impossible in this case. He contacted Hans Saalard. Hans is—was—one-hundred-percent honest. I'd swear to it."

Jon took a long moment to answer. Alex wanted to go back to the hotel. She didn't need this, didn't deserve it. Twice this evening she'd been the victim of potshots from men. And now Hans, who couldn't defend himself, was being subjected to doubts regarding his integrity.

"I didn't mean to imply that your friend wasn't honest. I'm sure he was simply acting on the assumption that Copple *was*. Unfortunately, he was anything but."

"But—"

"I'm sorry, but it's one of the given facts around a post that each one has a black marketeer."

Alex didn't pull away when Jon took her arm again. She was too lost in thought, too confused. "But if the artifacts are being sold on the black market..." She trailed off, appalled at both the unwanted knowledge that this man's opinion of her mattered and the realization that Hans had not only died senselessly, he had died for a stolen collection.

"Oh, my God," she said now, not noticing how tightly she was gripping Jon's arm, not caring. Her eyes met his.

He slowly nodded, no smile on his generous lips. "I think," he said reflectively, "the artifacts in your collection are *hot*."

Alex gulped the cold air, trying to steady her chaotic thoughts. The memory of the customs official rose to the surface. "The photographs. They'll think..."

"Slow down, Alex," Jon said, gripping her arm tightly. "You'll be in the clear. You'll just have to explain how you came by the photographs, then relinquish any claim to the collection."

He couldn't know there was more to it than that; he couldn't know that the Saalard family was depending on her. "Isn't there a chance Copple was operating legitimately for once?"

Jon said nothing, and Alex knew a moment's real despair. She fought the feeling of being on thin ice. "What did you say about Copple a minute ago? That he was in communications?"

"That's right."

"Not in the economics or commercial section?"

"That's right, why?"

"Because I've been the stupidest person on earth. I didn't even think to check him out. I know Hans. Knew him, anyway. And because of that, I didn't even check on Roger Copple. And Hans was so honest himself, he automatically assumed everyone else was."

She felt the knife blade of angry sorrow prick at her heart. She should have checked on the contact, should have called James to ask about Copple; she had already known—had known for years—that trust was never enough. As usual, someone had taken it on the chin for trusting too much. Hans was dead, and she was in deep trouble.

Now she said dully, "If Copple wasn't working in the econ-commercial section, he wouldn't have had the contact with the Soviets to even be considered as an intermediary for a sale like this one."

Jon's hand covered hers. "You didn't know," he said softly.

Alex glanced up at him, for a brief moment, snared by the sympathy in his golden gaze. She dragged her gaze away. "I should have known."

"Why?" he asked. He sounded half-surprised.

"Because you can't take anything on faith," she said.

"Nothing?" he asked, and she had the feeling he didn't mean her business—or anything remotely connected with it.

"Nothing," she answered grimly. But she was conscious of a stinging in her eyes. She looked to her left, willing the watery shadows to clear.

He let it pass, but gripped her hand tightly, and they walked in silence for a few minutes. Alex's thoughts were chaotic, her emotions churned to a white froth, but his steps matched hers, and his body was close enough for her to feel his warmth, steadying her, grounding her.

"Is this why you wanted to tell me about Roger Copple? To warn me that I might be involved in something rotten?" she asked finally.

"No," Jon said, not looking at her. "When I said that Copple was trying to deal items that were hot...I didn't only mean stolen goods."

Again Alex felt they were heading toward thin ice. She shook her head. "I don't understand. What did you mean?"

Jon stopped and met her gaze. "I meant that I think they are highly radioactive."

She could only stare at him.

"That's why I made that blunder about the black market a while ago. I couldn't care less about the black market. That's not what worries me."

She felt both cold and hot, afraid of his next words as much as she had ever been afraid of anything. She felt a long shudder work through her as she thought of the objects in the photographs, remembered the patterns embossed on the items. She felt as if she'd had all the pieces of a puzzle but had put them together to form the wrong picture. Now the pieces rearranged themselves into a new and frightening image.

"No-o-o," she said slowly.

"No what?"

"No, it's impossible."

"Why?" he asked, not as if he wanted to know, but as if he wanted her to confirm his suspicions. "Tell me why it's impossible." She knew he was asking for a proof she couldn't offer.

"It has to be," she said, clutching at his arm.

"But you know it isn't," he said slowly, as dully as she had spoken only moments earlier.

"Because the etchings on the gold aren't Armenian in design," she said, equally slowly.

He sighed and closed his eyes. "That's what I thought you said tonight."

"They're Ukrainian," she said with a note of awe. "Old, *old* Ukrainian. That would explain the Armenian influence."

"Exactly," he said, propelling her forward again.

"You think—" she began, then broke off, the suspicion too terrible to voice.

"Exactly," he said again. "Chernobyl."

Alex looked about helplessly, not believing this, not willing to believe it. She saw the man who had earlier lit his cigarette. He was on the opposite side of the street now, not looking at them, but reading a theater billing by the light from the street lamps.

"Is he following us?" she asked, nodding at the man.

Jon looked at the man, frowned and shrugged. "Probably."

"Why?" she asked.

"I'm with the embassy." Jon looked at her closely. "Does it frighten you?"

She considered his question for a moment, then shook her head. "It doesn't seem very important right now. Not in the wake of what we've been talking about." But she was only telling half of the truth; something about being followed did scare her.

"You agree with me, then?"

"Agree?" she asked.

"That the collection could come from the Chernobyl area."

She hesitated. "No-o. Oh, I don't know what to believe." She laughed shakily. Not knowing what to believe—or whom—was the bane of her existence.

"I'm having trouble with it myself. I couldn't think what Copple had done—or come in contact with—that would literally eat him alive. When I heard you talking about those photographs, when James told me you were looking for Copple, when you said the collection had a Ukrainian influence..."

"You put two and two together—"

"And may have come up with twenty-two. Who knows?"

"But you believe it," she said.

"I believe it," he agreed. "It makes a rather ghastly kind of sense."

Alex shuddered. He was right. It did. She glanced over her shoulder at the man still reading the theater boards. She stamped her feet and didn't argue as Jon took her arm again, leading her toward the street corner.

She was not unfamiliar with being tailed. She had been in Moscow often, not that her movements were usually of any interest to the KGB. She often associated with embassy people, however, and their movements were always of interest. James had told her a long time ago—in Germany, perhaps, or maybe it had been Israel—that embassy personnel in any country were closely tailed. In the Soviet Union it was a daily fact of life.

Jon glanced over his shoulder, then back at her. He rephrased his earlier question. "Does it bother you?"

Alex again considered the question. Jon's eyes held a bigger question behind the shadows. "The idea that the collection might come from around Chernobyl? Or the man following us?" she asked.

Jon smiled bitterly, dismissing the first question as obvious. "The tail," he said.

"Ye-es," she said, slowly. "I think it does. Not because I've got anything to hide, just because it violates my privacy."

"There's no word in Russian that means privacy," Jon said softly, and to Alex, the look in his eyes was sad. "There is only a word for being alone."

She nodded, surprised he knew that. "And to the Russian, the concept of being alone is the saddest thing possible," she answered.

"It can be," Jon said, his eyes linking with hers.

"I meant..." she began, but trailed away at the unexpected fire in his gaze. And yet there was gentleness there, too, making his need a flame that would warm but never destroy.

"I didn't," he said.

She felt the desire emanating from him. He wanted her, and that frightened her; he seemed to want more than just the surface Alex. He looked as though he were reading her soul. She tried pulling back a step, but he held her fast. Her heart beat in a painful rhythm; her head felt light. The snow looked like stars against his hair. His face was wreathed in the white of his own warm breath coming and going raggedly.

"Don't," she whispered, not at all certain what she was prohibiting, knowing only that his eyes asked too much.

"Alex," he murmured, her name a plea on his lips. His mouth twisted almost bitterly and lowered to hers.

His lips were cold, his breath like fire against her cheeks. She felt the feather-soft kiss start a chain reaction of sensation inside her. Even as her body came alive to his touch, her mind snapped shut. She felt pinned by a poignant stirring, a liquid reminder of long-forgotten desires. Her knees threatened to buckle, and weak with unfamiliar longing, she could only cling to his arms, drowning in his embrace.

She pulled back, more reluctantly than he could possibly have known. "No," she said firmly.

Whatever his intention had been when he kissed her, a blind for the man tailing them, a light test of the waters between them, it had gone awry for him. Somehow, with some stark inner honesty, she knew it was the kiss and not her pulling away that filled him with confusion. She could read it in his face, feel it through their heavy clothes, recognize it in his gripping hands.

He reached a hand to her cheek. The rough, cold touch of his glove against her face made her shiver. He lowered his hand, warming her, chilling her with his tenderness.

"James told you I was vulnerable," he said, misunderstanding her denial.

"Yes," she said, hoping he would leave it at that.

"So I am," he said. But what she saw in his eyes wasn't vulnerability.

"I . . ." she began, but trailed off, unwilling to feed him a lie about her need for freedom, but more than half-afraid he would see the truth.

"It's late," he said softly. "We'd better get back."

He took her arm and directed her across the street, as so-licitous of her safety now as his lips had been with the kiss.

"Alex?" he asked, and when she didn't answer, he sighed.

Alex turned her head away. He couldn't know how his sigh affected her. He couldn't know how difficult it was not to trust him, not to give in to the desire to believe he would be considerate of her heart.

"Tell me about your wife," she said.

"Keeping me at a distance?" he guessed, correctly. "She's dead," he said tersely.

"I know," she said. "James told me."

"The ubiquitous James."

"He's a friend," Alex said softly.

Jon looked as if he were about to speak, to ask her some-thing; then he sighed again. "Did he tell you how she was killed?"

"Terrorists, he said."

Jon paused beneath a street lamp, the light revealing a strain that had been absent earlier. Alex regretted having asked him, both for the tension she'd created in him and the sympathy she could feel stirring in her.

His eyes met hers. "Margaret hated Foreign Service life. Really hated it, I mean."

Alex said nothing.

"She kept begging me to stay in Washington." He looked away, and Alex glanced over her shoulder. The man who had been across the street from them was now about half a block behind them. If he was following them, he wasn't bothering to maintain even a pretense of innocence.

"How long were you married?" she asked Jon after sev-eral moments had passed.

"Ten years," he said. It seemed a lifetime to Alex; her marriage had lasted only six months, though the scars had lasted seven years.

"How long ago did she die?"

"Two years." He glanced down at her. "I'm over it, you know."

Suspecting he was lying, to himself if not to her, she struggled with an odd desire to erase the frown from his forehead with her finger.

"Have you been married?" he asked.

"Yes," she said, fighting the sense of panic the simple question produced in her.

"Don't like to talk about it?" he asked.

"I'm freezing, standing here like this," she said, moving out of the direct light and onto the broad sidewalk.

"Why did you pull back?" he asked.

She acted as if she hadn't heard him. He hesitated, then followed her, taking her arm again, linking it through his.

Alex glanced back. The man was walking again, maintaining the half-a-block distance behind them.

"Ignore him," Jon said. "Even though it's obvious, it isn't wise to play games with them."

"Play games?" she asked.

"Talk to them, offer cigarettes or a drink. Occasionally some hotshot will take it into his head to try to embarrass his tail. Not a good idea."

"Don't worry, I don't have any interest in a direct confrontation."

Jon smiled. "Good. I wouldn't dwell on it, either, though. It's better if you just accept it as a fact of life."

"Like confiscating those photographs," she said.

"I'd say that comes under a different heading, but yes, it's better to accept it, at least on the surface."

"James once told me about a woman here who couldn't handle the surveillance. Linda something."

"I'm fairly new here," Jon said. "I don't know who she is." Alex could hear the tension back in his voice. She wondered that she could read him so easily on such short acquaintance. Perhaps it had something to do with midnight walks and freezing temperatures. Maybe it was because he'd already knocked a small hole in her defenses.

"Linda was an embassy wife. She was thirty-three, a music graduate of Michigan State. She'd never been overseas before."

Snow crunched beneath their feet, and their steps matched the low rhythm of the street cleaners. She found herself letting the awareness of the man following them fade away. She talked while Jon said nothing.

"The first piece of furniture she asked for when she came to Moscow was a piano. James was there. He said she cried when it was delivered. She didn't speak Russian. She tried learning it when she arrived, taking the basic embassy-wife course. But she gave it up as hopeless."

Jon's arm jerked reflexively. Alex almost abandoned the story; she knew it was cutting close to the bone. Again she felt that empathy stirring between them.

"Go on," he said harshly.

"She hated shopping. She couldn't speak the language, couldn't bargain. Didn't understand the labels, didn't know what she was buying. She felt the Russian merchants were cheating her, but she couldn't argue with them. Pretty soon she had other embassy wives, who did speak Russian, doing all her shopping for her."

"Go on," he said again. His arm was a solid band of iron pressing hers tightly against his side. She could feel his quickened, painful breathing.

"Her husband worked long hours—typical embassy hours. Linda began withdrawing from what few friends she had. She played the piano all day, morning till night. She stopped going out. She played until her back and arms ached, then took aspirin and played some more."

"What happened?" he asked, though his voice told her that he already knew.

"James said one of the hammers on the piano broke."

"And she broke, too?" Jon asked, making the connection swiftly, too swiftly to let her believe the story hadn't painted an accurate sketch of his wife.

"Yes," Alex said softly. "They med-evac'ed her to a hospital in the States." Alex didn't have to wait long before Jon added to the portrait, three or four snow-muted steps.

"Margaret was afraid, too," he said. His eyes gazed straight ahead, but Alex knew he was seeing the past. "She begged me, over and over, not to go to Lebanon." He glanced at Alex, then away. His eyes were full of pain, self-recrimination. "She had been having an affair—" At Alex's sudden movement, he waved his free hand. "It wasn't serious. Not really." He shook his head. "I don't even think she had her heart in it. She was just so damn unhappy." Jon blew a white cloud of air into the night. "And that was probably my fault, too.

"I thought...I believed that taking her to Lebanon would pull her out of it. I thought she was suffering from guilt. You know, over the affair. I thought if we had a change of environment, if she could see I didn't want to end things over one stupid mistake, that things would get better."

"But they didn't," Alex asked.

Jon shook his head. "No. If anything, things got worse. Packing up your troubles and moving them halfway around the world doesn't make them disappear." He sighed again. "Like your Linda, Margaret didn't speak Arabic. She sat at home all day...."

Alex mentally supplied the unspoken words, *Adrift in a world she didn't understand.*

"She was afraid of everything. I worked long hours—" he nodded at her with a bitter smile "—the typical embassy hours. And then we had to entertain. Most of the guests didn't speak English, and Margaret would spend the whole evening either downing the contents of whatever bottle was closest or sitting silently in a corner, knitting something."

"You don't have to tell me this," Alex said.

"I know," he replied. "For some reason, maybe because you look like you've had to fight a devil or two yourself, I feel like telling you."

"Have you ever talked about this before?" she asked, startled by his words, stung by his confession. Afraid of his perception.

He stopped, then resumed walking. "No." Alex saw the flash of his quick smile. "I suppose I haven't needed to."

She felt a swift dagger point of alarm. She didn't want him to tell her any more. She didn't want to know. She didn't want his confidence. A confidence was a responsibility, and responsibility led to trust.

"Anyway," he said, stealing the moment when she might have stopped him, "she kept pulling further inside herself. Again, I thought all she needed was time. Every time we tried talking about it, she'd start crying, and—" he grinned half sheepishly "—I'm the kind of guy who gets totally unnerved by tears. I'd promise all kinds of things…the moon, the stars, easy things like that."

Alex smiled, but the reflex felt forced. She'd been promised the moon and stars so many times, but when the time came, all she'd been given were pain and loss.

"I finally suggested counseling, and she looked at me like…like I'd just told her I hated her. She looked betrayed. It was my fault, she said, not hers. I knew how to solve the problem, I just wouldn't."

Alex made an incoherent murmur of protest. Jon waved his free hand as if wiping the past away. "She was right. I could have set up a practice in the States. You know, shingle carved in wood, white picket fence, the whole bit. But I didn't. I just kept thinking that time would fix everything. That she'd see I didn't hold the past against her." He snorted. "I was too blind to see that was the last thing bothering her."

They walked another block before he continued. "I arranged a tour for her—you know, the moon and stars."

Alex felt the impending disaster of his wife's death approaching and tried girding herself against feeling his pain.

"She didn't want to go. She cried. She begged." His arm crushed Alex's unconsciously. "But I insisted. I was the doctor, I knew best." He shook his head. "I even packed her bags for her. I stood outside the tour bus and waved to her. She didn't see me. Her head was buried in her hands." Jon imitated the action, his hands drawing furrowed lines down his face. He dropped his hands and took Alex's arm again. He continued, his voice hollow. "She didn't see me because she was crying."

Alex felt a shudder work through the man beside her, felt its echo in her. "Don't," she murmured, but he ignored her.

"Terrorists destroyed the bus two days later in a pass near the Syrian border. They claimed responsibility in a public statement."

There were no words Alex could say that would take away his pain. She blinked away her sudden tears, and they turned to ice on her cheeks.

"I found her journals when I packed up her stuff. That's when I found out all the things that were really eating her up inside."

Alex swiped at her frozen face. Her motion seemed to call his attention back to her.

He stopped walking. "Sorry." His grin was strained. "I ask you for a walk, scare you half to death, then spill my guts." He lifted a hand to her cheek, smoothing away the frozen moisture. "And that wasn't why I came. That isn't why I'm here."

"Don't," she whispered again, more chilled by the story, by the tragedy of it, than he could ever know. For the first time, she wanted to tell her own story. James knew, because he had known Tony, because he'd been there. Hans had known, because he had known Marja, because he was the one who had interceded to stop that single, stark example of Alex's poor instincts.

But she had never confided her feeling to anyone. She had never spoken of the shock she'd felt, the helplessness, upon discovering that Marja bore the same last name as Tony. She had never told anyone about the gun.

"You're easy to talk to," he said, still not looking at her. "It was as if I knew you'd listen. Knew you'd understand." He chuckled. "Maybe it's just because it's late, the morning is coming, and you'll be gone in a few weeks."

"Secrets among strangers?" she asked, half understanding. Wasn't that one of the reasons why people sought psychiatrists? They could spill every drop of their anguish to a stranger. Wasn't that, to some degree, why it had crossed her mind to tell him?

He smiled wryly. "There are a lot of secrets floating around tonight."

She nodded, relieved the conversation was shifting elsewhere. "The collection of artifacts," she said.

"Copple's death."

"The photographs."

"Why you pulled away from that kiss." He said it as if they were discussing a dinner menu, and because he wasn't looking at her, he missed the spasm that crossed her features.

"Sorry," he said. "It's late, you've got jet lag, I've got appointments in the morning." He stopped, releasing her arm as if just realizing he'd been pressing it against his side.

Forcing her lips to curve into a smile, she met his gaze, unaware that her eyes were still luminous with unshed tears, aware only that he'd spoken to some hitherto untouched part of her.

"And we have a mystery to solve," she said.

"That's not your worry. You confirmed what I suspected. Tell the authorities—both Soviet and at the embassy—what you know. You'll be all right that way. I'll pass my suspicions on to the powers that be. It's the most either of us can do. And then, if you're smart, you'll clear out of Moscow."

Because of the art or because of you? she wanted to ask.

"I want to see it through," she said, meaning the mystery of the artifacts, not the mystery of the man beside her. "I owe it to Hans Saalard's family."

"What do you owe them?"

"It sounds silly," she said.

"Tell me."

"I want to create some meaning from his death," she said.

Jon didn't say anything, but his eyes focused on her sharply and he stilled.

"You can never find meaning in someone's death," he said softly. And Alex could see how long he'd searched for meaning in his wife's death. Then, as if the words were dragged from him, he asked, "Did you love him?"

"Hans?" she asked; then she realized that he meant her husband. "Yes," she said simply.

His expulsion of breath was audible. "You're no ice queen."

Her mind flew to James's nasty comment. She shook her head, rejecting the truth, rejecting Jon's perceptiveness.

He said nothing, merely raising an eyebrow, then led her around another corner, and there, looming out of the dark night, was her hotel.

"What are you going to do about the photographs?" he asked as they stopped before the large glass doors.

"Meet with the Ministry of Culture in the morning," she replied. "I know Andre Makarov, the minister. And now, I've got a few questions of my own."

He studied her for a long moment. "And this meeting doesn't scare you?"

She had dealt with the Minister of Culture on many occasions, but never over something like this. "A little," she lied.

He smiled. "I can imagine it might scare some people to death."

Thinking that his ideas about what someone would or wouldn't fear was strongly colored by his former wife's fears, she shook her head.

"And you're meeting with Ned tomorrow?"

"Yes," she said, smiling at this further evidence of his eavesdropping. "I can't keep any secrets from you."

"No?" he asked, lifting her hand and holding it for a moment against his chest, and then moving it to his lips. "I'm looking forward to the time when you don't."

Chapter 4

Alex took the metro to Derzhinskovo Ploshchad, Derzhinsky Square. Despite the midmorning hour, the subway was crowded with dark-scarved, heavy-coated shoppers. Babushkas, grandmothers, the real governing body within the Soviet Union, stared openly and distrustfully at Alex's lightweight but warm, silver-colored coat. They eyed her fashionable boots with disfavor, her gloves with expressions all too evident of their lack of faith in the gloves' ability to keep her hands warm. The only article of her clothing to pass inspection was her fur hat; it was Russian.

The air outside the ornate metro station was frigid, filled with pinpoint-sized snowflakes and permeated by the odors of diesel exhaust and cooked cabbage. A thousand murmured conversations mingled and hung in the air, blending with the ever-present sound of snow being scraped from the sidewalks.

Alex crossed the busy intersection via the tunneled crosswalk and entered the massive building housing the Ministry of Culture. She quelled a desire to turn around and leave. She wanted to know the real story of the collection's background. She owed that much to Hans's family. And she had her reputation to think about . . . and Hans's. She couldn't allow his family to hear any slurs against his name.

A squat woman wearing a tan wool hat and a red cardigan sweater sat at a small table in the very center of the cavernous hall. She looked up unsmilingly and held out her hand for Alex's papers.

Alex handed over her passport, her business credentials and the noted appointment time with Andre Nikolayevich Makarov, Minister of Culture, fine-arts division. The woman read each line of both the passport and credentials, then read the English scrawled on the small note several times, before nodding and opening a log book.

She entered the time, the date and Alex's name. "Reason for visit?" she asked.

"Request of the minister," Alex replied, collecting her papers.

A velvet voice spoke from behind her. "That's a neutral way of saying it."

Alex started, turned and met Jon Wyndham's warm eyes. A tightening that had nothing to do with the upcoming meeting made itself felt in her stomach. What was he doing there? Why had he come? Why was she so glad he had?

"It's embassy policy to have more than one Westerner in on every meeting," he said.

"I'm not embassy," she said breathlessly.

"I am," he replied, however illogically.

She couldn't help but smile, but his answering smile did nothing to ease her tension. If anything, it heightened it.

"Besides," he said, "I thought you wouldn't object to a little moral support."

She didn't object to the moral support, only to the man who was giving it; she couldn't think clearly if he was there. She couldn't seem to think at all. After the midnight walk, after that brief, but too intense moment when his lips had descended to hers, the last thing she needed to do was spend time in his company. She forced another smile to her lips, willing herself to accept this unwanted kindness on his part.

Why had she met this man now? A thousand years ago, a lifetime ago, she might have been able to trust him. He was the kind of man who urged trust, commanded respect. She sighed inwardly. He appeared so open, so genuine, yet she knew all too well how deceiving appearances could be.

"Your papers, *pazhaluista*," the receptionist asked Jon. He handed over his diplomatic card and suffered the close examination with a slight smile. He gave his reason for the visit as "American Embassy escort."

Alex studied his profile as he pocketed his identity card. The very quality that invited trust was the single most threatening thing about him, she thought. That and the attraction she felt for him, an indefinable chord of affinity, as if they had been born to match harmony to melody.

"Ready?" he asked, reaching for her arm.

Never, she thought, rejecting maybes. "Yes," she answered aloud. Together they walked the dark, empty hallways, their footsteps echoing hollowly. Alex thought her heart would probably sound the same. She looked away from him, unaccountably saddened.

They took the broad stairs of the old building, Jon gazing at the ornate decor with some interest. "I've never been in this building," he said, letting her lead the way. "It hasn't been renovated yet. Most of the others resemble army barracks." He pointed up at the high intricately designed ceiling.

Alex realized that his small talk had nothing to do with the architecture but was an attempt to set her at ease. Despite herself, she felt her heart warming toward him.

Another woman, wearing another tan, woolen hat, sitting behind another small table with a log book on top, took Alex's and Jon's names, papers and credentials, and soon escorted them into the minister's office.

Andre Makarov rose from behind his large wooden desk, hesitated for a brief moment on seeing that Alex was accompanied, then rushed Alex with the enthusiasm of a long-lost relative finding a cousin at a train station.

"Hello!" he called in English; then, switching to Russian, he repeated the greeting. *"Privyet,* Aleksandra Sergeyevna!"

Jon thought Andre Makarov looked like an American movie's portrayal of a Soviet official. The man stood some six feet tall—tall for a Soviet—had the broad shoulders of an athlete and the blond, smoothly combed hair of a forties' mobster.

Jon waited just inside the doorway as Makarov kissed Alex on both cheeks before waving her to one of two smallish teak chairs with green vinyl seats. He then extended his hand to Jon. "Welcome," he said in English, then repeated the phrase in Russian. *"Dobri pazhaulivats."*

Jon murmured the appropriate response, but he could discern no sign of welcome in Makarov's eyes. The man was displeased that Alex was escorted.

Alex performed the introductions, and Jon watched as Makarov's eyes grew even more wary.

"American Embassy doctor?" Makarov asked, sitting down. Jon heard the note of patronization in the minister's tone. Physicians in the Soviet Union were ranked just slightly above janitors. But American diplomats were all reputed to be wealthy, and that commanded serious respect on the part of most Soviets.

"New chairs?" Alex asked in Russian. Jon noted that she was careful to avoid the use of his name. She knew the man, so Jon knew that calling him Gospodin Makarov would have been an insult in the wake of their many years' acquaintance. And since she avoided his first name, Jon suspected she and Makarov had never progressed to the toast of friendship, a polite device that would have allowed them to call each other by their first names or nicknames. That left only the unwieldy patronymics, combining their first names with the gendered version of their fathers' first names.

Jon wondered how Alex would ask about the photographs. Bluntly? Or would she let Makarov bring them up?

"It has been a long time since we are of seeing you," Makarov said. Jon wondered if the English was for his benefit. He saw Alex frown slightly. He had already gathered, since she had spoken only Russian since they entered the room, that she preferred speaking Russian with Makarov. Jon could see why; her Russian was flawless, so there would be no possible chance of misunderstanding.

There was an almost palpable tension in the room, a feeling that many things were waiting in the wings. Jon turned a glance to Alex and was struck by her calm, unruffled appearance. She looked as though she attended such meetings daily, as if having photographs confiscated and being summoned to the Ministry of Culture were an ordinary occurrence. To his amusement, he felt a stab of pride in her.

Studying Makarov, Jon wondered if he were KGB, then wondered if it mattered. But the understated authority in the man did matter. He shifted position, and his eyes met Jon's. Makarov's lips smiled, but his eyes did not. His hands rested flat on his desk, as if telling Jon he had nothing up his sleeve—a notion that translated exactly from English to Russian.

Now that they were in Makarov's office, Alex was more grateful than she could have said for Jon's having come with her. Makarov was behaving in a very different manner than he normally did. The look in his eyes was cold, his gaze indirect.

They progressed slowly through the byways of polite Soviet conversation, the gradual lead-in chat-chat necessary prior to getting down to the business at hand.

Andre enquired after her health—a serious inquiry; Soviets were always serious when asking personal questions. She answered honestly and returned the question. He answered at some length about the cold he'd narrowly avoided and the drafty windows he would have to repair at his grandmother's summer dacha, a small cottagelike structure many Muscovites maintained in the country. He asked about her plane trip, and she answered less honestly, leaving out all mention of the now-missing photographs.

She asked about skating in Gorky Park, and he advised her on how best to rent a pair of skates. Alex was aware that Andre seldom glanced in Jon's direction, as if by ignoring him, he could ensure that Jon would not interfere in the conversation. For her part, she found Jon's solid form next to her as comforting as if he were holding her hand.

"It is best to be of going skating at night," Makarov said, his piercing eyes never leaving hers. "It is the most beautiful then. The air is being crisp and clean, and the paths are being lit with lantern light." He sighed heavily, and Alex tensed, knowing from his sigh that the moment of purpose had arrived.

"But you must be careful not to be of going alone down a dark path," he said softly; the words seemed ominous to Alex. "It may appear beautiful, but it could be deadly."

"I'll be careful," she said slowly, trying to ignore the double warning in his words. She drew a breath; two could play this game. "It's easier to be careful if one knows what obstacles are there."

"Ah," he said, the smile gone from his face, "but it is so difficult to be careful when one is following the trail of beauty."

Alex said nothing, feeling hemmed in by innuendo.

"We Soviets are proud of our beautiful things," he said reflectively.

"With good reason," Alex murmured diplomatically, cautiously.

"Yes," he said, nodding. "We like to keep them in the bosom of the Motherland."

If she had needed any confirmation regarding the status of the collection, she had it now. "That, too, is logical," she said. Her eyes met Jon's briefly. The warning in his eyes belied the calm on his face. She felt immeasurably stronger.

Makarov continued. "And we resist efforts to have these beautiful things removed from our great nation. It makes us feel...*ne-udobna,* how do you say that in English?"

"Not comfortable inside—more than uncomfortable...anxious, maybe," Alex translated, feeing more than a little uncomfortable herself. She smiled, hoping she was revealing none of her inner anxiety. "I hope you know me well enough by now to know that I'm not interested in purchasing anything the Soviet government wishes to remain in the Soviet Union," she said.

"Ah-h-h." His fingers drummed on his desk for a moment, once, twice, the third time, as if in decision. He pulled a file folder from a lower drawer, opened the cover and pulled out the confiscated photographs. He glanced up at her, a swift, hard look, one she'd never seen from him before. It spoke volumes, none of them good. "You were of carrying these with you?"

As she nodded, she could see Jon leaning forward slightly to see the photographs. Then he sat back, his expression a study in boredom. He hid a yawn with the tips of his fingers, his gesture clearly indicating he found the matter of little consequence. Again she was relieved that he'd joined her for the visit, as well as for the fact that he had alerted her the night before to the shady side of the situation.

"Yes, I had those photographs with me," she answered simply. She would have to wait and see what Andre said about them before elaborating. She could inadvertently implicate herself even more deeply than she already was.

"Yes," he repeated. "May I be of asking why, *dyevushka?*"

The use of the formal "girl" was enough to set Alex's internal alarm bells ringing; they had known each other too long for that title. "They were given to me by a man in Washington. I believe you have worked with him before . . . Hans Saalard?"

"Ah-h-h. Yes. Just so. I have met him many times before. Not a man, one would be of thinking, who would turn to the black market for pleasurable pursuits."

"No," Alex agreed. "I am sure he did nothing of the kind." Taking a deep breath, she continued. "You are saying these artifacts are being exported via the black market?"

Andre held up his hand. "You have seen them, yes?"

"Only the photographs," she said. "But I can assure you that Hans Saalard wouldn't have touched anything to do with the black market." She had her mouth open to add that she wouldn't, either, but Andre pounced on her words.

"But he is dead now, is he not?" Andre's eyes bored into hers. "So we will not be of knowing, will we?"

If Alex was surprised at Andre's knowledge of Saalard's death, she didn't dwell on it; she was more angry at the implied criticism. She had had enough of the parry and thrust. Jon's presence gave her the courage to voice some of her sense of outrage. "What's going on?" she asked, switching firmly to Russian. "What is this all about?"

Andre Makarov waved a hand at the photographs and donned an expression of surprised concern. "Nothing, we hope."

"If the Soviet government doesn't wish these pieces to be exported, I have no wish to acquire them."

"What—exactly—did Hans Saalard tell you about them?" he asked.

"Only that they were being sold to fund a new exchange program."

A smile of genuine amusement crossed Andre Makarov's face, and he spoke in English again. "And you were of believing this fantastic story?"

Alex felt cold. "I had no reason not to," she said. "Now I can see that he was told a lie."

"Ah, yes. And who told him this lie?" Andre asked.

Again Alex found herself grateful for Jon's company. She was unused to such attentiveness, though. It made her wonder what his expectations were. Meanwhile, as a diplomat, trained in the business at hand, he would know immediately how much to say, how much to hide. She didn't. She looked at him, and he nodded slowly.

"An employee at the American Embassy," Alex answered.

"Yes? And does this employee have a name?"

"Roger Copple," Jon answered for her. From Makarov's unblinking stare, she could see that Makarov already knew about Copple.

"So," Makarov said, leaning closer, his smile slipping from his lips, "the American Embassy is trying to sell precious Soviet art objects."

Jon snorted. The contemptuous sound expressed his reaction to such a crude attempt to twist words.

"Of course not," Alex countered in Russian. "I didn't say that." She was determined to keep her part of the dialogue in Russian; later, what she had said could not be misinterpreted.

With her hands clasped together in her lap, she told him what she knew. "Hans Saalard was contacted by Roger Copple, of the American Embassy in Moscow and told that the embassy was transacting the sale of these artifacts for the Soviets."

"He was contacted?" Makarov asked in obvious disbelief.

"Yes."

"But he is dead, yes?"

Alex nodded. It was obvious that he knew all this; why was he asking her about it? Unless he thought she knew more than she did? It seemed to confirm what Jon believed about the collection. Another suspicion began to dawn in Alex's mind.

Andre looked at her in some amusement. "A lot of people seem to be dying." He frowned suddenly. "What caused the death of this Copple?"

Jon rested his hands on his lap, loosely clasped. "He died of appendicitis," he said calmly, repeating the official embassy line.

"*Neuzheli?* Really?" Makarov's voice dripped with obvious disbelief.

"*Neuzheli,*" Jon answered coldly.

To Alex's surprise, Makarov laughed. "You are the physician," he said. "They would not have let us talk to him, anyway," Andre said, shrugging. "We have known about his activities on the black market for some time."

Deliberately, Alex used the patronymic. "Andre Nikolayevich, are these items officially restricted?" She pointed to the photographs.

"Oh, yes. Definitely." He folded the file closed and replaced it in the drawer. Alex shivered, hoping her candor had been appreciated, hoping it was enough to call a halt to any suspicion of her own involvement. And she hoped she had taken the conversation far enough away from Roger Copple's death that Makarov wouldn't pursue the subject any further.

Andre met Alex's gaze with a steady look. "The art objects in those photographs are among some of the most significant religious art in the U.S.S.R. today. The Armenians—and, indeed, all of the Soviet Union—would never allow them to leave the country."

The alarm bells that had run inside Alex earlier resumed their frantic peal. There were too many things wrong with Andre's statement: the items' religious significance, the Armenian involvement and something else, something Alex felt she should focus on, but couldn't.

The objects in the photographs were not particularly religious; it was a predominantly secular collection. And they were definitely not Armenian in origin. Andre Makarov was lying to her. And if he was lying about the objects, what else might he be lying about? And what was the elusive proof of his lies, the niggling, fluttering little thought on the edge of her mind? Something he had said? Something she had heard?

"I see," she said slowly, trying to draw the meeting to a conclusion. "Well, then, there is little reason for further discussion, is there?"

"It is always a pleasure to see you. I am sorry about this collection, of course. But perhaps, there will be other collections in the future." His tone was doubtful.

"I hope so," Alex said, rising. The something in her mind pressed for release. She drew a breath. "Such lovely things should be out for everyone to see."

Andre Makarov blanched. There was no mistaking the horror on his face at her notion. Alex felt a shaft of fear strike at her heart. She didn't dare look at Jon. He had been right. Oh, dear God, Jon had been right. The items were *hot* hot.

"There are many fine things on display at the Hermitage now," Makarov said smoothly, the color slowly returning to his face.

"But none like these," she stressed, trying to focus on what her subconscious was trying to tell her.

He smiled faintly.

"I wonder," she said as artlessly as she could, "would it be possible to at least see the artwork before I leave the Soviet Union? I assume you have it in your hands?"

When Andre Makarov said nothing, raising one hand in an almost helpless gesture, Alex shook her head. When Jon spoke, Alex realized he had reached the same conclusion she had, only quicker. "You don't know where they are, do you?" he asked softly. "You don't know where the artifacts are."

Makarov was under control almost immediately, the mantle of his position securely draped around him. "This is a difficult job. And I am much afraid you are mistaken about the seriousness of such a crime against the Soviet Union. If you are aware of anything regarding this collection, it would be wise to speak now."

"I know nothing except what I have told you," Alex answered. She wasn't exactly lying; supposition about the artifacts' potential danger wasn't *knowing*.

Andre stepped from behind his desk and opened the door for his guests. "Should you hear of anything else concerning the artifacts, I would ask that you report it to this office, please."

Alex bowed her head and passed through the door.

"Aleksandra Sergeyevna," Makarov said, detaining her. She turned, frowning slightly at the bad luck of talking over the threshold. "I have been meaning to ask you, how is your good aunt?"

Alex stiffened. Her great-aunt, sister of her mother's mother, still lived in the Soviet Union in a small village north of Riga in Latvia. To her certain knowledge, she and Andre Makarov had never spoken of the old woman. "She is in fine health," she answered coldly.

"That is good," he said with deadpan sincerity. Alex subdued a shudder. "Let us hope she continues to enjoy her years."

"Yes, let's," Alex said, dryly, hating him at that moment. Hating him for the thinly-veiled threat: leave this matter or your aunt's health will suffer. She had to look away from him lest he see the anger in her eyes. Her eyes met Jon's, and she could read a corresponding anger in his. With a dim shock, she realized his anger was not just for her feelings, it was broader than that. His was a seething hatred for Makarov's implied threat of harm to an old woman, a gut reaction of disgust at man's inhumanity to man.

And for some reason, perhaps because his reaction was not based solely on thoughts of her feelings, she found herself trusting that anger. In his anger, at least, he was a man of total integrity, a man whose compassion would require him to do the honorable thing. Her own anger ebbed as she allowed him to carry the weight of it.

"You will be leaving soon, then?" Makarov asked, stepping over the threshold.

"Fairly soon, yes," Alex said, retrieving her coat and hat.

He opened the outer door and held out his hand. "And I hope you will come back and visit with me," he said.

With reluctance, she shook the outstretched hand. "I will, thank you."

"And remember what I said about skating in Gorky Park."

The trail of beauty. "I will," she said wryly.

"And you will contact me immediately if anyone else should offer you precious religious art objects?"

"Of course," Alex said. With the door inches away, with Jon beside her, this was the opportunity to point out the discrepancies in his statements regarding the collection. "Especially if the objects are from Armenia. You did say that's where these came from?" She gave his hand a final pump, but did not release it. If he lied now, she would know it. In Western culture, it was considered difficult to lie while meeting another's eye. In Russia, it was considered impossible to lie while touching another.

Andre blinked at her, then looked down at their still-clasped hands. He released hers quickly. "Please be careful, Aleksandra Sergeyevna."

Alex smiled grimly. "I know," she said. "There are many dark paths."

He smiled, and to Alex's surprise, the smile seemed more wistful than ominous. "More than you can imagine."

"Settle down, Jon. You know we don't have a shred of proof that he died of radiation poisoning." Ned Sternberg's words echoed in the soundproof secured room.

"Come off it. What more proof do you want? His hair was falling out, he had sores all over his body, his liver failed, his white blood cell count was off the charts, his—"

"Could it have been AIDS?" the CIA chief interrupted calmly.

"What?" Jon asked blankly.

"I understand the symptoms are very similar."

"Oh, Lord, Ned!"

"Now, Jon, don't get excited. I was only offering it as a possibility."

"An *impossibility,* you mean. The white blood cell count drops in AIDS. That's the whole point of the disease. Copple's went sky high." Jon ran a hand through his hair and looked around the strange plastic room high in the embassy. It had been Ned Sternberg's suggestion that they discuss the Copple case in a totally secure room. It was bug-proof, surveillance-proof and smelled of cleaning fluid. He could see through the clear walls to the dingy structure of the old American Embassy building beyond. Lining the bubblelike structure were stacks of cardboard boxes, abandoned furniture and probably thousands of rubles' worth of Soviet electronic devices.

Finally Jon asked slowly, "Why is the embassy so intent on covering this up?" He thought of Alex, of her trembling hand in his as he had ushered her into the taxi. He thought of how troubled she'd looked the night before when he'd implied she was neck-deep in smuggling artwork. If there were less covering-up, she needn't be troubled.

Ned's friendly expression never wavered, but Jon had the distinct impression that the man behind the face had hardened. "Jon, if this episode should leak to the press—"

"It should!" Jon snapped. "Before someone else dies!"

"Think, Jon. We know Copple was dealing on the black market. He'd already been threatened with expulsion as it was. Yet he continued."

"And what he got his hands on—"

"Is irrelevant, from our standpoint. The Soviets were already breathing down our necks after Copple. He was an embarrassment to both sides." Ned raised his hand to prevent further interruptions from Jon. "He also worked in communications. He was the most likely candidate for heavy bombardment of microwave radiation."

"Well, isn't that enough to blow this whole thing wide open?" Jon asked, rising. There was no room to pace in the small space, and his head brushed the ceiling. He sat back down.

"Come off it, now, Jon. You know we can't do that."

"We've protested microwave bombardment in the past."

"That's right. But this time, it's not just a matter of not being sure—" he quirked a smile at Jon and nodded "—one-hundred-percent sure that's how Copple died. How much did we fill you in when you arrived at post?"

"About the microwaves?" Jon asked. At Ned's nod, he sighed. "The usual. I am the doctor, after all."

"I didn't think we'd told you much. Well, here it is. It isn't something we want to get out."

"Be careful, Ned. I may just run right out and tell the first reporter I see."

Ned Sternberg chuckled, but the sound didn't deceive Jon. The bureau chief was not amused. "The microwave radiation is a blocking device."

"What?"

"The Soviets are using microwaves to block *our* surveillance."

A twisted expression formed on Jon's face. He felt it. It was combined of a bad taste and bitter memories. "So we're doing it to ourselves."

"If you want to look at it that way, yes, in essence."

Jon looked at Ned as if he'd never seen him before. "Have you explained this—in essence—to the women who had miscarriages?"

Ned shook his head. "Come down from your white charger, Jon. What good would it serve to add to their tragedy? And there's no proof the miscarriages were caused by microwave bombardment."

"No? Statistics alone say it loudly enough. The microwave bombardment began in what—seventy-six? Seventy-seven?"

"In seventy-five."

"Whatever. I'm willing to bet you every cent I have that since that time, at least one American woman per year has miscarried."

"This is getting us nowhere."

"Maybe to you it isn't. But the facts are a little too obvious for my blood. First you cover up the fact that it's our own damn fault the embassy is being slammed with enough radiation to scramble eggs, then you want to cover up the fact that Roger Copple got his hands on something so hot, it literally burned him up."

"You're stretching, Jon."

"You're evading, Ned."

"What makes you so certain Copple was peddling something radioactive?"

"Common sense," Jon answered promptly. "He had classic radiation-burn marks around his hands and chest. His body carried every symptom—"

"Yes, but—"

"—and Alex Shashkevich says the objects she was offered—through Roger Copple, remember?—weren't Armenian, but Ukrainian."

"Oh, so you've discussed the matter with Ms. Shashkevich. How much did you tell her?"

Jon hesitated, thinking not of Roger Copple nor the collection of artifacts, but of Alex. Of the things he had told her. In her eyes, he saw the universe, an infinite array of splendor. There was so much about her that was fine, graceful. His mother would have called her an old soul. His mind flashed to the midnight walk and his own long tale of woe. He had seen the tears standing frozen on her cheeks, had seen the empathy in her eyes. And something more. He'd seen a shocking vulnerability, a yearning. It was as if another Alex were trapped inside of her, an Alex too frightened to do more than peek through tear-filled eyes. The impression had fled almost as soon as it had come, but it had made Jon conscious of a desire to coax that other Alex to come out, and, once free, to protect her.

He saw her serious contemplation of Andre Makarov's words, her spark of anger at the implication in the man's question about her aunt. And he'd seen the gratitude in her blue eyes when he'd supplied the information about Copple. But most of all, he clung to the light that had come into her eyes when he'd first stood by her side in the Ministry of Culture.

Ned Sternberg was waiting for an answer. Should he tell Ned about the visit with Makarov? "I asked her about the collection's origin."

The need to tell him about the meeting faded with the chief's next words. "You're thinking Chernobyl," Ned said heavily.

Even knowing Ned, the man's lightning-quick assessment was impressive. "Exactly," Jon answered.

"Impossible."

"Why?"

"Tell me how black marketeers would get their hands on stuff from Chernobyl? It was thoroughly cordoned off immediately after the disaster. Whatever was there is long buried."

"Who cares *how* they did, they *did!* Isn't that enough?"

"Yes. It's enough." Ned leaned forward, the smile gone from his face, his blue eyes twin chips of ice. "It's enough if you want to fly off half-cocked and create an international incident. It's enough if you want to find yourself persona non grata to both the U.S.S.R. and the embassy. It's enough if you want to wind up with that scrambled egg you were talking about all over your face."

Jon leaned back in his chair. He felt both cold and hot, both angry and amused. Persona non grata was embassy slang for being kicked out of the country. It meant going home with his tail neatly tucked between his legs, his career in tatters.

"Your threat is well taken," Jon said slowly.

"Jon, don't think I don't care. Expulsion isn't a pretty thought. But you need to think about this thing logically. Let my team do their thing."

"I take care of the sick, you take care of the subterfuge?"

Ned's eyes narrowed; then he smiled. "A little rough, maybe, but accurate."

"It just so happens that one of my sick coincides with some of your cloak-and-daggering."

"That's only supposition, Jon."

"Do me a favor, then."

"I'll try," Ned temporized.

"Start an investigation—as discreetly as you like—but start looking for this damned art collection." At Ned's frown, Jon lightly slapped the table. "You can do it. Or let me put it another way, since we're into exchanging friendly threats, do it or—"

"Or what, Jon? You'll sing? You'll go ahead and make a mountain out of this molehill of yours? You'll accuse the Soviet government of having lied about sealing off Chernobyl?"

"Ned, you didn't see how Copple looked at the end. We can't afford to let anyone else come in contact with whatever he did." A horrible thought struck him. Copple's girlfriend, Nancy Abernathy, had showed a high white-blood-cell count. And he hadn't seen her in a few days. "Ned, what about—"

Ned Sternberg sighed and suddenly looked his sixty-three years. He held up his hand. "All right. All right, we'll sweep for radiation." He stood, punched out the proper code sequence on the door and pulled the plastic door inward. Then he pressed the next sequence and pushed the heavy metal door outward. He stepped down the three short steps, turned back and met Jon's eyes. "But if we don't find anything, you owe me a kilo of caviar. Beluga."

"You're on," Jon said promptly, following Ned. He absently shut the doors behind him and heard the locks engage. "And if you do find something?"

Ned sighed again and walked down the narrow corridor leading to the next set of locked doors. Here he would knock and a Marine guard would allow them to exit. He rapped on the heavy door and turned to Jon. "If we do find something?" The door began its ponderous swing outward. "Then, may God help us all."

"Sir?" the young Marine asked.

"Nothing, Terry," Ned said. "Let's hope it's nothing at all."

Ned Sternberg was on the telephone when Alex arrived in his outer office. The secretary directed her to a chair, buzzed her boss and went back to her filing. Alex waited, surveying the small reception area, trying not to eavesdrop on Sternberg's conversation. That was more difficult than she would have imagined, for Sternberg was speaking near-perfect Russian and talking about Chernobyl. He asked several questions, all relating to the effects of radiation. He queried the person on the other end of the line about first-encounter burns, secondary contact and finally, long-term effects.

She hid any knowledge that she had heard anything, merely rising when he came through the office door calling his secretary's name.

If Alex had a difficult time hiding her thoughts, Ned Sternberg had no such problems. Although his eyebrows lifted slightly, his face was impassively pleasant.

"I knew someone was waiting for me, but I didn't realize it was you, my dear," he said. "Won't you come in? Sally, bring us some coffee, please—or would you rather have a soda?"

"Nothing, thank you," Alex said, smiling at the secretary.

"Never mind, then, Sally," Ned said, escorting Alex through the door and closing it behind him. He, like Makarov, waved her to a chair in front of his desk. The only difference in the chairs was that Sternberg's seats were covered in a rough woven fabric.

Ned asked her if she had enjoyed the party the night before. She asked him how long he'd been at post. He commented on her perfume and said he wished he were younger. If the smile accompanying his words had reached his eyes, she might have believed him.

Unlike Andre Makarov's conversational finesse, Ned cut through the polite chatter with the sure stroke of a surgeon wielding a scalpel.

"I have a few questions to ask you about those photographs you say the Soviets confiscated from you yesterday," he said.

Alex smiled grimly; this interview was taking on the resonance of the one she had just had with Andre Makarov. Only this time Jon wasn't with her. That she wanted him there came as a distinct surprise.

She shook her head, as much to clear it from thoughts of Jon as to contradict Ned Sternberg's misconception. "You can certainly ask any questions you'd like, but I want to correct something first."

"What's that?"

"I didn't just *say* the photographs were confiscated. They *were* confiscated. And Andre Makarov of the Ministry of Culture has them now."

"And how do you know this, Alex?"

"I saw them there this morning. He showed them to me."

Ned frowned. "And why did he do that?"

"I think for two reasons—one, to let me know he had them, and two, to warn me not to try any more to purchase the items." She wondered if she should mention that Jon had been with her.

Ned leaned back in his chair and twirled a pencil in his fingers. "How did he warn you about this?" he asked.

"It's rather complicated, but essentially, he was speaking of ice-skating and advised me that going down dark paths after beautiful things could be dangerous to my health."

A brief smiled flitted across Ned's face. "You're a remarkable young woman, Alex."

Alex lowered her eyes for a moment; his statement was just that—a statement. It neither hinted at approbation nor did it condemn. She raised her eyes and met his squarely. "Are you going to warn me about dark paths, too?"

Ned laughed as if he couldn't help it. For the first time amusement touched his eyes. "I was," he admitted. "I was certainly going to do just that. Perhaps not quite as poetically."

Alex relaxed somewhat. "But now?"

"Now I think I'd better enlist your aid."

"Enlist away," she said softly. "But I have to warn you, I've resisted recruitment opportunities before."

He smiled. "I'm sure that no recruiting officer in his right mind would have allowed someone like you, with your talent, brains and ability to speak Russian—not to mention your open-ended visa—to pass by unnoticed.''

Alex realized she'd been premature to relax. There was a message behind his words: we know all about you. She resented the knowledge, distrusted the implication. There had been a note in his voice that implied that she'd been passed over deliberately, that in some file in Langley, Virginia, her name was red flagged, her loyalty suspect.

Her jaw tightened.

''Why have you avoided recruitment?'' he asked, his tone pleasant but the smile absent from his lips, gone from his eyes.

Alex considered possible answers, then responded truthfully, not being particularly careful to withhold the disdain from her voice. ''I'm not very political. I prefer the world of art. In that world, what you see is literally what you get. Politics has too much gray for my taste.''

Her honesty didn't sit well with Ned Sternberg. He leaned forward. ''Your background is unusual.''

Alex waited.

He cocked his head and pursed his lips. ''Let's see, your parents are Soviet, correct?''

''Second generation,'' she said, then added, ''And they do not subscribe to communism.''

He smiled. ''And you travel back and forth to the Soviet Union frequently.''

She nodded, feeling the dislike of him uncoil in her. She felt as if they were playing strip poker and he held all the aces.

''And you are single,'' he said.

Alex sighed. She knew that to this man's mind, the fact that she was single implied that she was susceptible to sexual coercion, sexual blackmail. James had told her once that it was common knowledge that the desire for love often overcame the desire for patriotism. She shook her head, hating the implications, despising the notion. ''Yes,'' she said, letting the word express her weariness with his tactics.

But Ned Sternberg wasn't finished driving the point home. "And you have an aunt living in the Soviet Union, isn't that right?"

It was the final straw. If his intention in reciting her background had been to make her feel vulnerable, frightened of his omnipotence, he was far afield. She had been more afraid, more vulnerable, the night before, listening to Jon's story, wanting to tell him hers, than she would ever be to such heavy-handed tactics as this. She almost laughed.

"That's odd," she said coldly, and he frowned. "That's the second time this morning someone has asked me about my aunt."

"Andre Makarov?" Ned asked.

"Yes. And I didn't much care for it then, either." She didn't bother to hide her anger. Coming from a family whose escape had involved the sacrifices of leaving their homeland and relatives, whose entire departure had been necessitated by betrayal, she felt the weight of centuries, the mantle of familial protection, descend upon her shoulders.

He nodded, as if he were reading her mind. Perhaps, she thought, having made his point, he was satisfied. Whatever his reason, he changed the subject. "Jon Wyndham tells me you think these mysterious objects come from Chernobyl," he said.

Again Alex felt this interview was like the one with Makarov; she was being deliberately left in the dark to try to find ways to combat misconstrued words, surmises offered as fact. "Did he say that exactly?"

Ned smiled and lifted a finger in acknowledgement. "Well, no," he said. "I believe he said the Ukraine."

Alex nodded. She wouldn't play the game. He would have to spell out what he was after; then she would either correct him or cast doubt.

Ned sighed. "And *is* the collection from the Ukraine?"

Alex shrugged. "I'd have to see the objects to be positive.... Their markings are unusual, old enough to appear Armenian, but of a style more consistent with Ukrainian traditions."

"They could be from Kiev?"

"They could be from any number of villages in the Ukraine. The Ukraine is quite large, you know. It's roughly the size of Texas."

Ned nodded; then, not looking at her, he asked, "Did Jon talk to you about Roger Copple?"

Reminding herself that it was Jon who had advised her to tell the authorities everything she knew, she hesitated only a fraction of a second before replying. "Yes." Jon hadn't urged her to tell everything she *thought*, however, so she didn't elaborate.

"And what did he say?"

For some reason Alex was unable to fathom at the moment, perhaps due to her anger at Ned's callous recitation of her background, and still feeling puzzled by the gloves-off routine he was using with her, she wasn't going to offer Jon Wyndham up on the proverbial platter to this American official. It might be better to assume Jon had just told her the official line.

"He said Copple died of appendicitis," she answered, then took the offensive. "Why? Didn't he?"

Ned assumed a visage of surprised innocence and promptly lied to her. "Yes, of course. He died of appendicitis."

The uncomfortable thought crossed her mind that Jon Wyndham might have been the one who had lied to her. Her heart wrenched painfully while her mind called up his image, and her soul searched that image for the honesty, the kindness she had seen there. It *had* been there, hadn't it? She hadn't allowed herself to fall into the trap of trusting her unreliable instincts again, had she?

Ned, as if sensing her sudden doubt, tried to add to it. "Jon is fairly new here. He has a tendency to see a conspiracy under every fur hat." He chuckled.

"Oh?" Alex murmured noncommittally. She laid her palms flat against her thighs lest her fingers curl, clawlike. Ned's attempt to discredit Jon produced exactly the opposite reaction in Alex. Her heartbeat steadied. And she couldn't help but wonder why it had mattered so much.

Ned waved his hand, as if one hint had been enough. It had, she thought grimly. "That's not why I asked, my dear. I was curious to know if Jon mentioned anything about Roger's . . . er, extracurricular activities?"

She remembered lashing out at Jon for his inadvertent assumption that she knew about Copple's actions. "Andre Makarov made it fairly plain," Alex said, deliberately excluding Jon's name from the conversation. "I understand that your Mr. Copple was a player on the black market."

"You must see our position, then," he said. His smile was deprecatory.

Alex didn't know what position he was referring to, so she kept silent. Her stomach was knotted with ten kinds of emotion, not one of them pleasurable.

"I don't see that there's much more we can do about your confiscated photographs, Alex," he elaborated. "Considering where they originated."

She waved her hand, as if the matter were long past. Andre Makarov had the photographs, and it was only assumption that they had originated with Copple.

"Unless you'd like us to lodge a formal complaint?"

Alex drew a shallow breath. "No, if the items are black market, I don't want them, anyway," she said, then added, "as I told Mr. Makarov."

"Of course not," Ned said quickly. He rose from his chair and came around his desk, then held out his hand and drew Alex to her feet. She looked him square in the eye.

He led her to the door and opened it. She passed through; he remained inside. "Besides," he said from the other side of the threshold, causing a shiver to run through Alex's body, "with the exception of yourself, everyone connected with this collection is . . . dead."

She drew a sharp breath, her stomach constricting. Was there a threat in his words? Or was it just the truth of them suddenly striking home?

"Miss Shashkevich?" the secretary asked, stepping from around her desk. "I have a message for you." She handed Alex a standard phone-message form. "Dr. Wyndham is waiting for you downstairs."

Alex took the simple form with Jon's name and extension number on it, stared at it stupidly for several seconds, then slowly folded it. Her hands, she saw with a detachment she was far from feeling, were quite steady.

Why was he waiting for her? Her rapidly beating heart supplied one possible answer, while her mind rejected it out of hand. She turned to bid a farewell to Ned Sternberg. He wasn't looking at her, but rather at the note she held in her hand, a speculative expression on his solemn face.

He met her gaze. "Do be careful, my dear," he said softly.

Of what? she wanted to ask. Of dark paths or of Jon Wyndham?

Ned smiled then, opening the outer door. He waited until she had walked through. "The price in trusting the wrong people is very high," he said.

Alex schooled her features to reflect a polite question, though his words had cut with deadly accuracy. The Foreign Service was small, so he undoubtedly knew Tony Hamilton. Which meant that he knew about her, *all* about her.

"I'd hate to see you hurt," he said, and unexpectedly, his eyes softened, revealing a tinge of sympathy. He gave a half wave and shut the door.

Alex stared at the closed door for a few seconds, her thoughts skittering in a thousand different directions. Oddly, it was Sternberg's warning about the high price of trust that stuck in her mind.

No one knew that more than she. She had trusted her parents, and both of them had let her down. She had trusted Tony. And, once upon a time, she had trusted herself.

But that had been long ago. This was now, and Jon Wyndham was waiting for her downstairs. Alex sighed, wishing, with a piercing longing, that she could trust what she felt about *him*.

But she didn't dare. Did she?

Chapter 5

Alex's heart jerked once, painfully, as she stepped past the Marine guard. Jon was just beyond the central fourth-floor desk, sitting on the low sofa near the door. He was reading something attached to a clipboard. He wore thin, wire-framed half glasses.

Walking slowly, glad for an opportunity to study him without his being aware of her, she wondered at the rush of genuine pleasure she felt on seeing him. She thought he looked tired, but the impression could have been heightened by his white lab coat. And it could have been the lighting; everyone she'd met inside the embassy looked tired, even the eighteen-year-old Marines.

"Jon?" she asked softly. He looked up quickly, a light springing into his eyes. The impression she'd had of his being tired disappeared. A soft smile curved his full lips, and he disposed of his glasses, folding them carefully before tucking them in his breast pocket.

He rose, slipping the clipboard beneath one arm, the other reaching toward her. With no hesitation this time, she placed her hand in his. The sense of electrical current running between them was in no way lessened by continued contact, she noted. The thought both pleased and disturbed her.

"Finished already?" he asked, letting her know that he knew what she'd been through with Ned Sternberg. "Feel like some fresh air?"

She hesitated. She wanted fresh air—needed it, in fact. But she'd already lived through two tense meetings this morning; a walk with Dr. Jon Wyndham was unlikely to be anything but more of the same, albeit for different reasons.

"Just lunch?" he pursued.

"Excuse me, ma'am. Can you sign out, please?" the Marine guard behind the tall, imposing desk asked.

Relieved to have an excuse for delaying her answer, Alex took her time signing her name while quickly weighing the pros and cons of spending more time in Jon Wyndham's company. Everything in her urged her to accept his invitation and, perversely, it was this that almost made her say no. It came down to not being able to trust her own instincts. Every time she did, she was hurt. Therefore, logically, if she instinctively wanted to be in Jon's company, he should be suspect.

Knowing this, however, should be enough to help her guard against anything he might say or do to undermine her resolve to steer clear of any involvement with him. And, she thought with a tinge of shock, she simply wanted to be with him.

She turned back to Jon with a slight smile. It was one thing to argue with herself in logical fashion. It was an altogether different matter even trying to think while he stood smiling down at her.

Trust me, his smile said.

Perhaps for the moment, her reserve answered.

"Ready?" he asked.

"Yes," she lied.

He smiled, as if he knew she had been wrestling with herself, then took her hand and led her onto the elevator. As confined as the small square box was, he might as well have pulled her into his arms. The sudden drop in her stomach had little to do with the drop in floors.

She could almost feel his thoughts, as well as the heat emanating from him. She wouldn't meet his eyes, afraid that rather than a closed-door sign, he would read other things, things he made her feel, things she didn't want to feel again.

"You're not claustrophobic, are you?" he asked.

Her eyes met his, and he smiled slowly, a gentle smile, as if he'd been reading her mind and knew the turmoil raging within her. He had no idea, she thought, how that smile weakened her determination. She looked down at her hands.

"You look as though you've been reading my mind," he said, making her heart jump. "What did you see there?"

She shook her head. "Not in my repertoire, I'm afraid."

"Oh, I think it probably is."

She smiled somewhat bitterly. "If I had been a mind reader, I never would have gotten into half the things I have."

"Like your marriage, for instance?" he asked.

The elevator doors opened and Alex swiftly exited the too-small space, using the people waiting for their turn as an excuse not to answer.

"You're not going to answer my question, are you?" Jon asked, leading the way down a dim hall and up a narrow flight of stairs.

"What question?" she asked, turning an innocent face in his direction.

He pushed open the door to the clinic. "It'll keep," he said.

No smile curved his lips now and his voice carried the cadence of a vow.

Jon quickly changed from his lab coat to the hunting jacket he'd worn the night before. She remarked on the lack of a hat, and he grinned.

"It's American machismo. We men from the States like to pretend we're strong enough not to feel the cold. Soviet men do it, too, if you notice. They never lower their ear flaps."

Alex laughed, and together they departed the embassy for the busy Chaykovskova Street. They followed the curved highway, crossed under the tunnel and took the Krasno-presnenskaya metro route one stop to the old section of the city, an area known to dissidents, artists and philosophers, Arbat.

They talked easily on the way, another disarming sensation, Alex thought. It made her feel as if she were teetering on the edge of a trap, as if the ease with which they talked was only an interlude, and soon the probing questions would begin anew.

Jon asked her if she'd known the Arbat quarter before the recent Gorbachev reforms, and Alex nodded. "Yes, of course. It was my favorite area."

"And what do you think of it now?"

"It looks like a mall," she said, pointing out the blocked entrances to the streets, the new brick walkways, the small, still-leafless plants. "But it's still Arbat, home of writers and bookstores."

"And the odd restaurant," he said, leading her inside a noisy, crowded *pivliki*—shrimp—pub. The smell of dark beer and heavily-spiced steamed shrimp assaulted them, as did the roar of the crowd. Shrimp shells crunched beneath their boots. The warmth and camaraderie were palpable.

"You're the first person I've ever met at the embassy who would go inside one of these places," Alex called over the noise. For a moment, perhaps because of the cold wind escorting them into the room or, more likely, because of her English, the roar subsided. Dark, curious eyes turned toward them. One bundled-up woman nudged a man next to her, and they shifted around their small chest-high platform.

"Pazhaluista," the woman said shyly, nodding to the empty space at their already-crowded stand. The man added his voice to the invitation.

Jon said their thanks and led Alex to the cramped space. Shoulders brushing shoulders, legs pressed tightly against legs, the crowd inched sideways to allow them room to pass.

A few called greetings in beery, friendly voices; others made lewd comments about Alex's potential prowess in bed. Several speculated on the anatomical difference between Soviet and American males, tossing ruble notes onto the already littered tables.

The woman who had signaled them again nudged the man and spoke in his ear. He bellowed for the waiter to bring more shrimp and beer for the strangers.

"For us all," Jon yelled as the man's voice died. Alex raised an eyebrow. He had offered to buy for the entire table. Apparently he knew it, for he set down a stack of rubles. "If you will permit us?" he asked the group.

The man who had made room nodded and smiled. He appeared as shy as the woman. The woman hid her face in her hands and giggled.

"You speak Russian very well," Alex said softly to Jon, while the woman across from her whispered in the man's ear.

"Foreign Service Institute in Rosslyn," Jon replied.

"Still," Alex persisted, "you have the accent and the grammar. That's amazing, from just a course."

"It's a fairly intensive course," Jon said with a broad smile. "And I was in Yugoslavia for three years. Serbo-Croatian and Russian are similar. And you? Do you speak other languages besides Russian and English?"

Alex nodded, grinned ruefully and waggled her hand in the so-so gesture.

"From your travels abroad? Or from your earlier days? I understand your ex-husband was a diplomat . . . ?"

Alex was grateful for the blast of cold air that accompanied the front doors opening. She didn't answer, turning with the rest of the room to look at the source of the chill. A man hesitated in the doorway. He was larger than most Soviet men, filling the doorframe with his bulk. His eyebrows matched his dark coat and dark fur hat. His hands were clad in the half gloves common to soldiers and frontiersmen—and modern punk rockers. As before, when she and Jon had first entered, the room grew quiet, all eyes on the newcomer. Then he raised his arm and called to someone in the back. Noise, laughter and people's bodies soon swallowed him as if the brief silence had never been.

The shy woman lightly touched Alex's arm, and the stream of questions flooding from the rest of the group took up the remaining portion of the convivial meal. Where are you from? Why are you here? Where did you buy that coat? Are you rich? Have you any family? Where did you learn your Russian? Do you like Moscow? Do you like President Bush? Have you seen Gorky Park? Did you like the music there? Have you ridden the metro? Have you seen the new improvements in the city? Have you ever been to Sokolniki? Do you like Palekh boxes? Will you still be here for Easter? It is too bad that they will not be selling Ukrainian Easter eggs for some time to come. Have you ever seen them?

And on and on, over the smell of spiced shrimp, the steadily rising sound of laughter and the sound of a hundred heavy beer bottles clinking against tall, thick mugs. To the floor fell the shells, as was customary; to the waiter went the rubles, the glasses for refills and the scanty—except in Jon's case—gratuity.

Back outside, the air was fresh and to Alex, it seemed brighter and cleaner than it ever had before. After the sharp tang of spices and beer in the *pivliki* hall, the cold air was a relief. Breathing deeply, thoroughly relaxed, smiling broadly, she turned to Jon.

"That was wonderful," she said. "I haven't been in an old-fashioned Russian beer hall in years. Lifetimes. It brought back a thousand memories."

Jon looked at her curiously for a moment, his hand covering the small one clutching his sleeve. "You really love it here, don't you?"

Alex, warmed by the beer and the camaraderie, and forgetful of her resolve to stay aloof, smiled and pushed the hair from her face. She linked her hand through his arm and led him across the main street of the Arbat section. "Oh, yes," she answered finally. "But when I'm in Israel, I like it just as well. And there's a little island off Greece . . ." She sighed happily. "They're all home, and they're all beautiful. I'm a hopeless wanderer."

Jon was silent long enough that she paused and looked up at him. He was studying her intently.

Instantly, she grappled for her ever-present guard. Treat it lightly, she cautioned herself. "What?" she asked. "Do I have shrimp on my face?"

He smiled, but he didn't laugh. Had he read something in her tone, in her smile, that let him hope for something that could never be? "No. You look beautiful." His smile faded. "Very beautiful."

His words had been a caress, and her heart had responded to them. He wasn't flirting; his words had held a note of deep sincerity. *No,* she thought. He was too dangerous.

"Don't close up on me," he said softly, taking her hand again and linking it through his arm. "Every time I start to break through that shell of yours, you don a new one."

"You should quit trying to break through, then," she said, and wondered why she hoped he wouldn't listen to her.

"I've never been too crazy about enigmas," he said, unknowingly pricking her heart. "But something about you makes me want to keep trying."

She looked away quickly, lest he see the unconscious longing in her eyes. If she weren't careful, this man would storm the castle of her heart and take the vulnerable part of her as prisoner. And then what would she be left with? More pain? Another trip down the disillusionment road? She had survived other trips, but she had a vague suspicion that this one would be different . . . a pain too intense to be endured.

But why did he make her want to believe that the light she saw in his eyes was the light of hope?

He pulled her arm tighter against his body. "I'm going to kiss you, Alex."

Her heart skipped a beat. She felt as if her senses were at war as she both leaned forward and tried stepping back at the same time. "Soviets never kiss in public," she said through suddenly dry lips. She was finding it difficult to draw air.

"I'm not a Soviet," he said softly. "And neither are you." His free hand pulled her around to face him. Slowly, as if telling her that he would take his time but brook no refusal, he lowered his cold lips to hers.

Knowing how his lips felt against hers didn't make Alex want Jon less. If anything, this second kiss, tasting of paprika and dark beer, only deepened her desire to know him, weakened her resolve to run from these new sensations. The gentle, soft, questing inspired a liquid softness in her, a warming that she'd never encountered before.

Just as slowly, he raised his head. His eyes were cloudy, bemused. His breathing was irregular and his hand, as it lightly stroked her hair, was trembling. Somehow the intensity of his reaction to her wrenched her more than his kiss.

"Dyevushka," a grandmother said from Alex's elbow, "it is not permitted to have public display of affection."

"I told you," Alex said, all too aware of the breathless note in her voice.

"It was worth it," Jon responded. He turned to the militant babushka and said in extremely broken Russian, "I am so sorry. I not speaking language. You speak Chinese?"

Alex sputtered with laughter, which she only just managed to turn into a cough. The grandmother glared at her for a moment, before spying another person breaking another unwritten rule. *"Dyevushka,"* she called as she moved away, "it is not permitted to be feeding the baby ice cream. It will give him a sore throat."

Alex met Jon's amused gaze. She shook her head. "You are—"

"Irresistible," he supplied. "I know." He sighed heavily. "It's a curse."

Alex couldn't help but chuckle at the long-suffering expression on his face. But behind it, lurking in his eyes, she sensed that he had been as shaken by that kiss as she had.

"Under my spell, yet?" Despite the jesting note, his eyes were as warm as ever, almost as if he were deliberately making things light to smooth over the moment, as if he were giving her time to get her bearings back. Time to don another shell.

Grateful, Alex pulled ahead of him, breaking the mood, and led them across the street. Once on the other side, she turned to look back at the young woman who had been feeding the baby ice cream. A crowd of five or six babushkas had gathered around her, each with an ailment brought on by ice cream, each with a personal story of the ills of ice cream feeding, all with censure on their lined faces.

"Of all the things about living here, it isn't the bugging devices, the tailing or the constant sense of being watched that would bother me—"

"Finally," he interrupted, "I meet an exhibitionist."

Alex choked on a laugh, but continued as if he hadn't said anything, "—It's the millions of unwritten rules, governed by the babushkas. Elevator rules, standing-in-line rules, how to test the bread rules, how many buttons you can leave unfastened, whether you can or can't clap at a performance— and then, how to clap properly."

"Use the back of the spoon, top button closed, clap in rhythm with everyone else? Those?"

"Precisely. And never face the baby carriage forward when entering or exiting an elevator—rule fourteen. And it is not permitted to take the baby into a store if the baby is dressed for the outdoors. And it is not permitted to take a baby outside unless it is dressed for the outdoors."

Jon chuckled, but grew serious quickly. "Oh, I imagine the surveillance would get to you pretty quickly. It gets to everyone."

"I've heard a few stories about surveillance teams actually helping people."

Jon looked over his shoulder and back at Alex. She wondered if he'd spotted their day's tail. "Such as?" he asked.

"You didn't know the Forresters. They would have been gone before you arrived. But he was the usual cowboy type of security officer, guns at the ready, you know?"

Jon smiled. "I know the type, yes."

"He spoke limited Russian, and his wife spoke none. They had a small baby, and the baby got the croup. Anyway, they put a vaporizer in the baby's bedroom, hooked up to a transformer. To make a long story short the transformer caught on fire. They burst into the baby's bedroom, yelling and screaming. Peggy grabbed the baby, and Tom beat out the flames with a blanket. The noise had no sooner died down than the phone rang. Peggy answered it, still in tears, and a man asked something in Russian. She said she didn't understand and started to hang up.

"Then the man asked, in heavily-accented English, if she wanted him to call the fire department for her, and was the baby okay?"

Alex looked at Jon. His expression was a combination of faint amusement and dismay. "And you find that acceptable?"

"Well, if you're going to have someone listening to your every move, I think it's pretty decent if he's willing to help when the going gets rough."

Jon laughed. "An optimist, too." His smile faded. "I still contend you'd feel differently if it were an everyday occurrence."

"Maybe," Alex conceded, thinking that Margaret had done a lot more damage than anyone could guess; the woman had managed to implant the notion that her fears were rational and that everyone must feel that way, and then she'd died, sealing those ideas in Jon's mind. The realization that, in worrying about his past, she was rapidly becoming more involved with him than she would ever have allowed before didn't stem her concern, didn't make Alex pull away. Instead she took a cautious step closer to him.

He pressed her hand to his side, as if acknowledging her gesture. He didn't comment on it, however, and deftly turned the subject. "I talked Ned Sternberg into running an investigation on the collection. The embassy's involved, right up to our necks. We can't ignore it anymore," Jon said.

Alex felt that quiver of responsibility work through her. "Does anyone know who Copple's contact might have been—on the Soviet side, I mean?"

Jon shook his head and shrugged. "Not a clue. For all that everyone pretty well knew about his—" Jon tipped a sardonic smile her way "—unorthodox activities . . . he was fairly closed-mouthed about his contacts. Maybe Nancy knows," he added thoughtfully.

"Nancy?"

"Copple's girlfriend. At least, scuttlebutt has it that they'd been seeing quite a bit of each other."

Alex noted Jon's stiffening and wondered at it. His voice had sounded distant, thoughtful. Even worried. His eyes met hers and he shook off whatever was bothering him. "Did Ned give you the full treatment this morning?"

"Yes, he did," Alex said. She almost added that she wished Jon had been there, but she held the words in, half-afraid of their implication.

She was surprised to see a sheepish expression on Jon's face. "I didn't tell him about going with you to Makarov's office."

"I didn't, either," she offered. "Was that wrong?"

"Not for you, no. For me, yes. I should have mentioned it."

"Why didn't you?" she asked, truly curious.

Again his demeanor looked sheepish. "Embassy gossip," he said somewhat obliquely, but Alex thought she understood.

"Gossip about you and me?" she asked. "But how could there be any? We haven't done anything."

His eyes met hers. For a moment, she felt pinned by his gaze, stunned by the depth of his desire. Awed by the degree to which she returned that desire. Suddenly she understood how anyone could gossip about them. All anyone would have to do was see them exchanging a glance like this one.

"Yes," he said finally. "People know you're James Bowden's friend."

Was he asking her about her feelings for James? Nothing showed on his face. Suddenly, inexplicably, it was important to her that he know there was nothing between James and her. "We're just friends."

"He knew your husband . . . ?"

"Yes," she said tersely. She quickly shifted the subject before he could ask any more questions. "Do you think Andre Makarov believed Copple died of appendicitis?"

"No. Do you?"

"I think he knows what Copple died of. I think that's what's worrying him."

"Does that surprise you?" Jon asked. He halted in front of an antiquarian book store. Mounds and mounds of fraying books were stacked in the window.

"Not if what we suspect is true," Alex said softly. She raised a hand to the window. "Wouldn't you just love to have a few weeks to sort through the stacks of books in there?" She sighed. "I'll bet there's an original Dostoyevski under that pile. Or maybe some Tolstoy works the Western world has never seen."

"Dyevushka?" a male voice asked at her side. Alex turned, and gasped. She gasped not at his presence, but at his condition.

A thin man of indeterminate years stood beside her, his face a travesty of tortured flesh, his eyes hidden in darkened, hollowed sockets, open sores around his lips, shaking fingers reaching for her arm. She flinched from him even as Jon's hands jerked her back against his solid frame.

"Dyevushka, please," the man said. His voice was wheezy, his tone frantic. He stepped closer, close enough that Alex could smell death on him, close enough for her to read the pain and fear in his bloodshot eyes. "There is danger."

Jon pulled her sharply behind him, out of the path of the apparition. The man scarcely seemed human.

"Dyevushka, understand!" the man groaned in Russian, his reddened eyes blearily following her movements. "Lis-

ten to me carefully. They must be taken care of. Listen. Ivan. Eleven. Forty-three.''

For once, Alex's Russian threatened to desert her. She barely heard the numbers, and understood them even less. The man slumped against the window of the bookstore for a moment, but when he saw Jon pushing Alex backward, farther away from him, his ravaged face hardened. ''Listen to me. It is vital you understand. You are the only one who can help me now. Please . . .''

He lurched toward them, his footing uncertain. Jon shoved Alex out of the way, but the doctor in him was already moving toward the man.

The man said something indistinguishable, then, ''. . . He will kill me anyway. He knows I have hidden—'' A paroxysm of coughing shook the thin frame. ''Kill me now,'' the man said, a tear running down his ravaged face as his cracked lips bled. His eyes pleaded with Alex. She dropped her eyes, afraid of his gaze, afraid of the desire to accommodate his wish—if she could understand it. His hand moved and she was amazed to see that when it lifted, the bony fingers held a thin stiletto. The sharp blade caught a random ray of sunlight and shimmered as it waved shakily toward Jon.

Alex had a flash of melded images: Jon wounded, his blood flowing from his warm body; the ten thousand dollars snugly and foolishly resting in her wallet; a black-and-white photograph of Hans Saalard's face in the newspaper; Jon's shadowed face as he told her that Roger Copple had died of radiation poisoning.

''No . . .'' she said, her eyes rising, meeting the maddened eyes of the man before her.

He lurched another step nearer, the knife swinging wildly. ''He told me to get them out. . . . I believed him. I believed I was doing . . . the right thing. But I am damned. And he that was dead—'' He wheezed. He staggered toward her, the knife thrusting outward.

But whatever he'd planned, whatever the knife had been intended to do, was halted by the loud cry of a man from somewhere behind them. The sick man whirled at the shout, then stumbled, the knife blade wavering in the cold air, like a heat-seeking missile uncertain of its destination.

Jon's hands suddenly wrapped around her shoulders, tightening painfully and wrenching Alex to the sidewalk. He rolled over her, forcing her beneath him. Over the sound of his ragged breathing, his hammering heartbeat, she heard the dull roar of a gun, a shrill woman's scream—*herself?*— and the shouts of passersby.

Slowly, Jon pulled himself off of her, letting her breathe. "Are you all right?" he asked gruffly, his eyes searching her face, her body. "Are you hurt?"

Alex shook her head. She felt strangely numb. Her eyes traveled past Jon to the crumpled figure now lying on the sidewalk not five feet from them. The deadly knife was slowly spinning on a patch of ice, the glint of the blade sending light refracting off the bookstore window. It was harmless now, but still seemed ominous, even so.

A large man in a black coat and black fur hat approached the body and knelt over it, one hand inside the breast of the old man's coat. He did not touch the body itself.

He looked up and met Alex's gaze. With a dim, dizzy feeling, Alex realized he was the same man she'd seen in the doorway of the *pivliki* hall. Jon had been right; it was an entirely different matter when you met your tail face-to-face.

"Did he hurt you?" the man asked in a gruff voice.

"No," Jon answered for them. Alex's voice seemed to have frozen inside her. Jon pushed himself to his feet and absently brushed his trousers. He reached a hand down for Alex, and she took it gratefully.

Standing over the dead man, seeing just how small he was, just how helpless, Alex felt as if the world had shifted on its axis. One moment, they had been laughing about treasures in the bookstore, the next, a knife was being brandished in their faces, and now the man—the menace— was dead. Or, if she looked at it another way, the pathetic creature had received the death he'd asked for.

A crowd had already gathered around them. The voices were muted, whispering, pointing out the Americans, their rescuer, the now-still knife. A militiaman pushed his way through the crowd, asking what the trouble was, demanding to know who was responsible for disorder on this street. His voice, which had been loud and punctuated with aggressiveness, trailed off when he caught sight of the large man and the two Americans standing over the body. The expression on his face changed so swiftly that a few of the disaster watchers actually giggled. He looked as if he wished he could be anywhere else on earth but right there.

"This man was a *huligani*," the large man said. "He was trying to rob these foreigners." His head jerked toward Alex and Jon.

The unfortunate militiaman, uncomfortably aware that he had stumbled onto a case involving foreigners—which meant it involved the KGB—looked at Jon with no small measure of supplication.

Jon nodded at the dead man. "He brandished a knife at us," he said in calm, clear Russian. Only Alex, her hand gripped painfully in Jon's, knew the tension that surged in him.

"Ah, yes," the militiaman said, his expression lightening. He turned to the large man. "How did he die?"

The large man rose ponderously to his feet. He gave a sideways jerk of his head and the militiaman walked to the doorway of the bookstore with him. Standing in the shadows of the door, he and the large man conferred.

"KGB?" Alex asked Jon softly, looking at their rescuer. Jon nodded, his face tense. His eyes searched her face, as if he still needed to be sure she was unhurt. His breath came lightly, shallowly, his mouth parted slightly, his lips drawn inward, as if in anger. Alex wondered what he was thinking, and then knew, with a certainty that seemed to come directly from his mind to hers, that he was shaken by the depth of concern he felt.

As shaken as she was.

Alex watched as the KGB man handed the militia officer some documents. She repressed a smile as the militiaman handed them back quickly, as if they were on fire.

The militia officer approached Jon and Alex. He cleared his throat twice, glared at the noisy crowd and proceeded to apologize, in English, for their inconvenience. "And I am afraid I will have to be adding to this day's troubles. You will have to be coming with me to my precinct office. There we can take your report and settle this unfortunate incident."

"That's impossible," Jon said firmly. His stance told everyone in the crowd that the two Americans were not going anywhere, with anyone.

The KGB man stepped forward. "Excuse me," he said. "It will be for just a few minutes. Routine. Then you may go. It is only necessary for paperwork. You did nothing wrong. You are accused of nothing. It falls upon my shoulders for the shooting of this man. He was nothing, a *huligani*. It will be over in minutes."

Jon glanced down at Alex. The look was far from indecisive. He nodded at her, as if they were exchanging messages. Perhaps they were, she thought. She had never trusted anyone more than she trusted him right at that moment.

"Permit me to telephone my embassy. Then I will accompany you," he said.

The militiaman looked to the KGB man, who looked at the nearest telephone booth, then slowly nodded.

Jon strode to the telephone stall, not letting go of Alex's hand. He dug in his pants pocket for a telephone token. Alex scarcely heard his terse conversation, her eyes and ears on the scene behind them, her mind on the dead *huligani*.

Within moments Jon replaced the receiver. He turned, his face less strained, his lips relaxing into a smile for Alex. "James is duty officer. He's on his way," he said, leading her back to the crowd.

"Please?" the militiaman asked, waving his hand toward the opposite side of the street.

The KGB man tapped the militia officer on the shoulder. "Take them to the station, then send some people to pick this man up," he murmured. Alex looked away, but listened closely to the swift exchange. "Tell them to wear gloves and then to burn them. Do not take this man to the city morgue. Nor to the morgue at Vagankovskoye Cemetery. Take him to the crematorium at Donskoy Monastery. Tell them to cremate him—and all his clothes—at once. No questions, no mistakes. I will wait here for your men."

The militia officer nodded and stepped forward hurriedly. Alex looked back down at the frail body as they stepped from the curb. If she hadn't misunderstood the reasoning behind the KGB official's words, the man would have died before long, anyway.

She and Jon trailed behind the nervous militia officer for about a block and a half, with a portion of the crowd following them as if the officer were the Pied Piper and they the children of Hamlin.

"Did you understand what the big guy was whispering there at the end?" Jon asked quietly.

"Yes," Alex said, and translated in a low voice.

Jon whistled softly. "That tears it," he said. "I was right. Did you understand what the man with the knife was saying to you?"

"I understood the words, but not what he meant," Alex said.

"My Russian totally failed me. What did he say? Numbers?"

"Yes, he said—"

The militiaman stopped abruptly in front of a narrow doorway. A large, black Zil, the limousine of high officialdom, stood at the curb, its hood steaming in the cool air, testimony to its recent arrival. Alex and Jon exchanged glances, and Alex drew comfort from Jon's slow nod.

The militiaman waved them inside, looking impatient to be rid of this unwanted responsibility. "Please," he said, gruffly, gesturing toward the dark interior of the building.

As she had at the airport, Alex knew the pressing weight of fear, recognizing and trying to swallow her terror of an authority so strong, so persuasive, it had killed more than eight million people in the name of one mad ruler. Telling herself that Stalin no longer ruled didn't mitigate the fear one iota.

But the pressure of Jon's hand around hers did.

Several of the occupants of the room spoke to their escort, all heads jerking toward the back of the building, where *he* was waiting. Their words meant little to Alex, since no one specified who the waiting *"he"* was.

"Please," the *militzianyer*—militiaman—said again, this time pointing the way along a narrow pathway between small, paper-strewn desks to a doorway down the hall. "It will be more comfortable this way."

Alex met Jon's eyes for a pregnant moment. His held a flicker of amusement. Nothing, his expression said, could be comfortable at the moment. That he could find anything amusing at that particular moment both amazed her and gave her confidence.

Alex led the way, the corridor seeming more confining with every step. Standing back, the militia officer motioned at the last door along the hallway. It stood ajar. A commotion sounded behind them, and Alex turned in relief, recognizing James Bowden's unmistakable accent. Jon turned around, too, and started forward.

"Jon! Alex! What on earth is this all about?" James called from the exterior doorway. His usually smooth hair was ruffled and his chest was heaving, as if he'd run to meet them instead of taking the car they could both see through the door. Ivan, the chauffeur, stood behind him.

"I didn't think I'd ever be so glad to see anyone," Jon said, grasping the other diplomat's hand with both of his own.

Even as Alex stepped forward, prepared to follow, a hand closed around her arm and drew her through the half-opened door, into the room beyond it. Just as swiftly, the door was closed—and locked behind her.

Jon whirled at the sound of the door closing, his heart constricting as he saw that Alex no longer occupied the hallway.

"Alex!" he called, crossing the distance in a single stride. "Alex!"

The doorway at the end of the hallway was now closed. He wrenched the doorknob, and when it didn't give, he pounded on the door with his fist. "Alex!"

What the hell was going on? An icy chill worked through his veins, freezing him to the marrow. What had they done with Alex…and why? His mind flashed to his last image of Margaret, then to the image of Alex as she had pointed to the books in the window of the store in Arbat.

He whirled to face James, a terrible fear gripping him. *Not Alex.* He could see the confusion in the other man's face. "They've got Alex in there!"

"That's impossible," James said, striding to the door. "Try the door again." He, like Jon, tried the doorknob in both directions. "It's locked," he said, a stunned expression on his face. He rapped smartly on the door. "This is the American Embassy. I demand immediate consultation with Aleksandra Shashkevich, American citizen."

No answer came.

James turned to Jon, his face a study in stupefaction. "What should we do?"

Jon willed his temper to stay in check, forced himself to remember that Alex was no frail, weak woman, that she would be able to handle whatever was happening on the other side of the door. And he tried remembering that James Bowden was, in Alex's own words, just a friend.

He turned from James and, leaning back against the far wall, hunched his left shoulder tightly against his jaw.

"What *we're* going to do is go get her," he said calmly, before lunging for the door.

Almost as soon as the door closed behind her and she wrenched free of the grip on her arm, Alex heard Jon's voice calling her name. She tried the door herself, and when it didn't give, looked up to meet Andre Makarov's half-apologetic gaze. He held the key in his hand.

"Alex!" she heard Jon call, then heard James's voice demanding to see her.

"Ignore them," a deep voice ordered from behind her. Alex whirled to see a complete stranger seated at a small table in the center of the room. From his military-style clothing, she guessed he was some sort of intelligence officer. His cold eyes made her shiver.

"Alex!" Jon's presence on the other side of the door gave her a courage she was far from actually feeling.

Andre Makarov crossed the room to sit at the table beside the cold-eyed man. The stranger paid no attention to the pounding on the door, nor to Andre Makarov's whispered comments. His cold, dark eyes watched Alex with an intensity that made her acutely uncomfortable.

"What is this?" she demanded. "Why did you drag me in here? Unlock this door." She hoped she sounded more forceful than she felt.

Andre waved his hand. "Please, Aleksandra Sergeyevna, this will only take a moment. If you permit?"

"I do *not* permit," Alex said, and Jon's pounding on the door punctuated her refusal.

The uniformed man gestured to a stack of file folders on the small table before the two men. One of the folders was open and held the confiscated photographs.

"Quickly, *dyevushka,* tell us where the artifacts are."

"Alex!" Jon called from the doorway. Alex jumped when the door shuddered with a tremendous impact. Jon was planning on joining her, but at what cost to his shoulder?

"I don't have the foggiest idea where they are," Alex answered truthfully. "Now, will you open this door?"

"What did Apraskin say to you?"

With an explosive sound, the door once again shuddered, and all in the room heard Jon's groaned imprecation.

"I don't know any Apraskin," Alex said as she tried the door again.

"Let us not play games. Apraskin is the man who died on the streets a few minutes ago."

Somehow giving the man a name made his death more real and more tragic. Alex shrugged helplessly. "I can't tell you anything," she said.

"He said something to you. What?"

Alex could hear Jon and James talking in the hall, but couldn't make out their words.

The stranger's eyes were twin chips of ice, and Alex suspected his heart was a perfect match.

"Aleksandra!" Andre snapped at her, making the quantum leap from patronymic to first name. "It is vital that you tell us what that man said. We know he said something to you. The man who shot him radioed to us before he approached the body. We must know what it is the dead man said. There is no time to waste."

"I—"

The uniformed officer made a gesture of impatience. "She's not with the embassy," he said. "We can detain her."

"I don't think—" Andre began, only to be cut off by the officer's swift slapping of the table. The pictures slid from the folder to the floor.

"I don't care what you think! Your department has botched this entire affair. It is time for action, not thinking. I had the man—" He broke off suddenly, as if he had said more than he intended.

Alex cleared her throat. She heard Jon call her name, his voice more frantic now; he must have heard the hand slammed on the table. Again she heard a quick conference but couldn't make out the words. Then she heard a scuffle, other voices calling, footsteps running. The sounds echoed in the small chamber.

The two men in the room turned their eyes to her, one set with a plea in the dark depths, the other menacing. The uniformed man rose and stepped around the small table. *"Dyevushka?"* he prodded, coming toward her.

Alex pressed back against the bare wall. "He was practically incoherent," she said quickly, before the man could advance any farther. "He said something about danger, then he said 'Ivan.' Then the number eleven, then forty-three. That was all he said."

"Nothing else? You are absolutely certain?"

The noise outside the room suddenly stilled and Alex turned to the door in fear. Had Jon been hurt? Had James?

Even as she wondered, she heard two thunderous steps, a loud shout and the door crashed open. Jon spilled into the room at a half run, his hand already going to his shoulder. James tumbled in on his heels.

"You all right?" Jon gasped, his glittering eyes locked with hers. A message, a thousand questions, shone in the depths of his gaze.

She nodded, oddly breathless.

"Good," he said, his hands on his shoulder.

The uniformed man moved swiftly to Alex, taking her arm in a painful grasp. "What else?" he said.

"What is the meaning of this outrage?" James demanded, his chest heaving, his words breathless. His eyes were round with emotion, his eyes on the hand hurting Alex's arm.

But it was Jon who snapped, "Let her go!"

Alex would never have imagined that gentle face could look so menacing, so deadly. She had no doubts whatsoever that he could kill the man holding her. It gave her a shot of pure power, of courage.

Apparently the stranger had no doubts, either. He released her, but with obvious ill grace. He turned to Andre. "Detain her," he said coldly.

Jon stepped between Alex and the men at the center of the room. "I wouldn't even try it," he said. Though he spoke in a reasonable tone, Alex could see from his profile that his eyes were as cold as the stranger's, and a muscle was working in his tightly clenched jaw.

"She is not a diplomat. The Geneva Convention does not apply," the uniformed man said dismissively, as casually as if they had been discussing a visa request.

Jon flicked a glance at James. Alex followed his gaze. James was standing totally still, as if any movement he made would trigger an explosion. The expression on his face told Alex that he was completely overwhelmed, out of his league. James opened his mouth, then shut it again.

Andre Makarov stepped forward, his eyes darting from the three Americans to the unnamed officer. They remained on the stranger. "Please," he said, with an obsequious note in his voice, "I do not believe this to be a good plan."

Somehow that added a notch of fear to Alex's already tightly stretched nerves. It told her just how high-ranking an official this man must be. If a minister of culture was kowtowing to him, she had little hope of changing the outcome.

But Jon had no such qualms. One look from his eyes warned Alex to be silent. The fact that he was aware she was watching his every move stole whatever voice she might have had.

"Detain her and you'll have to detain me, as well. And, believe me, you'll be getting more than you bargained for."

"Jon—" James began warningly, but Jon cut him off with a wave of his hand.

Alex stared at Jon, listening carefully to his every word.

"I don't know what possible grounds you think you have for detaining her. . . ." He paused, not as if he were at a loss for words, but as though the anger in him was difficult to subdue.

Alex's hand unconsciously went to his shoulder. He shivered at her touch, almost as if it had been a hot brand she placed there. He drew a shuddering breath. She realized she had touched him not to contain him, but to spur him on.

No, said her mind. Her hand gripped his shoulder more tightly. Telling him to let it go, to relax. Not to attack these men. His career was at stake. His life. And even as her fingers dug into his jacket, she wondered why he was doing it for *her*.

Why?

As if her thoughts had winged to him, he stiffened. "There were enough witnesses out in that street to fill the Hermitage. And *I* was a witness. Do you want to detain me, as well?" He shook free of Alex's grip. "Detaining her won't answer any of your questions." He looked not at the stranger but at Andre Makarov.

At his words, Alex felt her legs grow weak and her insides swoop as if she were on the downhill of a roller coaster. Why was Jon Wyndham doing this for her?

"She hasn't told us everything she knows," the uniformed officer said. He glanced at Alex, then down to the photographs still scattered on the floor.

"There isn't anything to tell," Alex protested.

"Detain her and have the entire American contingent breathing down your neck," Jon snapped, pushing her behind him. "I don't know what's going on here and frankly, I don't care to. But you hold her, and whatever it is you're so worried about will show up on the front page of every Western newspaper. I'll personally guarantee it."

The stranger's eyes bored into Makarov's.

"Tell him, Makarov. Tell him I'm right," Jon said.

Andre sighed. "It's possible," he said. "He could do that. And you know the embassy will protest." He bent closer to the officer and hissed, "We know what Apraskin said. We don't need her."

"And if she lies?"

Andre turned, ignoring Jon's sudden protective gesture and James's indistinct murmur of protest, and held out his hand, looking at Alex meaningfully. Alex touched his cool fingers.

"Tell me, Aleksandra. Were you telling the truth?" His eyes met hers, no longer the subservient flunky. A message lurked in his direct gaze.

Solemnly, feeling intense relief wash over her, Alex nodded, understanding. While they were touching, it was impossible to lie. She had tried it on him. He knew she understood it. The *truth*.

Her hand gripped his. "I was telling the truth, Andre." She deliberately used his first name in answer. She saw the flicker of acknowledgement in his eyes. Drawing a shuddering breath, she faced the uniformed officer. "I was telling the truth," she repeated.

"Yury Dimitrovich?" Andre asked, cocking his head at the door.

The uniformed man waved his hand in disgust. "Let her go," he barked, but he turned to Alex. "Don't try to leave the Soviet Union, *dyevushka*. It would not be good for your health."

Jon turned suddenly, his no longer golden eyes meeting hers. He took her hands, and for a split second, she felt an understanding pass between them. *I'll be there....*

"We can go?" James asked, looking from Jon to Alex. His eyes narrowed, and he turned an outraged gaze on the two men who had detained Alex. "Gentlemen," he said, making the word an insult, "you will receive a formal protest of these proceedings. I protest the locked door, the interrogation without acknowledgement of proper channels and the harassment of Ms. Shashkevich. While I am aware that Ms. Shashkevich is not directly connected with the American Embassy, she is an American citizen and is considered very much a friend of the embassy. Washington does not look kindly upon those who unlawfully detain its friends and citizens."

He turned on his last clipped words and, with a slight get-moving gesture, ushered Jon and Alex from the room.

The ride to the embassy was a silent one. James looked pointedly at the back of Ivan's head. He occasionally shot Alex a look that seemed half apologetic, half condemnatory. Jon sat quietly looking out the window, his hand crushing Alex's.

Once at the embassy, all three of them were whisked to the fourth floor, and together with Ned Sternberg and the sen-

or security officer, Tom Kenyon, were ushered to the secure room.

In a session not unlike the one she'd just undergone at the police station, the embassy officers fired questions at her. After both she and Jon had described and redescribed the events of the afternoon in detail, the three embassy officials talked across them as if they weren't present.

"Yury Dimitrovich...that must be Yury Dimitrovich Tursunov, Internal Affairs."

"It would fit."

"He knew who the man was...this Apraskin," Ned said. He nodded at James. "Get me everything you know on Tursunov and Apraskin."

"Apraskin must be the link...Copple's connection."

"And it's clear that Tursunov and Makarov don't know where the collection is."

"And equally clear that they believe Ms. Shashkevich knows where it might be." All eyes turned to Alex.

"I don't, though," she said, a shade defiantly in view of the questions in their eyes.

No one answered.

"I think, after this interrogation, after what the uniform said, we'd better get her out of the country," the security office said.

"I agree," James said. "They've already confiscated the photographs she was carrying. Then a man was murdered right in front of her. And to top it all off, they held her against her will." His arguments made sense but his eyes were focused narrowly on Jon.

"Wait—" Alex began.

Ned Sternberg raised his hand, forestalling all speech.

"I think you gentlemen are forgetting that Ms. Shashkevich is not embassy personnel." He paused for a moment while the two men digested this. "Contrary to popular belief, we can't tell her what to do. We can advise...but we can't order." He turned to Alex. "All we can do is pick up the pieces should there be any repercussions from all this."

No one said anything for a moment, though Alex could feel their thoughts. Her eyes met Jon's. His carried a message, half determination, half apology. She frowned a question at him.

"I disagree," he said firmly, his eyes still on hers. "She should stay here." A muscle worked in his jaw.

Ned shook his head. Alex again saw a speculative element in his eyes as he looked from Jon to her. His frosty smile flickered. "It might not be such a bad idea for her to leave. There have been a number of alarming events revolving around those photographs of hers."

"Yes," Jon said, his full lips set in a firm line. "And Hans Saalard—the man who gave her those pictures—*died* in Washington."

"There's nothing to indicate any connection," Ned countered swiftly.

"No?" Jon asked, but let the point drop. "Here—" he nodded at Alex "—she has the long arm of the embassy to protect her, not to mention the KGB. If she leaves and there really is some danger—and I'd say that, if nothing else, possible detention at the airport for going against that creep's orders would constitute danger—then she's safer right here."

Alex released her breath in an audible puff. Jon's speech had been forceful, persuasive and direct. She could read the other men's acceptance of his logic. She herself felt suddenly uncertain.

In the worry over the dead Apraskin, she had almost forgotten the command not to leave the country. Jon hadn't. She had dismissed any connection between Hans Saalard's death and the photographs. He hadn't.

Or did his impassioned speech spring from other sources, sources more basic than mere logic? He met her gaze and she read a measure of triumph. And behind it she could see the belated reassurance, *Trust me.*

Fighting the sensation that she was caught in a web of his creation, she could only look at him helplessly.

"Trust me," he said aloud, his words a command. But in his eyes, she read a plea.

It was the unspoken message in his eyes that made her agree, the plea that made her nod.

Chapter 6

After much discussion, the embassy officials finally hammered out what they considered a workable plan. Alex's own opinions carried no weight; in fact, she was scarcely given an opportunity to voice any. She was to be accompanied at all times by one of the four men present. No one else, inside or outside the embassy community, was to know the details of what had occurred that afternoon. There was little hope of squelching the news of Apraskin, but everyone concerned would simply allow people to believe he had been a *huligani,* the story provided by the KGB.

James, Ned and Tom Kenyon would get to work on tracking down information on Apraskin: had he been Copple's contact? Did he have any family? Had his words been a clue to the collection's location? Jon was assigned the role of unofficial bodyguard, a task that drew frowns from both James and Alex.

Alex's residency at the hotel caused the greatest amount of argument: a two-way split in favor of embassy guest quarters or actually becoming a houseguest of one of the four men in the room. This was the only argument in which they actually listened to Alex's wishes. Over James's objection, and despite the quick frown on Jon's face, Alex chose the embassy guest quarters.

These quarters proved to be in the old embassy building, on the second floor, north wing.

"Same floor as the infirmary," Jon said, leading her into the elevator. "If you'll wait until I get through measles inoculations, I'll run you back to your hotel, then help you get settled in the apartment."

Up until that moment, though she'd known he was a doctor, she had only associated him as being with the embassy in a supervisory role. He had attended Copple, but she hadn't really pictured him *doctoring* the man. The offhand comment about measles inoculations brought home to her, as nothing else could have done, that he had tasks and responsibilities far removed from her mysterious art collection.

"Wouldn't you know the vaccine would arrive today?" he muttered. "We've been waiting for it for weeks. I've got six two-year-olds whose mothers are ready to go into seclusion for fear of measles."

Alex didn't say anything, struck by the prosaic reality of mothers worrying about shots while she had been worrying about a man being shot in front of her and people dying of radiation poisoning, poisoning possibly caused by a collection she had been prepared to purchase.

Jon's demeanor changed as they crossed the threshold of the clinic. Alex couldn't quite define the difference until he lifted a curly-haired two-year-old to his hip and chatted idly with the child's mother. Then she understood it. His face had relaxed. He was in his element. Bursting through doors, rolling her to the pavement, impassioned speeches . . . these were anomalous to Jon Wyndham's day-to-day personality. Those moments, those actions, had been borne of necessity, of concern for her. This was the real Jon Wyndham. A doctor, a man whose warmth and concern touched everyone in the room, a man who, for all she fought it, touched her.

He turned to her, and his smile held no hint of triumph now. No steely determination shone from his eyes; no muscle jumped in his jaw. It was just a simple smile...but it pierced through the years of armor and struck home. As if compelled, and as easily as the child he carried, she smiled back.

While she waited, Alex reviewed the last twenty-four hours, finding it almost incredible that she'd only arrived in Moscow the evening before. She found herself separating the sequences of events into two categories: those involving the artifacts and those involving Jon.

He had accused her of donning a new shell every time he started breaking through the old one. He had been right and wrong at the same time. Her heart was well-protected, not inside a shell, but, rather, inside a brick tower, its mortar made of pain and tears. She'd begun work on it while still she was a child, when her father had died. And she had added to it, brick by brick, in the years and hurts, relationships and betrayals since.

Until Jon, until now, she had believed the tower was impervious, too high to be scaled, too strong to be stormed. But he knew a magic others apparently lacked. He could see the weak spots in the layers of mortar. His smile, his eyes, the touch of his hand, his fierce protectiveness, the bemused vulnerability he readily admitted to, all of them combined to work at her self-imposed resistance to any form of warmth. He made her want to trust him.

Restless, she paced the small waiting room, stepping over other two-year-olds and avoiding the curious gazes of their mothers. From the narrow, screen-covered window, she could see the new embassy building, a tall, rectangular memorial to years of arrant stupidity. American designed and contracted, it had been Soviet subcontracted. And when the ten-year building project had been completed, the ribbon cut and speeches made, a routine sweep of the facility had revealed thousands of bugging devices. Too many to count, too many to remove without tearing down the entire structure.

So now it stood empty, unused, untenanted...another brick tower waiting to be torn down. It was useless, yet everyone concerned resisted having the tower razed. It represented years of spent dreams and hard work. It was a mistake, but one everyone was familiar with. No one wanted to see the crane with the heavy ball shattering walls, windows and doors.

Was she clinging to her own tower for similar reasons? More than for mere self-protection, was she holding fast to it because it was familiar? Because life was easier, safer, within its mortared walls?

One by one, the two-year-olds came and went, going in to see Jon with nervous smiles, coming out with tear-filled eyes and suckers grasped in chubby fists. Each time, Jon accompanied them to the waiting room and each time, he would meet her eyes and smile. And each time, her heart turned over. What was he doing to her? Why now? Why couldn't he have entered her life a decade ago, when she'd still been trusting enough to act on her instincts, instead of squelching them?

He was called to the phone once, in between children, and Alex could see that the conversation involved her. His eyes flashed to her, then away, and his face was thoughtful when he rang off. But he said nothing, merely scooping up the next child and escorting the mother to the back.

"The down side of doctoring," Jon said after ushering the last crying two-year-old and his mother from the waiting room and into the hallway outside the clinic. He removed his glasses and rubbed the bridge of his nose. "It's hard to get kids to trust you when you're coming at them with a needle."

With all the thoughts of Jon storming her defenses, she felt she could thoroughly sympathize with the children.

"It's almost six," he said. "What say we escape the embassy for a while?"

"To get my things?" she asked.

"Not until later, if that's okay by you."

"Last time we escaped the embassy, we got into trouble," Alex said, smiling. She realized she'd said it just to see his broad face relax into a grin.

"So we did," he said. "But how about the circus?"

"The circus?" she asked, surprised. Somehow it sounded too lighthearted an adventure after the day's events. Prosaic... like the measles inoculations. It sounded too simple, too ordinary... like the reading glasses tucked in Jon's pocket. Was this part of the man's charm? The fact that he was exciting and *normal*. He was *real*.

She smiled. "Sounds good," she said sincerely.

"Apraskin's son is one of the performers," Jon added, pulling on his jacket and dashing the idea that this was an ordinary excursion.

They swung by Jon's apartment so he could change his clothes. Alex was surprised that he wasn't housed nearer the clinic but in the new two-story, town-house-style compound near the new, empty, embassy. Like the empty building, these apartments were undoubtedly riddled with listening devices, but in these, where nothing of a secure nature need be discussed, embassy families lived, loved and withstood the constant attention.

James had told her once that people within the embassy were told, during the initial security briefing, what they could talk about inside their apartments and what they could leave lying around for the KGB to read. The list of things they couldn't talk about was extensive: no arguments, no mention of financial difficulty, no discussion of sexual relations—good or bad—avoid referring to family members by both first and last names, no talk about embassy activities, and on and on. Letters from home containing any material that could potentially be a subject for blackmail—which ranged from advice on any subject to the political situation in Zanzibar—should be locked in an embassy safe, and all other correspondence should be read carefully, then destroyed.

But while James was extremely conscious of the rules, it appeared that Jon didn't adhere to every detail. In fact, she thought, he acted as if he didn't care about any of them. He gestured her toward the bar while he tossed his coat to one of the armchairs and kicked his shoes toward a closet. If this wasn't enough, the untidiness of the rest of the apartment provided testimony to his habits. Half-finished books covered the end tables, folded facedown on the undusted surfaces. Newspapers fully hid the top of the dining table. The remains of a solitary meal sat on the counter, an indication not of slovenly habits but a single, busy man.

His apartment was well-furnished, with adequate space and neutral colored carpeting and walls, as were all the American apartments. Artifacts collected on his travels kept the apartment from appearing sterile and showed Alex another side of Jon Wyndham. African masks hung on the wall beside delicate watercolors of Budapest. An Azerbaijan oriental rug—a deep blue Kuba-Shirvan—lay on the floor at right angles to a pale dhurrie. Baskets, large wooden figures and *zarfs*—the small Arab coffee sets with ornate brass pitchers—were placed around the apartment, while the bookshelves were stuffed with smaller, more expensive items, such as Palekh boxes, exquisitely decorated Ukrainian Easter eggs, miniatures of St. Basil's Cathedral and chunks of carved amber.

As Alex studied his things, Jon dressed quickly, scarcely speaking. He didn't appear to be uncomfortable with her presence in his home, but *she* was. She felt she was seeing too many sides of Jon Wyndham. Somehow, by seeing him in the clinic, then in this apartment, seeing how he worked, then how he lived, she felt she had stepped through a doorway that led to intimacy.

Seeing his dining table littered with newspapers and forbidden correspondence, she felt hemmed in by the tiny things that made up a person's life. And seeing them, she felt the unwanted tug of desire for the little things that made two people a unit. Things like passing the cream, sharing the paper on Sunday mornings, watering the lawn after a spring mowing, laughing during a water fight. As if they were displayed in front of her, all those simple mundane intimacies worked at the mortar that protected her heart.

She hugged her coat tighter, feeling a chill at variance with the room's temperature.

Watching her standing too close to the front door, one slender hand clutching her coat's lapels, Jon took in her nervousness and wondered at its cause. Instinctively, he knew it had little, if anything, to do with the afternoon's bizarre events. It had something to do with being in his apartment, something to do with him.

Still, if she had any idea of the things she stirred in him, she would probably run full tilt back to the States. She couldn't know she conjured dreams of things he'd thought long buried, long past. He wanted her with an intensity that startled him. And yet, he wanted her trust even more. In the short time he'd known her, he'd already come to recognize her alarm at probing questions. In his arms, her lips against his, she'd responded with a passion that had almost surprised him, then pulled back, a shutter clicking down, end of frame, end of quest.

What he had told her was true; he was not much of a person for mystery. But with Alex, as much as he wanted her, he wanted to know why she shrank from getting close. She wanted to, he could feel it. Whatever he felt for her was matched in the ease with which her lips had met his. Still she resisted. She remained aloof. But her blue eyes, eyes the color of the late-night sky, had pleaded with him to try, to persevere.

He wished he had met her under different circumstances, wished they'd simply met at a cocktail party one evening, chatted and discovered they had a few things in common, then gone off for a cup of coffee and, six months later, decided they were good together.

He pulled on his jacket, smiling, thinking how different the reality was from the fantasy. He'd known her a mere earth's rotation . . . and in her company, he suspected he could actually feel the earth moving. The unusual circumstances had forced them to a greater intimacy, a swifter knowledge. But still, he would have to tread warily, he decided. He would move slowly, for her sake, but also for his.

Because he was already aware of the fact that he didn't want to let her go. It was why he'd argued to have her remain in Moscow. It was why he'd slammed through that door with his shoulder. He wanted her. And he had the odd feeling that he wanted her for a lot more than a mere night, a week, even a year.

He held out his hand to her and smiled when her lips parted unconsciously, wondering how much of his thinking she could read in his eyes.

The strange events that had begun in Washington with Hans Saalard's death and continued until a man lay dead at her feet on the streets of Moscow began to lose their sharp focus for Alex. They seemed impossible beneath the colored lights of the Malyy Circus, listening to the American-style rock music, watching the unique, fur-ruffed bears walking on their hind legs, jumping through hoops of fire and holding out their paws to the audience for treats.

Like a blend between a fancy night club act and a stuntman's reunion, the intimate little circus caught and held Alex's attention. The performers, whether walking the high wire or performing back flips on horseback, were all dressed in sexy, bright-colored costumes. The lights went up, and a woman was revealed, draped around a pole. A man danced out to her and played out a romance for the audience. A single acrobat swung down from the ceiling singing a Russian folksong, and the audience joined in.

Just as the mood of the circus invaded Alex's senses, so did Jon's proximity. While he sat neither too close to her nor too far away, he looked at her as if trying to read her mind, her heart. Every time their eyes met, her heart seemed to skip a beat; her throat felt hot and dry, but her legs were liquid. His eyes... she thought a little wildly. He asks questions with his eyes.

And she answered with her own: No.

Maybe.

When next his eyes met hers, they carried no hidden message, no ulterior designs. And as he laughed easily at the bears' antics, his laughter urging her to do the same, she wondered if she hadn't misunderstood his earlier glances, the questions in his golden gaze. She wondered if perhaps she were seeing not reality but what she wanted to see. If only she could trust her instincts, if only she could be sure.

Jon laughed especially hard at a sketch in which the bears imitated children learning their school lessons, and during intermission she asked him why.

He grinned. "Those bears acted exactly the way my cousins and I did when we were kids." He shook his head, and the simple gesture and the sigh that accompanied it told her more about his love for his family than any words could have. She must have had that look once, long before her father had died.

"My uncle was a minister—a very strict one," Jon said. "Every Sunday after church, all the kids, from the biggest to the smallest, would have to recite verses from the Bible. And we were just as much trouble as those bears."

Jon chuckled again, and the sound played along Alex's spine, creating a tingling warmth in her chest. Though they were discussing only a random memory, Alex felt as if the moment was very important, as if, in catching this glimpse of his past, she was seeing yet another facet of the man beside her. If she saw enough, would she trust her liking of him?

"What my uncle never realized—or maybe he did and felt the end justified the means—was that we would spend the whole week on a frantic search for the shortest biblical verse. My Cousin Frank finally outdid us all. He came up with 'Jesus wept.' It's from the Book of John, somewhere."

"You still remember the verse," Alex said, smiling, oddly touched by the frank affection she saw on his features.

"Tell me about your family," he said, his smile guileless, his eyes curious.

Alex's mind flew not to her family, but to her marriage.

"When you were a kid," Jon amended, as if understanding her hesitation.

Alex willed herself to relax. Telling a simple story wouldn't commit her to him, and not telling one would be churlish. She took her cue from him and focused not on her marriage to Tony nor on her father, but on her father's sister. "I have an aunt—her name is Natalya. Even though she's far too young to actually be called White Russian, she nonetheless plays it to the hilt. She acts like she's expecting the Tsar for sherry and crumpets at any moment. She only speaks French—the language of the upper crust, you know—and we always had high tea on Saturday afternoons. Since none of us spoke French, except to say hello, goodbye and thank you for the day, Aunt Natalya, the afternoons had their hilarious moments."

"She sounds great."

"She sounds nuts," Alex corrected, but with a smile. She hadn't thought of Aunt Natalya in years.

"And your folks?" Jon asked.

Had his gaze sharpened? "They're both dead," Alex said, half resenting the question's intrusion into the evening and wholly hating herself for answering so shortly.

Jon didn't let the matter drop. "They must have been very young. Were they killed in an accident?"

As if the words were being pulled from her, Alex answered, editing her life as if rewriting the events. "They didn't die at the same time. My father died when I was a child, my mother only a few years ago." She shrugged.

"That's tough. I'm sorry."

His response was a common one, yet something in his tone made it different. Warmer. More sincere. She met his eyes. "It was a long time ago," she said softly. And for perhaps the first time in her life, it really did seem a long time in the past. If only she hadn't met Jon now. If only she'd somehow managed to meet him years ago, when she was younger...before Tony, before discovering Marja.

She sighed. But without Marja, she never would have met Hans Saalard. And without Hans, she wouldn't be sitting here, wondering about Jon, about the feelings he inspired in her. She shivered, caught up in a spiral of connecting lives, connecting loves.

The overhead lights dimmed abruptly, signaling the second half of the evening's entertainment, and Alex felt the reprieve. Jon had been prepared to ask more questions, she was sure of that. Instead, he reached for her hand.

As she felt his broad hand encircle hers, she had the sensation that they were the only two people in a night-dark limbo. She couldn't see him, yet she felt his touch. The music's roar precluded speech, yet his grip said everything.

The noise in the center ring indicated some fantastic new sight. Alex clasped Jon's hand tighter, half in anticipation of the next act, half in response to his presence.

"Citizens and comrades..." the voice over the microphone announced from the dark. "Never before in any part of the world have such amazing feats of daring been attempted...!" The rich voice continued to expound on the wonders of the next performer while a spotlight swept the crowd, the center ring and the pitched circus ceiling. "Sasha the Incredible!"

The colored lights flickered on, casting an eerie red-green glow over the single ring. Sasha the Incredible stood to the right of Jon and Alex at the edge of the ring, his dress that of a Gypsy, his demeanor that of a thirties hood. He coughed, a choking paroxysm that made him double over. As someone moved toward him from the curtained enclosure, he waved them aside impatiently, turning to face a blond woman strapped to a large wheel on the other side of the ring.

"I don't like the sound of that cough," Jon said thoughtfully, his forehead furrowing.

"I don't like this whole thing," Alex murmured, knowing the wheel would be spun and the amazing Sasha would throw knives at the helpless woman.

The frown disappeared from Jon's brow and he smiled down at her. "It's okay. If he hits her, I can probably fix her." His hand squeezed hers, compelling Alex to share the joke. She chuckled feebly. "Besides, he's why we're here. Sasha the Incredible is really Alexander Apraskin, Junior."

As she had anticipated, the wheel was spun and the woman strapped to it whirled around and around, her arms becoming twenty arms, her legs up, then down, twenty of them, as well. Sasha the Incredible began throwing knives with almost careless ease. His face was relaxed, his lips smiling faintly. The only sound in the room was the high-pitched thunk of the knives as they connected with the wheel. Alex held her breath and was grateful for Jon's hand so tightly clasping hers.

The lights dimmed, except for a spotlight on the still-whirling blonde. The announcer's whisper echoed throughout the circus. "Watch very closely now, as Sasha the Incredible performs the single-most dangerous stunt ever attempted in a circus arena."

A brief drum roll was followed by the spotlight, focused on Sasha. Another cough, this one less intense, shook him. The woman was in the dark, totally invisible except for her glittering costume, which shimmered as if it were iridescent. The glow of her skimpy suit showed that she was no longer spinning around.

Alexander Apraskin turned his back on the woman, and after a bow and a cocky grin at the audience, he raised a fistful of knives for the crowd to see. Alex's eyes focused on the hairy hand. She had seen that hand before.

And then, before the spectators could do more than half raise their hands to applaud, the amazing Sasha, in rapid-fire succession, sent each of the knives over his shoulder and into the darkness, all without looking at the glowing costume.

Someone screamed and the crowd as a whole surged to its feet. The lights rose, as did the music. Sasha the Incredible spread his hands widely and walked in a large circle around the ring, his right hand indicating the unscathed woman. Circus hands released her and Sasha helped her step down and into the center of the ring. On the wheel, testimony to his talent, was the complete outline of her body.

Applause burst out around Alex and Jon, deafening, thunderous and, in Russian style, in unison. Mesmerized by the sharp blades reflecting the multicolored lights, Alex was struck not by the knife thrower's skill, but by a profound relief that his father had apparently not shared that talent. If he had, it wouldn't have been a matter of the knife spinning on the patch of ice, but her world spinning to an end.

As if following her thoughts, Jon also didn't applaud. His eyes were also on the knives on the now-still wheel. He leaned down to Alex's ears. "Let's head backstage and see if we can find out anything about the incredible Sasha's father."

In that instant, Alex remembered where she'd seen the man's hand before. It had been Sasha Apraskin who had held the ruler in the photographs, the ruler that showed the size of each artifact.

The man who had died in front of them that afternoon wasn't the only connection with the deadly collection.

Alex nodded, stepping from the short aisle and down the two broad steps leading to the side curtains. They were eyed with surprise by the still-applauding audience—who would leave in the middle of the circus?—and with suspicion by the curtain attendants.

Alex quickly whispered her surety that Sasha the Incredible was the owner of the hand in the photographs. Jon stared at her for a few seconds, a frown gathering on his brow. He turned and looked at the ring, now occupied by cavorting dancers.

"That explains the cough," he said reflectively.

Alex felt a hot shiver work down her spine. How many more people would die before this ended?

Despite Jon's finesse, they were denied access to the dressing rooms.

"It is not permitted," the man at the curtain said. *"Nilsya."*

Jon asked if Sasha Apraskin would come talk with them, then.

"Nilsya," the man said again, with less apology in his voice this time.

"We'll wait," Jon said.

"Nilsya!" the circus attendant said, signaling for assistance. "You must go now. Your seats or the door. Your choice."

To all Jon's questions—Where does he live, then? Where can we reach him? Does he have a telephone?—the attendant turned a deaf ear. All but the question about the telephone. To that one he merely snorted. Of course, he didn't have a telephone. No one without connections and a two-year supply of rubles had a telephone. The man did, however, accept one of Jon's cards, shoving it incuriously into his sweater pocket before dismissing them with a quick gesture of his hand toward the outside door.

It had begun to snow again while they were inside, and the sidewalk was dusted with a thin white layer that would be black with coal dust by morning. But now the tiny flakes cleansed the air, melted on their eyelashes and stung their exposed cheeks to a red that glowed in the lights from the street lamps.

The street was silent, as most of the audience remained within and the hour was late. Street cleaners, the nighttime rhythm of their brooms slower, swept the corners clear, ignoring Alex and Jon, ignoring the dark figure with the gray fur hat who stood in the doorway of a bread store, shoulders hunched against the cold, a cigarette glowing in his hand.

Alex saw him. So did Jon. The man standing in the cold, watching them, waiting for them, was part and parcel of the day's bizarre events: tense meetings, veiled and not-so-veiled threats, a rowdy beer hall, a man dying before their eyes, measles inoculations, the circus and this not-so-subtle reminder that all was not well.

Instinctively, Alex pressed closer to Jon, as if the cold outside emanated from the dark form in the dim doorway. Jon's arm stretched around her shoulders and drew her tightly against him.

"Time to call it a day," he said with that uncanny ability he had to read her thoughts. "Let's go retrieve your things from the hotel and get back to the embassy."

"I can just stay there," she said, meaning the hotel.

"Not a chance," he said. And his tone brooked no arguments. "Not without a resident bodyguard."

Alex looked up and met his gaze. His brown eyes were black in the uncertain light and his lips were unsmiling. Yet she had the feeling he was half teasing her, gauging her reaction, testing.

She shook her head slightly, denying not his words but the question behind them, saying no, not to the bodyguard, but to the idea of such intimacy. But perhaps her lips betrayed her or her eyes or even her racing heartbeat, so loud she was sure he would be able to hear it, for he stopped and drew her into his arms.

He studied her for a long moment, as if memorizing her features, as if giving her time to pull away. Alex felt she couldn't have moved if her life depended on it. His eyes held her prisoner, his arms supporting her.

"I want you, Alex," he said finally. Quietly. So sincerely and so simply that she felt her knees threaten to give way.

She wanted him, too. She wanted him, and yet knew she couldn't trust her own desire. Desire led to need, to dependence, and then to ruin. But her body...her instincts...kept her still, feeling his warm breath play over her cold face, fearing his sincerity, yet drawn to it.

"You know, when Margaret died, I swore I'd never get involved with anyone again."

Alex made some sound. Perhaps it was protest; more likely it was because his words cut too closely to her own vow, her own truth.

"Then you came along." He looked up at the snow-sprinkled night sky. "Like the spring."

Alex inhaled with difficulty. The confusion on his features more than matched her own.

"Like the spring," he repeated, and looked back down at her. His lips twisted in a wry smile. "And I hadn't even noticed how much I missed the warmth." His mouth lowered to hers, capturing it, tasting, letting her know how honestly he'd spoken, how deeply she moved him.

And she, stunned by the intensity of her own desire for him, was, for once, able to quell the doubts, subdue the weighty arguments of her heart and mind. She gave herself to his kiss, as moved as he, as desirous as he…and as lonely.

Jon felt the change in her, felt it through her lips, felt it in the sudden relaxation of her body. A wild exultation swept through him; she wanted him every bit as much as he wanted her. No holding back here, no skittering behind the shadows he read in her amazing eyes.

Instead she leaned into him, returning quest for quest, ache for ache, her sweet mouth passionate, her heart truly open to him for a timeless moment. He knew he was undone. He couldn't go back now. He couldn't let Alex slip away from him. She was more now than the mere hope of spring, she was life itself. He could taste it on her tongue, recognize it in her cold, gloved hands softly exploring his face.

And behind the kiss, behind the touch, he could feel the worries, the demons that haunted her. He knew that whatever they were, they couldn't be driven away by moving too quickly, by pressing too swiftly. And so it was he who pulled back, with a reluctance she might never even guess. He clasped her tightly against him, willing his body to submit to his mind, drawing in the cold air, forcing it to chill his heat.

"I have time," he said, though whether it was to reassure himself or to let her know he would wait, he couldn't have said.

When she shook her head, he released her, saddened when she didn't meet his eyes, heartened when she fell into step beside him, her hand linked through his arm.

She was silent during the drive to the hotel. Glancing at her occasionally, Jon wondered what she was thinking, hoped she was thinking of him. As he pulled into the bright drive of the hotel, he was startled to hear her laugh.

"What?" he asked, wholly perplexed, though her laugh sparked an answering smile.

"I was thinking about that poor KGB man assigned as our tail. He has to stand around in cold doorways watching us kiss."

The relief that coursed through Jon felt all out of proportion. Whatever her demons were, they weren't those of repression. She had been able to think about, review and see an amusing side to their kiss. The passion he had felt from her had been neither manufactured nor regretted.

Though she still refused to meet his eyes, Jon sensed that she wasn't as distant from him as she had been before. Something in their kiss had touched her. And from the expression on her face, he guessed it had touched her deeply. Remembering his own reaction, he wasn't surprised. They had exchanged far more than a hint of desire.

She took the key from the sleepy *dijournaya* and led the way to her room. At the door, handing him the key, her eyes met his briefly. With speculation? With fear?

He inserted the key into the lock, half wishing it were a metaphor and the tumblers clicking were those of her heart.

"Thanks," she said, stepping past him into the room. "I won't be lo—"

She had pushed the door open, then bitten off her words on a gasp. Instinctively, Jon pulled her back into the hall and stepped in front of her.

The protection was unnecessary. Whoever had been in her room was no longer present. But that someone had been there was obvious. Alex's room looked like a scene from a spy movie, clothing and bedding strewn about in wild abandon, mattress askew, pillows ripped and spewing feathers.

With a giddy sense of having been thrust into another profession, Jon wrenched open the door to the small lavatory. It, too, was empty, though it had obviously been visited. Whatever the culprit had been after was small enough, seemingly, to fit inside a shampoo or cosmetics containers, for the contents had been emptied directly onto the floor and the bottles discarded into the sink.

"Get the *dijournaya*," Jon told Alex as he rejoined her. "She has some explaining to do."

Alex looked from the room to Jon. "I don't think I can take much more of this," she said.

"You're doing fine," he answered, though privately, he agreed with her. Her eyes were too wide, her mouth tightly drawn, her skin pale. "We'll have you out of here in a few minutes. Fetch the *dijournaya*."

Alex looked at him for a long moment, and Jon had the disquieting feeling that she was assessing him, judging him, and he was relieved when she nodded and turned away.

He would have been even more relieved—and perhaps encouraged—had he known Alex's thoughts as she approached the *dijournaya*. For the first time in years, Alex had looked straight into a man's eyes and decided to trust him. This could all be an elaborate game—his reactions were much more appropriate for a professional agent than a doctor. Yet his honesty earlier, and the protective surge she felt in him now, said she should trust him. But more than what she saw or felt from him, the truth was that she had decided in that moment that she could trust her own instinctive desire to place her faith in him.

"There is some trouble in my room," she told the *dijournaya*, and quickly reviewed her room's condition for the disgruntled woman. As she led the way to her room, she hoped her instincts wouldn't be proven wrong.

Again.

Chapter 7

The *dijournaya* was of little help. If she was to be believed, she had been readying the samovar for the nightly tea and had seen no one but a heavyset man visiting someone down the hall from Alex's room. She had served him a cup of tea.

Jon's mind immediately flashed to the figure in the darkened doorway and to the man who had shot Apraskin that afternoon. Unwilling to delay Alex's departure, Jon let the tepid explanation ride. He had seen for himself how willing the *dijournaya* had been to accept a bribe; Alex had given her one that first evening. He refused the offer of a different room, not bothering to explain that Alex would have been checking out of this one anyway.

Despite the mess, it didn't take Jon and Alex long to gather her things and transfer them to his car. They drove in relative silence to the embassy. Instead of pulling into the secured entrance of the old building, Jon drove to the newer American compound and pulled into his parking slot.

At Alex's questioning look, he said, "You're staying at my place." He hoped the words sounded firm and decisive.

After the chaos in her hotel room, he didn't want her staying alone, even under the protection of the American Embassy. He also hoped he had managed to keep an almost-eager note from his voice, because the fact was that he was glad events had conspired to place her directly in his custody.

"I'll be fine in the guest quarters..." Alex said quietly, yet the tenor of her voice suggested doubt.

"You'll be better here," he answered, getting out of the car. As he went around for her, he again cautioned himself to go slowly, to hold no expectations.

Seeing Alex's confused face gave him a moment's severe struggle. He wanted to pull her into his arms, not play the courteous diplomat offering shelter for the night. And seeing her shed her coat in his living room, her eyes looking at his walls, his table—anything but him—made him want to carry her to his bedroom, not play the considerate host.

He saw her tentative glance at the stairwell.

"The bedrooms are upstairs," he said softly. He had the impression that if he had spoken loudly, she would have jumped.

She smiled; it was an obvious effort. "Your apartment is large," she said. Had she said it hopefully?

"By Russian standards," he replied. It was true. Two Soviet families, complete with grandmothers, parents, two children and the classic pet, the Great Dane—the word in Russian was *dog*, with a long *O*—could easily have lived in this apartment and would have been deemed rich by Soviet standards. But not many diplomats, with attendant families, would have tolerated any Soviet apartment. The truth was, this space was small by American diplomatic standards.

"How about a nightcap first?" he said. "I think we could both probably use one tonight."

She shook her head and ran a hand across her forehead. In the gesture, he could see how near she was to total exhaustion. For a moment, he hesitated; he'd seen that look often enough in his marriage to know how little his reassurances and offers of comfort would mean. But this was Alex, and if he ignored the pain on her face, it would hurt no one but himself. He stepped closer, warily.

She half turned to him, a sigh on her lips, confusion in her eyes. It was too much for him to stand; he couldn't keep from drawing her into his arms, willing her to accept the comfort he was offering, aching for her to relax in his embrace.

Confused, tired, overwhelmed by the events of the day and her conflicting thoughts about Jon, Alex at first stiffened when he drew her into his embrace. But he made no move to kiss her and despite the desire she felt from him— for him—he contained himself so that no gesture gave his need away, so she relaxed into his gentle, firm hold.

Even as she relaxed into his embrace, even as she cherished the comfort he tendered, her wayward heart accelerated and her lips parted. Her body and heart were betraying her mind. She could relax, comforted, but if she didn't draw away from him now it would be herself, and not him, who betrayed the moment. She pulled away, but never had she withdrawn from an embrace with such difficulty.

He let her go easily, so easily that she felt a stab of pique. She immediately chided herself for the irritation; she didn't want anything else from him . . . did she?

She followed him upstairs to the guest bedroom. Unlike the rest of the house, it was tidy, almost too tidy. She knew instinctively that no one had ever stayed there. For some reason, the thought saddened her. For all that she had withheld giving her love to anyone, her guest room was usually filled with friends. And that thought made her think of Hans Saalard and his standing refusal to stay at her house . . . a refusal that had resulted in his death. For the second time that day, she wondered if Hans's death had any connection with the collection. The damned collection.

Trying to drag her mind from the thought of Hans, she focused on the double bed flanked by two Danish end tables holding small ceramic lamps. The comforter was of

Norwegian design and only served to further remind her of Hans. *How she would miss him.*

In her pang of sorrow, in the wake of the past two days, she discovered a resolve. She had been frightened today in so many more ways than mere physical danger, but now she felt strong. She would not allow fright to steal the good name of her friend—it had been made obvious by both the Soviet and American powers that be that Hans Saalard's involvement was suspect—and, now that a commission from the sale of the artifacts was distinctly out, if there were some way to compensate the family for his death, she would find it.

"All right?" Jon asked from behind her. She had no idea how much time had passed while she had arranged the day's events into order in her mind.

"Fine," she answered, turning. "And, Jon?"

"Yes?" he asked. She felt a vague pleasure at the wistful note in his voice.

"Thanks," she said simply, and stretched out her hand. It was only at the quicksilver realignment of his features that she realized she was not holding out her hand for him to shake but rather as an offering. He looked down, but he made no move to take it. She felt her stomach tighten. There was no wistfulness on his face now, only primitive desire. It struck her forcibly, like a touch.

Then he waved his hand, dismissing her apology, dismissing her handshake, checking his mood, controlling his emotions. She was close enough to him that his motion displaced the air and she felt the soft, Jon-scented breeze.

"Well...good night," he said, shoving his hands into his pockets. He rocked on his heels for a moment, as if stalling the inevitable, then turned to leave. At the doorway, he paused. "Do you want to sleep in, or should I wake you when I get up?"

Alex smiled. "When you do, please," she said.

His face was shadowed by the dark hallway, but his eyes caught the lamp's reflection. They locked with hers for an eternal split second. She felt dizzy by the time he looked away. In the depths of his eyes was a world she had never known, a world comprised of dreams, promises and possible futures. It was a world she didn't dare consider exploring.

However much he made her want to.

"Good night, then," he said, crossing the threshold and pulling the door closed behind him.

Alex released her breath in an audible sigh. "Good night," she echoed softly, knowing he couldn't hear, but needing to say it anyway. She stood in the center of the room for several moments, her mind on the man who threatened to challenge every defense she had.

The strange happenings of the past two days crowded Jon's mind and drove sleep from his body. He tossed in one direction, then another. He read for a while, then turned out the light and lay in the dark, trying desperately not to think about the woman lying less than thirty feet away. Twice he heard the soft squeak of the bedsprings and wondered if she was having trouble sleeping, too. Once he thought he heard her call out and got out of bed to see if she was having a nightmare. But her door was firmly closed, the space beneath it dark, the silence in the hallway complete.

It must have been after three when he finally abandoned the frustrating attempt to sleep, rising and donning a thick terry-cloth robe he'd picked up last time he was in the States. He would have that nightcap he'd foolishly rejected, then return to lie awake for the few remaining hours of the night.

He crept past her doorway, determined not to inflict his insomnia on her. He was already to the stairs before he realized her door had been open. Instead of the shadowed white door, a yawning hole led into her room.

It was curiosity more than anything else—so he told himself—that compelled him to turn around and investigate.

Her room was dark, but in the light from his own bedroom down the hall he could dimly make out her slender form on the bed. His chest seemed too tight for his rapidly beating heart. He felt like the worst kind of voyeur, watching her sleep, liking the way her small frame made the bed seem large, wondering if she had opened the door because she was frightened, wishing he could see into her dreams, wishing she was awake.

"You can't sleep, either?" her contralto voice asked, startling him, quickening his heartbeat even further. Her voice played on his skin like a concert pianist with a finely-tuned instrument.

"No," he said. Even to himself, his voice sounded harsh. His eyes strained against the dark to see her face, to read her thoughts.

"I heard you outside my door earlier," she said. It was a statement, not a question.

His hand gripped the doorjamb. This was pure hell, he thought. "I thought I heard you cry out," he said. The harsh note still rang in his voice.

"You don't have to be worried about me," she said.

"I wasn't," he said truthfully. Too truthfully. He heard her quick intake of air. Abruptly, unable to withstand the torture of her proximity, the agony of knowing she was lying half-dressed not seven feet from him, he pushed himself away from the wall and turned to go downstairs.

"Jon?"

He stopped, as if her voice had a physical connection with his body. Perhaps it did. He turned, the war within him consuming his thoughts, racking his body.

She was sitting up, the covers loosely draped across her lap. The soft folds of her nightgown concealed, yet more than hinted at her full, rounded breasts and narrow waist.

Jon reached for the doorjamb, but never connected with it. Instead, he crossed the threshold and advanced into the room. His body blocked the light, throwing his own shadow across her bed, onto her lap. The image was too much, the illusion too strong. Throwing all his own advice to the cold Moscow night, he continued to walk toward her.

He half imagined he could hear her heartbeat, but realized it was his own, thundering in his chest, echoing in his ears. Slowly, he cautioned. *Faster,* his body demanded.

He stood beside the bed, his gaze locking with hers. Her blue eyes held his own image in their widened depths. Slowly, aching with his need of her, he reached a hand to her face and cupped her cheek. Her skin was warm from the pillow; her hair, spilling over his hand, was as soft as satin and as dark and full of color as mink.

She parted her lips as if to speak, but he silenced her with his own lips, swallowing her words, demanding her permission, exhorting her own need.

From the moment he had stood in her doorway, in the door she'd accidentally—or had it been deliberately?—left open, Alex's heart had taken over. Her mind raged at her, threatening her, pleading with her, urging her to caution, trying to make her remember her past, her own inability to rely on the very things that Jon Wyndham made her want to try...things like trust, instinct—love. But her heart, upon seeing him, had taken precedence.

She'd seen his struggle in the doorway, had heard the ragged edge in his voice. Though his face had been shadowed, she'd felt his gaze, so searing it had seemed to burn her.

And when he turned away, his hand a tight fist, his face a rigid mask, her heart had constricted in a well-understood, wholly sympathetic pain.

It's bad luck to talk across a threshold.

She'd called him back. *No,* her mind had cried; *yes,* her heart had argued...and won. And now, with his lips on hers, his warm, trembling hand against her face, she didn't care which had ascendancy...her heart or her mind. He was kissing her as she had never been kissed before, with passion, with untold desire and with something else, something gentle, almost reverent.

There was a vulnerability in his kiss, a touching vulnerability. He was confident, yet not arrogant. His touch was sure, yet he trembled. As he lowered himself to the side of the bed, his arms sliding around her, drawing her close against him, his assault on her lips never paused, yet his lips eased, gentled, letting her know all she had to do was say no and he would stop.

She leaned into his embrace and returned his kiss with an ardor she'd never totally allowed free rein before. He shuddered against her and groaned.

The feel of her, of her lips beneath his, her soft, warm breath playing on his face, on his neck, against his temples, aroused him as nothing else had ever done, made him feel he'd been searching for something for a million years and had just that moment discovered what he'd been looking for. He was filled with a sense of wonder and an odd feeling of profound relief. *He'd found her.* As easily as this, he'd found her. Any doubts he might have had, any inner warnings, fled, driven away by her searing touch. Tomorrow was as insignificant as yesterday; her lips promised *now*. He felt as if he'd been asleep for years and had just awakened.

His hands slid beneath the fabric of her nightgown to the soft flesh of her breasts. His moan drowned hers as his fingers curled around one taut nipple. She arched toward him—unconsciously, he knew—allowing him to explore her more fully, urging him to continue this foray.

Whether he shifted her or they moved together in a dance as ancient as the midnight sun, she would never know, but she accepted the bed's firm embrace as readily as she accepted Jon's lips pressed against her bare throat.

His hands, she discovered, had the same texture as his voice: as mellow and soft as a fine wine, as fiery and strong as brandy. And his lips were liquid velvet. He murmured her name and spoke in the language of lovers everywhere, but the things he said were meant for her alone.

With deft fingers, he slid her gown from her shoulders, baring her breasts. Then he shifted, letting the dim light from his distant bedroom fall on her. She felt his eyes on her and held her breath at the expression on his face. It was not mere pleasure, not mere acknowledgement of her looks; he was gazing down at her exposed flesh with bemused wonder.

Slowly, as if he knew his touch could burn, he caressed her bared breasts, his eyes rising to meet hers. "Alex," he said, his voice husky with emotion, "I've imagined this so many times, but I didn't even dream how beautiful you really are."

Had his gaze not held hers so steadily, she might have dismissed his words, thinking them a creation only of the moment. But his face was serious, his words sincere.

She had no answer for him, save in her touch and her kiss. She drew his head to hers and let her tongue tell him that she felt the same way about him. With a deft motion, he half lifted her and swept the covers from beneath her. And then her gown. The terry of his robe brushed her hot-cold skin and, tuned to her, he shrugged free of it, pressing his own hot, fully-aroused body to hers.

There was no turning back now, she thought, nor did she want to. She couldn't have. And, miraculously, for this one night, this one moment, she needn't.

His skin was as smooth as his lips, his broad shoulders muscled and taut. He lay perfectly still for a long moment, then slowly, easily, stretched against her, letting her know what she already knew, that he wanted her. But when he murmured her name, his lips capturing a straining nipple, she knew he also needed for her to want him equally, as fully and deeply as he wanted her; he needed her heart and mind, not merely her body.

Gasping, arching against him, she could no more have withheld her need from him than she could have risen and walked away. Caught by him, trapped in an embrace she wouldn't relinquish for all the freedom on earth, she knew that for now, for tonight, he could have her trust, he could have her heart. Yes, for the present, he could have all of her. All . . . because he asked for it and because he gave nothing less than all of himself.

And because for once, for one achingly glorious moment, he made her see rainbows in winter, made her believe in tomorrows, made her believe dreams were real, that hoping was enough.

His lips and tongue teased at her breasts, suckling, laving, urging her to fly with him, while his hands roamed her curves, her legs, the hollows of her throat. Her legs parted at his touch, and her back arched, instinctively, to allow him access to her inner secrets.

She moved, clay beneath the sculptor's hands, craving his touch, matching his need with a hunger of her own. His fingers probed expertly, promising even greater magic, while his name formed on her lips and she told him of her need of, him with her fingers across his broad back.

When she thought she would die from his searing touch, he rose, poised above her, all man, all desire. His body glistened in the dim light, his powerful frame awesome in its intent. And yet it was his eyes that held her mesmerized. How had she ever thought them merely warm? They were hot with promise. Her heart constricted painfully.

Slowly, his eyes still locked with hers, feeling her inner heat envelop him, he lowered his body into hers. Never had anything felt so right before; never had he had to fight so hard for control. Watching her lips part, her incredible eyes glass over, he swallowed an urge to confess his growing need for her, letting his body say it for him. If he said it aloud, she would run. He knew that instinctively, just as his hands and mouth seemed to know where to touch her dewy skin to make her moan.

He felt her hands slide to his shoulders and grip them, her touch both soothing and a torture. As she arched against him, her breathing growing ragged, her lower lip caught between her teeth, he gave up his internal struggle and gave in to the demand her body made.

His body matched hers in an aching rhythm, rocking, thrusting, parrying, motion causing action, touch causing caress. He never wanted this moment to end. But her low murmured cry triggered a chain reaction in him, releasing a drive as ancient as birch forests, winter sunsets and ocean waves. Softly, as easily as the rocking of a sled through deep snow, as tenderly as an old love ballad, yet as intensely as a rogue hurricane, they loved.

Time became meaningless; all other concerns faded. Pleasure grew, ebbed, grew even deeper as they moaned each other's names and whispered soft words neither one could hear over the pounding of their hearts. Each touch became a new delight, each kiss a treasure.

His mouth beseeched her, trailing heat against her skin. His hands implored. His body demanded. Faster and swifter, harder and deeper, stronger and stronger, until she cried his name aloud.

The world seemed to implode, all parts of the earth entering her, drawn inward, whirling into the deeper universe within her. She held him as if he were the only anchor in a vortex and dimly heard him cry out her name, then felt him cling to her helplessly as shudders racked his body. In that moment, in the clarity of a universe far removed from rational, everyday thought, she knew they had joined in a union so intense that neither of them would ever be the same again.

Jon held her to him, crushing her, his lips pressed against her temple. He hoped she would understand that there were no words that could fill the void their passion had created. There were no sentences, no reassurances that could ever be uttered that would add anything to their joining, and nothing could be said that would ever set the world back to the way it was.

Life had changed. It was that simple.

And that complicated.

For the now was over and tomorrow had arrived. As suddenly as the dawn, as quickly as the robin's first song in spring, Jon understood that he couldn't go back to lonely nights and even lonelier mornings. He wanted Alex.

"Jon?" she murmured, and he felt her voice to his core. He pressed his lips to her still-quivering mouth in answer.

He didn't let her speak, didn't give her the chance to take away the new promise he'd discovered. She'd given herself to him fully, he knew that. But in the aftermath, when her mind denied what her heart had found to be true, she might reject that perfection, might find a way to turn her back on the bright hope, and he, for the moment, would stall that thought. He held her, rocking her slowly, bringing her back to the night world of his guest bedroom, trying to tell her that there was time.

And after her breathing had steadied and her heartbeat had slowed, Jon lay holding her close to him, his eyes open and dry, wondering how he could get her to forget the past and think of the future.

When she felt his breathing change, when his body had shifted to more easily accommodate sleep, Alex stirred. She slid from the bed carefully, leaving the covers over him. She shrugged into his housecoat, the first thing that came to hand, and moved to a chair near the bed. Enveloped in his soft, warm robe, surrounded by his scent, she hugged the collar to her throat as she studied him.

With his hair disarrayed, his lips parted in sleep, his fiery eyes closed, Jon seemed a far cry from the threat he posed in her mind, and yet the very fact that he could sleep disarmed her. His broad and gentle hand lay against her pillow, cupped, somehow seeking her presence even in sleep. Did he have any idea how much he had moved her? How much he disturbed her?

Curling up on the chair, drawing her knees to her chest, she watched him sleep, seeing yet another facet of Jon Wyndham. Would the different phases of his personality never cease? Would she want them to?

She shivered slightly, both from lack of warmth and from the turmoil he created in her. She was sitting on this chair, away from him, because she felt the need for distance, an atavistic need to stand free of him. She had tried to tell him some of that need, but his kisses had silenced her, his stroking hand had soothed the words away. As if he had known what she would say, as if he had known she wouldn't listen to her heart.

"Come back to bed," he said sleepily, making her jump, making her wonder how long he'd been awake, watching her watching him.

"Jon..."

"Mmm?"

In the darkness between them, in the distance created by the few feet between the chair and the bed, Alex was able to draw on a reserve of honesty within her. "I'm afraid," she said, and though that seemed inadequate, it somehow said everything.

He sat up, not quickly, not rushing to her side, merely propping his body on one elbow. She couldn't read his expression in the dim light. "Of the recent events...or me? Us?"

"Me," she said quickly, then added, "You. Us. All of it."

"I know," he said, and though his words also might have seemed less than satisfactory, they, too, said everything. "We have time, Alex," he said.

She shook her head, thinking not of the present but of the long-distant past...of her father and of her ruined marriage.

"Trust me," Jon said, holding out his free hand.

"I can't," she replied. And to her own ears, the words sounded like the cry of a little girl.

"For now, you can," he said. "Come back to bed. You can't be hurt here." He turned the covers down on her side of the bed.

As if his voice were a drug, she felt some of the worry slide from her. She rose and crossed the few steps to the bed.

"It's okay, Alex. Everybody has the right to be afraid. Even you."

She released the belt of the housecoat and feeling ridiculously shy, slid beneath the covers, drawing them almost to her chin. "You don't seem very frightened," she said.

He chuckled ruefully. "Don't kid yourself. I'm terrified." The admission served to further relax her.

"Of what?" she murmured, half fearing his answer.

He was silent for a long moment, then slowly, his voice almost devoid of emotion, he said, "Of having to go back to winter now that I've tasted spring." He drew her into his arms, cupping her back to his flat stomach. His lips pressed against her shoulder.

Alex digested his words, tasting the bittersweet loneliness inherent in them, feeling as if they had been wrenched from some inner part of herself. How long had she been lonely, too? How long had she been trying to deny it?

"Will you tell me about it?" he asked softly, his breath shifting the hair at the base of her neck.

She shook her head slightly and heard his sigh.

"Alex, trust isn't something that happens overnight. Not to everyone, anyway." He half chuckled and drew her even closer. "Sometimes it has to be proven. Who knows?"

"It's not you I don't trust . . . exactly," Alex said softly, stung by his caring for her feelings, feeling flayed by his warmth and his honesty.

"What, then?" he asked, his baritone voice vibrating against her.

"Me," she said. "I can't trust myself."

"To do what?" he asked cautiously.

"What?" she echoed, blankly.

"You said you couldn't trust yourself. That implies you can't trust yourself to do something. . . ."

Alex had never thought of trust in that light before, of its having to *do* something, anything. She told him this, hesitantly, and waited for a reply that was several seconds in coming.

"Alex," he said finally, his tone tender and somewhat sad, "trust isn't like falling in love. It's more like loving itself." When she didn't say anything, he continued. "Every aspect of trust—whether it's trust in yourself, trust in someone else or simply a belief that the sun's going to come up the next day—every single aspect requires an action of some kind."

"I don't understand what you're saying," Alex said.

"Yes, you do," he argued. "Trust without action is like harmony without a melody."

She mulled that over for several heartbeats, then half turned in his arms. "Do you trust yourself?"

"I *have* to trust myself," he answered swiftly. "It's like taking responsibility."

"Responsibility," she mused, but he suspected she thought of it negatively. "Isn't that the whole trouble?"

"The trouble?"

"Once you've admitted responsibility—and you know you've chosen wrongly—how can you ever trust yourself again?"

At the almost-tearful note in her voice, Jon realized the barrier she had raised between them was higher than he had ever imagined. He didn't say anything in response, trying to catch the meanings behind the meaning.

"What if you make the wrong choices?" she asked.

Jon hesitated before answering. Wrong choices? Finally, willing his hands to be still, forcing a bracing note into his voice, he answered, "You still made a choice. *I* still made a choice. I have to trust myself that every choice is a good one."

"But they aren't—always good choices, I mean. Some of them are horrible."

Jon realized she wasn't speaking about any choice he might have made, but about choices of her own. And he understood that tonight wasn't being considered... yet. "Remember what William Shakespeare wrote?" he asked, and felt her shake her head. He quoted, " 'There is nothing either good or bad, but thinking makes it so.' "

She paused before answering. He felt her steady breathing, questioned her suddenly chill skin and rapid heartbeat. It was as if he could feel her mind probing his words.

"And you feel that way?" she said, a question, not a statement.

He nodded, then added, "There are no wrong choices, only choices."

"And you really believe that? No good... no bad?"

He hesitated again. "I believe the consequences can be unfortunate—or at least seemingly so—at the time. But in the long run, I believe we are what we are based on the choices we make."

Like her thoughts at the circus, the spiral of connections, she thought. We are what we know, who we know, what and who we choose.

Jon's soft voice continued. "I trust in my ability to choose. I trust in yours." His words brought the discussion to the moment, to the hours spent in his arms. She'd chosen them, he was telling her. Was he asking her if she felt she'd chosen unwisely?

Alex was silent for so long that Jon thought she might have drifted to sleep. But then he felt her sigh. "I don't know," she said. "I just don't know. I've distrusted my own instincts for so long now."

"What about your gallery?"

"That's different," she said swiftly.

"How so?"

"I—" she began, then stopped. "It's just different."

"Every situation is," he said, gently stroking her arm with his forefinger, pressing his lips to her shoulder. He hoped she knew he wasn't lecturing her. He hoped she understood that his words came from a very real place inside him.

He knew that she'd held the notion of her own inability to trust for so long that his few words couldn't begin to break down her wall of reserve. But maybe, just maybe, he'd knocked a stone loose. Of all things, he would hate it if she regretted this night's events. She had trusted him enough to allow him to come to her bed. Would she trust herself enough in the morning light not to hate herself for it?

Jon sighed and cupped her body to his. With his arms around her, his breath warming, half tickling her neck, she found herself wishing things were different, wishing she could picture trust as simply as he did, wishing she could trust him and her feelings for him, as fully as he made her want to.

"Don't run away, Alex," he said, placing a finger against her jaw and propelling her face back until their eyes met.

Caught by his gaze, she could only stare at him in mute entreaty. Tears quickened in her eyes, and she tried blinking them away. When had anyone bothered to care so much? When had anyone cared even half as deeply as she could see that he did?

The past hammered at her mind, the note her father had left: *Caring isn't enough.* The last words she'd exchanged with Tony: *I'll always care, honey. It's just too bad there's two of you to care for.*

But Jon was here now, his eyes holding hers, his full lips lowering to hers. His hands gripped her shoulders so tightly that she might have assumed he was angry had she not felt the tenderness in his kiss. He raised his head. His eyes, more shadowed than ever, still shone down on her.

The tears his kiss had driven away sprang back to her eyes and stayed. They stayed as his hands swept her body and demanded her full awareness. *I'm here, now,* his caresses said.

Her tears remained as her body begged for his knowledge. They remained as the world again spiraled and coalesced to form that new universe their joining created. They remained until he kissed them away, his arms holding her tightly, his body shuddering over hers.

She kissed *him,* then. No tears stood in his eyes, but she felt the ache, the unshed tears, inside him, and with her lips and her touch, she tried drying them as he had dried hers.

His grip eased as sleep overtook him, yet he retained his clasp of her hand, and if she moved, his hand would press hers closer to his chest.

Her mind spinning, her heart torn, Alex drifted into an uneasy sleep, where her dreams were filled with memories and a thousand reasons not to let her heart dictate her life. A thousand reasons why she should run from Jon Wyndham . . . should hate him for making her look at herself so probingly, dredging up old hurts, hinting at new dreams.

But most of all, in her dreams, in her half-waking moments, when he turned or touched her, she chafed at the knowledge that, in letting her see that he was a man capable of giving so much, he was breaking through her carefully constructed walls.

But the thought that tortured her the most was the knowledge that she had already chosen. That once again she had trusted her instincts, once again she was committing her heart to a man.

What on earth was she going to do when he let her down?

Chapter 8

Lack of sleep and too many unresolved questions left Jon's eyes gritty and feeling as if he hadn't rested for days. The dim light from the window, showing another gray and cloudy day in Moscow, did nothing to cheer his gloomy thoughts.

Alex was already gone from the bed when he rose, and when he'd joined her in the smallish kitchen, she had refused to meet his eyes. He had reached for her, but without seeming to sidestep him, she nonetheless avoided his touch, holding up her steaming coffee cup as an excuse.

"Alex," he said finally, hating the need for the confrontation, not wanting to force her to think about the ramifications of the night before, "we've got to talk."

"About what?" she murmured, her hands suddenly still, her entire body poised as if for flight.

"It's still just me," he said. "I haven't changed overnight."

Her eyes flicked to his, then away. She sighed heavily. "I know," she said softly. "I know." She stared down into the creamy-brown liquid. "Jon—" She broke off.

"What?"

Still not looking at him, she waved a hand as if to tell him that he should glean what she wanted to say from the warm air of his kitchen. When he didn't say anything, she glanced at him again, her eyes sad.

"You don't know me," she said finally, wearily, sitting down at his table.

"I don't have to know your past," he said. "It's the Alex I know now that matters."

"You don't understand," she said almost desperately. "There are things about me ... things about my past ..."

"Those choices you talked about last night?"

She shook her head, though Jon suspected he'd guessed correctly. "It's no use," she said. "It's not any good."

Jon didn't answer. In his mind, James Bowden's words that first night played over and over again, like a record needle snagged on a piece of lint. *Don't make him fall in love with you, Alex.*

"Alex," he said finally, "whatever happened in the past doesn't matter a tinker's damn to me."

She stood suddenly, sloshing coffee on the table, her eyes all but blazing at him. "Well, it should! It will." Her breath caught on a half sob. "It has to." She whirled on her last mumbled words and ran from the room.

Safely locked in the bathroom, her chest heaving, her cheeks flushed, Alex leaned against the sink, trying to steady her unruly emotions. She had tried to tell him, she assured herself, but he'd misunderstood. He'd waved the past aside as if it were no more than a pile of autumn leaves, but it wasn't that simple.

As he had implied the night before, she was who she was because of that past. He couldn't have one without the other. And once he knew, once he knew just how terrible her judgment was, how untrustworthy her instincts had proved—and had proved throughout her family's history—he couldn't want the woman she was.

Could he?

She took a deep breath and straightened her shoulders. She would tell him. This morning. She owed him that. After last night, she had to tell him. She would tell him the whole truth.

She heard his shower running, and a short time later she heard him leaving the apartment. She should have felt relief when she knew he was gone, but instead, perversely, she was saddened. Would the past never leave her alone? He had given her a chance to let it slip away, toss it out like dirty dish water.

But if she took that way out, it would be like lying. She would be cheating him. He had to know. He had to choose for himself. That was what they'd been talking about, wasn't it? Choices?

She met her own eyes in the mirror. But, dear God, it wasn't like telling him she was Russian. It wasn't like telling him she knew the artifacts weren't Armenian. . . .

She stopped, her hand reaching blindly for the sink. Andre Makarov had said point-blank that the Armenians would not allow the export of the artifacts. But she had never told him that Hans Saalard had told her that the artifacts were Armenian. That was what her mind had been trying to focus on. That had been the niggling discrepancy in his words that first day.

She would have to tell Jon.

She didn't stop to consider the sudden lift of her spirits. She only knew she had to hurry to the embassy.

To see Jon.

Jon walked the long way to the embassy, around the four long city blocks, his feet crunching through knee-deep snowdrifts the street cleaners had never cleared. He pulled at the cold air almost gratefully, wishing it would chill the fire that burned in him.

He'd suspected Alex might regret the night in the cold light of morning. But, he thought grimly, he'd be damned if she'd make him regret it, too. With that thought, his steps slowed. *Regret.* That was what labeling choices as either good or bad did. The very process produced regret.

Last night, with Alex in his arms, her skin gone dewy at his touch, her eyes soft and luminous, had been something he would never regret. Never.

But her reaction this morning made him pause. It didn't make him want her any less, but it did raise some questions he wasn't certain he could answer.

He realized that it was one thing to spout half-baked ideas about good and bad choices in the middle of the night, and an entirely different matter to look one's choice directly in the face in the stark glare of the fluorescent kitchen lights. Not that she suffered from the light; on the contrary, she was as beautiful in the light of day as by the uncertain light of midnight loving. It was her uncertainty he didn't want to see. Didn't want to face.

In some ways, despite his lack of regret, his words made him feel foolish, as if she were slapping him for the intimacy, hitting him for having seen a vulnerable side of Alex Shashkevich. And it saddened him that the night before had been no guarantee. She might be his choice, but she'd made it fairly obvious that he wasn't necessarily hers. And now her demon past was trying to block any hope of a future.

What on earth could she have done to warrant such a flogging now?

She was no fragile, frightened woman, as Margaret had been. If Alex but knew it, her very doubts over her own mistakes spoke of her strength. She didn't doubt others, didn't withhold her trust out of any misguided notion that she'd been let down too often, but rather, from a fear that she would place it incorrectly, that her own instincts were at fault. And that told of a hard-pressed need to see life for what it really was, to live it on her own terms. Simple and clear self-protection.

Unfortunately, it didn't make things any easier to know she was strong. If anything, it presented a greater problem. How would he be able to convince her that she could trust herself with him? That she would be stronger with him? He had failed with Margaret; he had given her no strength at all. Did he even have it left in him to try with Alex?

He felt drawn to her, as a child was pulled to brightly-colored toys, an old man captured by a box of old photographs. She was something—someone—he needed. Wanted. As her lips had moistened and parted, as her thick lashes had drooped and her hands had gone lax with languor, he had felt the distance between them shorten, then disappear altogether.

She had moaned his name, her face drawn, as if in pain. And he suspected the pain was real . . . not physical, perhaps, but mental, or even an emotional burning. She wanted him and if he was right, there was a part of her, a part long denied and ignored, that also needed him. And later she had cried—soft, slow tears—when their union reached its height, as if her body and soul had melded so thoroughly in that intense climax that some further release was necessary. He had soothed her with his hands, her tears mingling with his sweat and drying on his shoulder. But he'd had no words with which to comfort her; even now, he didn't know exactly what she'd wanted from him.

He suspected that, like himself, she had been unprepared for the intensity that sparked between them. That the events that had thrust them together—that he had used to keep them together—had taken her to a place where she never intended to be. James had implied she was a woman for *now,* a today person. One touch, one taste, had told Jon otherwise. But was she a woman for tomorrow? And was he fair to ask it of her? Perhaps he didn't have that in him anymore, either.

And yet, he thought, his mind flipping sides, playing devil's advocate to his wayward heart, Alex had also felt it. And he'd felt her doubts, heard them in her late-night questions. Could she handle the thought of a shared future? Would she be willing to try? Instead of flaying herself with her past, would she share it with him, let him show her that it didn't matter.

What had she done?

And if he did convince her, what did he have that she would want, anyway? A track record of a marriage that had failed even before Margaret died. A history of selfishness that had resulted in the death of the only person who should have mattered, but somehow never did.

He walked blindly past the lines at the bread store, at the dairy store, at the meat store. He sidestepped heavily-coated people avidly reading the newspapers spread in the glass-windowed cases lining the sidewalk. Alex fit in here, he thought. She would fit in anywhere, sprinkling her calm acceptance of the world—if not of herself—the way the fairy-tale Snow Princess dusted the world with sparkling frost.

In pursuing Alex he had nothing to lose but his loneliness. And he had everything to gain. But Alex?

He thought of the foreign-service wives who, like camp followers, dogged their husbands' flighty tracks, trying with world-weary smiles to create a home in whatever achingly lonely part of the world their colorful husbands chose to light.

Jon smiled wryly. What kind of a fool was he? Here he was, just a few days after meeting her, wanting to ask Alex to join him for that sort of struggle. Which was why, as he approached the embassy, he felt no clearer in heart or mind than when he'd left her. The handwriting was clear, and the words spelled no chance.

But what could she have done that was so terrible?

The young and vaguely pretty visa officer from the consular section, Nancy Abernathy, was waiting in his clinic lobby. She was the woman who had been keeping company with Roger Copple, the one Jon had worried about yesterday. Looking at her now, Jon cursed himself for not calling her into his office then. Whatever Roger Copple had touched had touched Nancy, as well.

His nurse said Nancy had been waiting for over an hour. Jon shook the snow from his coat, donned a smile and called the woman in.

He had noticed the slightly haggard expression on her face the day after Copple's coffin was flown back to the States, but had attributed it to grief over Roger Copple's death. Now he wondered, as he should have wondered then.

Abruptly, damningly, Alex's words of the night before came to his mind: *What if you make the wrong choices?*

Nancy coughed as she entered the room, making the welcoming smile on his face fade. He waved her to a stool, feeling a cold dismay. At such close proximity, he could see the dramatic changes in Nancy Abernathy. Her skin was tightly drawn across sharp cheekbones; her eyes seemed lost in dark, bruised-looking circles. Her mouth was limned with cold sores.

"Doctor—" she began, the remainder of her sentence obscured by a fresh series of coughs.

He rose from his desk, handed her a tissue and placed the back of his hand against her hot, dry brow. "How long has this been going on?" he asked.

"A while...now," she said between coughing spasms. "I feel as if I've been sick for weeks."

"Stomach?"

"Cramps," she said. "I've lost nearly fifteen pounds." Her lips drew back in a pitiful attempt at a smile. "Not that I'm complaining about that, you understand...."

She should, he thought grimly; she looked anorexic.

After a quick check of her throat, ears and respiration, Jon escorted Nancy to the dressing room, handed her a hospital gown and called the nurse in for a blood-and-urine series. He phoned Ned Sternberg while he waited, telling the older man that he didn't want to sound alarmist, but Nancy Abernathy appeared to have all the symptoms Roger Copple had.

"Appendicitis?" Ned asked pointedly.

Catching the inherent warning in the older man's words, Jon couched his words carefully. "The blood test isn't completed yet. We don't have the kind of facilities that allow us to make an instant diagnosis. But, from the initial examination, I'd have to say she's a very sick young woman."

"How soon will you know?"

"Definitely? Tomorrow, at the earliest. Taking all factors into account, however, I'd say we've got a positive."

"Damn," Ned said. "They'd been seeing each other for quite a while, hadn't they?"

"That's the rumor, but it's fairly irrelevant. *Appendicitis* isn't contagious."

Ned sighed. "I know. I'm afraid you're going to have to ask her some questions, Jon."

Jon didn't need to ask what questions.

Lying on the narrow table, swathed in a worn hospital gown and a thin sheet, Nancy looked even more pathetic than she had earlier. And as Jon began his questioning, her face began to register fear.

She didn't know what "deal" the doctor was talking about, she said.

"The only artifact I know about is this ring. Roger gave it to me." She held out her thin hand to show the doctor and nurse the large gold band with lapis lazuli inlaid in an intricate design. "About three weeks ago, he showed me a collection of things he'd purchased. He told me to pick out something for myself. I picked this."

Feeling torn by both hope—that they had at last discovered the artifacts—and despair—knowing Nancy was to undergo a lengthy, uncertain healing process—Jon shook his head. "Did you touch anything else?"

"Yes, why?" Nancy asked, and her coughing resumed. "There was a pretty candelabra and a chalice or two. They were beautiful." Her eyes teared. "Roger and I drank a toast from the chalice."

She closed her eyes, presumably with the pain of remembering, and so missed the spasm of fear Jon felt cross his face.

"But the ring...I thought it would...let Roger see where I stood.... You know, ring...marriage?" The tears slowly spilled from her eyes and edged in narrow tracks down her temples.

"Were they—" she paused and coughed "—black market?"

Jon shook his head, silently cursing the dead Roger Copple. What on earth had the man been thinking of to involve Nancy Abernathy? What kind of love was that? It was criminality on a far broader scale than mere thievery. It was tantamount to murder.

"I thought it was so pretty," Nancy said, another tear trickling down her cheek as she turned her hand in the air, letting the ring catch the light from the fluorescents overhead.

The nurse reached for the ring, but Jon jerked her hand back.

"Don't! Don't touch it," he said. He was immediately sorry he'd reacted so quickly because both women stared at him with frightened eyes.

Trying to maintain a calm he was far from feeling, he advised a now openly-sobbing Nancy of his suspicion that the ring was "tainted" and that she'd be much better without it. The poignant irony of his words cut him to the quick.

Such was her state and such the command in his eyes that when he held out a plastic bag, she tipped her hand obediently, allowing the ring to slide easily from her too-thin finger and drop with a soft whisper into the waiting bag. The skin where the ring had been was burned and bruised looking. Holding the tips of her fingers, he turned her hand up and down, studying the tell-tale marks of radiation burn.

The immediacy of the burn, the direct cause and effect, told Jon the artifacts had not been out of their original burial site for long. They had to be found, and found quickly. They were spreading death in a radioactive epidemic.

With a sigh, he sealed the plastic bag and again called Ned.

"In order to make a *proper* diagnosis," he said cautiously, "I'll need a lead-lined container." Knowing Ned would understand why he needed a container that would prevent radiation leakage, he hung up the phone without waiting for a reply.

Ned brought the container himself. He watched solemnly as Jon dropped the plastic bag into the container and shook his head as he sealed it.

"How is she?"

Jon stared at him for a moment, wondering if the man was as coldhearted as he sounded. He bit back the harsh words he wanted to say. "She's sick," he said simply. "Not as bad off as Copple was, but she's sick. It's not a field of medicine too many doctors are familiar with—me included—which probably says a lot for man's stupidity in playing with dangerous toys."

"Can I talk with her?" Ned asked.

"Of course, but I don't think she knows anything about all of this."

"She had the ring," Ned said, his eyes on the lead-lined container. He looked up and met Jon's eyes.

The bleak expression made Jon reconsider his opinion of the man. He'd been wrong to assume he was coldhearted. He was scared. He was worried. He was thinking of a thousand implications that Jon, a nonpolitical figure, couldn't begin to dream of. But he wasn't coldhearted.

Watching him approach Nancy Abernathy, seeing the shock of the older man's reaction to Nancy's debilitated state, Jon couldn't help but think that had Copple not died when he did, Alex might have held something similar in her hands, might have worn some piece of deadly jewelry. The thought of Alex's clear skin blotching and tightening, bruises appearing beneath her eyes, sores ringing her lips, settled like a canker in his heart.

"Doctor?" His nurse tapped him on the shoulder, making Jon start slightly. "Miss Shashkevich is here." She pointed to the waiting room.

Instinctively, his heart constricting with a wild hope, Jon started to walk toward the waiting room, but he stopped short of the doorway. He wanted to walk straight through, wanted to take her in his arms and shake the shadows of the past from her eyes. But he had Nancy and Ned waiting for him, too. For a brief second, he almost abandoned them, but duty held him fast. He reluctantly told his nurse to have Alex wait. "I'll be with her as soon as I'm done."

Jon stepped into the small room where Nancy Abernathy lay, and studied Ned. The older man's face was tired and in the harsh light of the clinic, drawn and gray. Nancy had not yet seen the older man; her head was turned away, silent tears etching her pallid skin.

Like Ned, Jon closed his eyes momentarily, trying to blot out the fact that her breathing was far too loud, too labored, her features pale and overemphasized by her loss of weight and the sickness eating at her.

Ned cleared his throat. Though it was a habit with him, Jon knew that this time, the clearing was an effort. "Nancy, the doctor tells me you're a pretty sick young woman."

Jon noted with a bitter smile that Ned was staying well away from the table where Nancy lay.

Nancy's eyes widened in fear at Ned's appearance in the room. They shifted to Jon for reassurance. "Am I going to die?" she asked.

Jon shook his head, "I don't believe so, Nancy. But I'm not going to kid you by telling you that you're not very ill. You're in a pretty bad way right now."

"What is it? Is it appendicitis, like Roger had?"

Again Jon shook his head, despite Ned's warning glance. "No, Nancy," he said, knowing the time for hiding the truth was past. It was as if the doubts and questions he felt in Alex now shaded this conversation, as well. But here, he had no doubts. Here, in the light of day, with Nancy looking twenty years older than she should, it was time for the absolute truth. Let security hang. "I believe it's radiation poisoning."

"What?"

"Jon—"

"Damn it, Ned, the woman's got a right to know what's going on. She's the one who's got to fight this."

Ned expelled an audible gust of air. "Is this room secure?" he asked.

Jon chuckled humorlessly. "As secure as any embassy room." Which was to say, not at all.

Ned sighed again but turned to Nancy. Jon was relieved to see the man's expression soften. "Apparently Roger Copple was trying to move some very hot items on the black market."

"No," Nancy said weakly, and Jon realized that despite Roger's commonly-acknowledged proclivities, despite his death, despite the evidence Jon had removed from her finger, Nancy didn't want to think about Roger's involvement with the black market.

There were no guarantees, were there? he thought with a glumness that went core deep. The strange life-style and loneliness of living in a restricted environment left women like Nancy Abernathy—and men like himself?—oddly vulnerable to the wrong kinds of love. The wrong people. They all took love where they could find it, no matter how wrong for them that love might prove to be.

Was that part of the reason Alex adhered so tenaciously to the belief that she had to choose wisely, that her own instincts were too often at fault? Fear of the wrong kinds of love, the wrong kinds of people? The thought saddened him even beyond the sorrow he felt for Nancy's condition.

He remembered Alex's shock on learning that Copple played in the black-market arena. Nancy, though saddened, didn't appear shocked. Somehow that seemed even more tragic to Jon than the concept of having chosen unwisely; she had known, however unconsciously, and yet had still continued to see the man. Well, it all had to come out now. She would have to see Roger for what he'd been. Jon hoped Ned would at least try to spare her feelings.

"Nancy, I'm afraid Roger was very active on the black market," Ned said, but not without sympathy. "If you didn't know about this, I'm sorry for you. But he was being watched closely because of those very activities." He glanced at Jon. "Unfortunately—for both him and every-one else involved—he wasn't watched closely enough."

"What are you saying?" Nancy asked peevishly. "Roger didn't need to die? But he died of appendicitis."

"No, my dear," Ned said, looking not at her but at the lead-lined container sitting in silent rebuke on the counter-top. "Roger Copple died of greed." He raised a hand to prevent Jon from speaking. Then, throwing his own edict of caution to the winds, he said, "We believe he may have been trying to peddle objects removed from the Chernobyl area."

"Oh, no!" Nancy cried, and held up her burned hand. "The ring he gave me? It was from there?"

"We believe it may have been, yes."

"Oh, my God," she moaned, holding her hand away from her, as if denying its connection to her body. "Did he die of—of radiation poisoning?"

"We believe so, yes," Jon answered, stepping over to her. He took her hand and applied ointment to the burn mark on her finger. Then he lightly wrapped the hand in gauze and laid it gently on the table. "How long did you wear the ring, Nancy?" he asked softly.

"Three—no, almost four weeks."

"Did he tell you where it came from?" Ned asked.

"No," Nancy murmured. "He only said it was old and very valuable."

Ned snorted in disgust. "Where did you see this collection, Nancy?"

"It was at a man's house."

"Where, Nancy? Where was this house?"

She shook her head. "I don't know. Roger drove. It was dark."

"North? South? Was it out of the city?"

"I don't know," she said fretfully. "I don't know. I told you. It was dark. North, I think. Out in the country. There were lots of trees. It was a dacha. The man's country cabin. Or maybe it wasn't his.... It was empty, except for the crate. The things were on top of the crate. And Roger had wine." She began to cry in dry, wheezy sobs. "The other man was sick. He kept coughing. . . ." She trailed off, then looked up at Jon with new hope. "He was sick. Couldn't it be the flu or something?"

"I don't think so, Nancy," Jon answered sadly. There was no point in deluding her about the seriousness of her problem.

"He drank the wine with us." Her voice caught on a ragged cough. "Oh, God, I didn't know," she said. "I didn't know."

Ned asked her if the man's name was Apraskin. She shook her head and said she wasn't sure. "Something like that. He was going to take the things somewhere."

"Where? Do you know?" Ned's voice was sharp.

Nancy shook her head helplessly. "I don't know." Her body convulsed in another spasm of coughing.

Jon shook his head at Ned and laid his hand on Nancy's shoulder. "Why didn't you remove the ring when it began to cause you pain?" His question made him think of Alex waiting in the lobby. Could things that caused pain be removed so easily?

Nancy cried out, as if betrayed. In a very real sense, Jon knew she had been. "I wanted to," she cried. "It itched. At first it was just annoying, then it began to hurt." She hiccoughed. "But then Roger died. And I didn't want to take it off. It was all I had of him, you know? I guess . . . I felt it would be . . . disloyal . . . or something." Her voice broke completely, then, and her frail body convulsed with sobs.

"I'm afraid, Nancy," Jon said, patting her shoulder, bitterly looking at Ned, "that he's given you more than that to remember him by."

"But I . . . w-will I live?"

"Yes," Jon said. "We're going to med-evac you to our facility in Wiesbaden, West Germany, today."

"But, Jon—" Ned began.

"Today," Jon stated, his eyes locked with Ned's. "I'll make the arrangements now."

Ned followed him from the room. Jon pulled the door closed, and his eyes went to the door separating them from Alex.

"Jon, we're not even sure that—"

"Ned, go back in there, look at that girl and tell me you're not gut positive. Tell me we should treat her here. We've already had one person die. Do you want another?" Until he'd said the words, he hadn't realized how personally responsible he felt for Roger's death. Hadn't realized why he was so intent on finding that collection and seeing it buried, once and for all. And why he needed to see that Alex never touched that collection of artifacts with death so beautifully etched in every line.

Ned held up his hands in the classic no-more-arguments gesture. "All right. But we keep it under wraps."

"Why? So somebody else Copple gave a little present to can come in here in a few weeks? He showed the collection to Nancy. Gave her a piece from it. Who else might he have let glimpse a little death? We know Apraskin must have come in contact with it. Nancy said he was supposed to move it somewhere. Maybe that's what he was trying to tell Alex and me yesterday."

"But his words made no sense."

"Maybe they do, if we think of them as a location."

"Like what?"

"I don't know. But he obviously thought Alex and I would understand."

"You're not going to talk with Alex about this, are you?"

Again Jon glanced at the closed door before answering. "She's involved, Ned."

Ned swept a hand through his hair. "This is getting out of control. Tom Kenyon is going to have a fit."

Jon met Ned's eyes and said slowly, "We're talking about some very hot art here."

Ned's eyes sharpened, and Jon knew he was thinking about Nancy Abernathy. "And then what?"

"I tried talking with Apraskin's son last night. I left my card for him. Maybe we can get him to tell us something."

"I should have done something about Copple months ago," Ned said, not entirely irrelevantly.

"That's water under the proverbial bridge," Jon said. Why was it, he thought, that everything today centered on choices?

Ned sighed. "Do what you think is best, Doctor," he said wearily.

Jon half smiled, less than grateful for having the problem shifted to his shoulders. "The powers that be obviously expected some sort of contact. They were there fast enough after the man was shot yesterday. And they followed us to the circus last night," he said.

Ned raised an eyebrow. "Yes? Then whatever 'Ivan, eleven, forty-three' means must be important. I don't think they know any more than we do about this. Except, perhaps, when it started and how in blazes they're going to keep it from becoming an international incident."

"I'd like to talk to Andre Makarov about this," Jon said.

Ned stared at him as if he'd lost his mind.

Jon added quickly, "The other man, Tursunov, made it pretty clear that Makarov was in big trouble. I think he'd probably bend over backward to locate that collection—if only to save his own neck."

Ned stared into Jon's eyes for a long moment, seeming to consider his words. It was impossible for Jon to guess the man's thoughts. Finally Ned nodded, though he looked far from happy. "On one condition. You don't go unaccompanied. And I want a mem-con." His eyes locked pointedly with Jon's. "And I'm going to assign a tail."

Jon nodded slowly. He hated the detailed Memoranda of Conversation, recalling every word and nuance of a meeting or chance encounter. It read like a script, only it was usually boring enough to put him to sleep.

Ned reached for the waiting room door. "And another thing—" He turned the knob but didn't pull the door open "—I don't want to see a word of this on the front page of any western newspaper. The embassy is involved in a potentially explosive situation. Remember that Copple wasn't getting these things at the local commission store, he was *fencing* them."

"The important thing is to find those artifacts," Jon said. "Nancy only had a *ring*—a little, insignificant ring—on her finger for three or four weeks. She drank a toast from a glow-in-the-dark chalice. We'll be lucky to pull her through. And if we do, we won't know the aftereffects for years. This stuff isn't just tainted, Ned. It's *death!*"

Ned sighed heavily. "Just try to keep it out of the press, okay?"

Jon shook his head. He knew Ned wasn't missing the point, yet the man's training in secrecy was so ingrained, he was having difficulty with the concept of Jon's talking with Makarov and even more trouble considering letting information leak to the press. "Okay, Ned, okay."

Ned shook his head and jerked the door open, then turned weary eyes back to Jon. A sad smile curved his lips. "I think a lot about a house I have in Annapolis," he said. "It overlooks the water and has flower boxes at the windows. I bought it years ago, a little place to retire to when I wanted out of this business. Lately I find I can't seem to get it out of my mind."

Ned hesitated in the threshold as he saw who was waiting for Jon. He gave Jon a sour smile, nodded at Alex and crossed the room with hand outstretched.

His heart quickening at Alex's reserved smile, Jon followed, positioning himself at her side.

After their greetings, Jon turned to Alex and softly told her about Nancy Abernathy.

"She was wearing a ring she said Copple let her choose from a large collection of artifacts."

Ned asked Alex if she was certain a ring had been part of the collection.

Alex nodded, but said she couldn't be sure it was the same ring unless she saw it.

"In this case," Ned said, leaning his head toward the inner clinic door, "I think we can assume it was."

"Will she be all right?" Alex asked.

Jon shrugged and spread his hands. "I hope so," he said. "She's not as far gone as Copple was." He told Alex what he'd already told Ned about the relative lack of knowledge about the problem of radiation poisoning.

"Alex," Ned said, "Nancy said Apraskin was going to move the artifacts somewhere. We now believe he may have been trying to tell you where."

"But he hardly said anything, and what he did say makes no sense."

"But apparently he thought it would to you."

"But why me?" she asked.

For a moment, Ned's eyes narrowed; then he shrugged. "Who knows? Maybe Copple told him you were the potential buyer."

Unconsciously, Alex stepped closer to Jon.

Ned turned toward the outer door. He paused and looked over his shoulder at Jon. "Remember what I said."

"Goodbye, Ned," Jon said with irony.

Alex hadn't touched the lead-lined container, only stared at it for a long time before speaking. "We've got to take this to Andre Makarov," she said. She'd already told Jon of the final discrepancy she'd discovered in Makarov's earlier statements. But she still felt the contents of the canister belonged with the Soviets.

Jon didn't answer for a moment and she turned on the stool to look at him. He was polishing his glasses, apparently in deep thought. She wanted to smooth the frown from his brow and thought that if circumstances had been different that morning, he would have been frowning over something else, her past, her faulty judgment, not Roger Copple's.

"We've got to take that ring to Andre," Alex repeated.

"Hmm?"

"The ring inside this container isn't the property of the United States," Alex persisted, pointing to the deadly object Ned had left in Jon's office. "It happens to belong to the Soviets. It's theirs and they should take care of it."

Jon sighed wearily. The day had been a long one, reassuring Nancy, arranging her departure and briefing the army specialists in Wiesbaden. One leak and the entire fiasco would blow sky-high.

And, on top of everything, Jon thought wearily, Ned had left it up to him to dispose of the damn canister. Alex had assumed Ned had forgotten it. Jon knew better than that; Ned never forgot anything. "As it happens," he said finally, "I agree with you" He held up his hand. "You call Makarov's office, I'll call Ned."

He was surprised when her hand lightly stroked his cheek. He covered her hand with his and met her gaze. The confusion and doubts he read in the blue depths of her eyes had little to do with the missing collection of deadly art. It had to do with the night before, with choices made, past and present. He drew her into his arms and held her tightly against him, remembering his earlier thoughts, remembering the burned ring around Nancy's finger, the sores on her lips. Never Alex. Never.

For a moment, Alex allowed the embrace to drive away the doubts she harbored about the two of them. Last night, everything had been easy; loving him had been easy. Today, her fears were back, this time not for herself, but for him.

Tell him now, her mind urged. Tell him now.

But he pulled away before her lips could move. "Let's get this over with," he said, and the weary note in his voice chased her meager courage away. He had enough on his plate right now; he didn't need to have her unpalatable past set before him. He didn't need to know why she couldn't love him as she wanted to, and, more importantly, why he couldn't be allowed to love her.

He reached for her hand, then raised it to his lips. His eyes met hers and stayed there, telling her something, something warm and easy.

A wave of sorrow rippled through her. Nothing was that easy, she thought, shaking her head. Nothing was easy at all.

How could she tell him? What words could she use? He blamed himself for his wife's death. She could start there, telling that at least he hadn't tried to cause that death.

She couldn't say the same about herself.

Chapter 9

"What is this?" Andre Makarov demanded, pointing at the lead-lined canister Jon set on his desk. The canister gleamed dully, reflecting the light from the single bare bulb in Makarov's office.

"There's a ring inside it," Jon said. "We believe it came from that collection of art that's been causing so much trouble lately." He reached for Alex's hand. The pressure urged her to relax, to trust him. Her hand fluttered in his as her heart fluttered in her chest.

Makarov paled, eyeing the canister as the policeman the day before had eyed the dead man on the street. Slowly, as though in shock, he lowered himself into his chair. His eyes never left the canister.

"Where did you get it?" he croaked. "Did you get the rest of the collection?" He looked up finally, his wide eyes focusing on Alex. "Did you touch it?" His voice rose to a squeak.

Alex shook her head after exchanging a glance with Jon. If she had harbored any doubts about the origin of the collection or about the danger surrounding it, she had them no longer. Makarov's panicked tone gave away just how deadly those artifacts were.

Jon took over the interview.

"The ring came from Nancy Abernathy, a visa officer at the embassy."

"A visa officer?" Makarov said blankly; then his eyes narrowed. "Roger Copple's lover." He shifted his gaze back to the canister. "Is she ill?"

"She is," Jon answered tersely. When Makarov said nothing, Jon leaned forward. "And I think it's time we pooled our information about this."

Makarov looked up at that, suspicion clouding his features. "That is impossible."

When Alex saw Jon's jaw tighten, she laid a hand on his arm and spoke in his stead. "Please, Andre Nikolayevich, three men are dead and one woman is very ill."

Makarov's face became rigid, half in repudiation of her words, half, she thought, in fear. Alex felt she was about to plunge into icy water. "Roger Copple didn't die of appendicitis. He died of radiation poisoning."

"Is the embassy trying to say—"

Jon snapped, "The embassy is saying he died of appendicitis. *I'm* saying to *you* that he died of radiation poisoning. And I think he contacted some—shall we say *hot*—artifacts. Art to literally die for. I think he was fencing something that made him sick. I think it killed him. Just as I think it killed that man yesterday."

"This is preposterous," Andre said, but his expression said it wasn't preposterous at all. "That man yesterday was a *huligani*. He was shot."

Alex ignored the comment. "I think you want to know where the missing artifacts are just as much as the embassy wants them found."

"And what does the American Embassy care about all of this? Why are they getting involved in a matter of strictly Soviet concern?" Andre asked, seemingly unaware that he was admitting he knew of the artifacts' missing status and, possibly, of their radioactivity.

"Because Copple worked for us," Jon said simply. "And therefore, the Americans are implicated in a potential international incident."

Makarov shook his head. "If this should get out..."

"It won't," Jon said firmly.

"You don't understand—"

"It's you who doesn't understand," Jon interrupted. "Both the Soviets and the Americans are going to be in big trouble over this."

Makarov looked from Jon to Alex, as if trying to see through the Iron Curtain itself. Finally he all but whispered, "Have you found out where they are?"

"No," Alex said simply, to Andre's obvious disappointment. "But with all of us working together, we may be able to find them."

Andre Makarov sighed. He stood and stepped around his desk. "Go home, Aleksandra Sergeyevna. Forget all about this."

"I can't, Andre," Alex said, shortening his name even further, pushing him to accept her goodwill. "Hans Saalard was my friend."

Makarov flinched at that, but whether it was from her usage of his first name or from the reference to Hans, she didn't know. His next words told her.

"He wasn't supposed to die," he said.

Alex felt her blood chilling. "Hans?"

Makarov met her eyes, then shook his head as if waking. "No. No. You misunderstand. Apraskin. The priest, Apraskin." He sighed and ran a hand over his face. "I cannot tell you anything." At her look of skepticism, he shook his head. "Not because I don't know. But because you will be talking with the embassy personnel. If this poured out— is that how you are of saying it? No? Leaked out, yes. If this leaked out, it would be causing irreparable damage to the Soviet Union."

"If the artifacts *leak out,* how much damage then, Makarov?" Jon asked softly.

Andre leaned against his desk, his attitude dejected. *"Bog znayet,"* he murmured. God knows.

"Apraskin was a priest?" Jon asked musingly. Alex noticed an odd expression on his face.

"Is that significant?" she asked.

Makarov answered for him. "Apraskin was the curator of a museum church outside of Kiev. Not a real priest, not a priest of the old Church. But a self-styled priest."

"A museum church outside of Kiev. Near Chernobyl, you mean," Jon clarified.

"Near Chernobyl, yes." Makarov had aged ten years since they had walked through the door.

"And you think it started with him?" Jon asked.

Makarov nodded, though his features still carried the stamp of doubt. "He protested the initial cordon, then strenuously objected when the artifacts were to be disposed of along with all the other tainted material surrounding Chernobyl." He held up his hands. "He was removed from the area and assigned to a small church in Moscow."

"Which one?" Jon asked quickly.

"The chapel at Novedyevichy. It doesn't matter. The artifacts are not there."

"You've made a radiation sweep?"

"Of course," Makarov said wearily. "And of the apartment he shares with his son."

"The circus performer?"

Makarov showed no surprise at Jon's knowledge. "Yes. We were worried because the son's wife has recently had a baby."

Alex knew that to the average Soviet, a baby was the single most prized possession. There was nothing more important than a baby. Yes, they would have checked the apartment.

"We tried to see Sasha Apraskin last night," Jon said, his eyes turning to Alex. She saw with a dim shock that he, too, had been struck by the realization that so much had transpired in so little time.

"He would be too frightened to speak with foreigners right now," Makarov said, with a wry smile.

"Because of his father?"

"Because of his black-market activities," Makarov answered, apparently having decided to throw security to the four winds.

"The *son* is the black-market connection?" Jon asked.

Makarov nodded.

"Why did you lie to me that first day, Andre?" Alex asked when the silence had stretched for several seconds.

He looked away, out the small window behind him. His eyes roamed the spired buildings in the distance. "What would you have me do?" he asked quietly. "These are dangerous things. Not things to be talked about, discussed." He turned to her. "You have not seen the ruin of Chernobyl. You have not see the death that stalked the streets of the small villages. You have only seen one man—maybe two. You didn't know what you were dealing with."

He paused, his eyes far away, a nervous tic making a muscle in his jaw jump spasmodically. "One old priest in a museum temple. One old priest. The church was located only three kilometers from the Chernobyl plant." His gaze met Alex's, a plea in their dark depths.

"We must find that godforsaken art and bury it in the ruins of Chernobyl," he said finally. Heavily.

The sky was moonless and cloud obscured. The dark was a palpable presence, lit only by the headlights of their car and the orange glow of Ivan's hair reflected in the windshield.

Alex felt as if the dark was an extension of her thoughts, as if her worries and concerns were being projected outward. She turned toward Jon, surprised again to see him in such elegant dress. It didn't suit him, somehow; formal clothing hardened him, made him seem colder, more distant.

Part of that distance had been engendered by his actions of the evening. But most of it stemmed from her fear of telling him about the past, her sure knowledge that the light in his eyes would darken and then fade completely, that the tender look he often gave her would turn to disgust.

Then there was his abstraction. Several times, she'd had the feeling he was about to say something to her, but then he would half smile, shake his head and turn away.

His face was turned toward the window now, and his gaze was turned inward. What was he thinking?

Tell him, her mind urged, and her heart took up the litany. But her throat closed over the damning words. She felt too fragile, too vulnerable in the wake of their lovemaking, in the wake of these strange few days. He'd touched some part of her that she'd shown no man. How could she bring herself to tell him the very thing that would turn him from her?

He'd so frankly accepted her, playing no games, as starkly honest in his lovemaking as he was in his daily life. His heart and soul talked to her. And for one completely free moment, she had been able to answer. She had known a brief, wholly rapturous recognition of what love could be like, what a life free of the past could feel like.

But she wasn't free of the past. Couldn't be.

Tell him now, her heart urged. "Jon?" she said softly.

He turned toward her, the same odd expression on his face that had been there when Makarov had mentioned that Apraskin was a priest. "Yes?" he asked, but his thoughts were miles away. His hand took hers absently.

Tell him now.

"When I said that you didn't know me—"

"Makarov said the man was a priest," Jon interrupted. His voice was slow, his words reflective.

Alex stifled a sigh. Here she'd finally screwed up her courage to tell him everything, and his mind was who knew where.

"Yes," she answered, not hiding her annoyance.

He blinked then, as if seeing her for the first time. "Are you okay?" he asked. "Tired? Would you rather not to go the ballet tonight?"

She shook her head, a ripple of amusement shaking her. She'd spent years of holding in the terrible truth about herself and when she'd tried to tell someone, he hadn't even noticed. The thought of what his reaction would have been if he *had* been listening sobered her immediately. Her moment of courage had flown; her heart shrank from seizing the moment and ruining the fragile feelings of love she was beginning to nurture.

"We don't have to go, you know," he said. But already his mind was slipping away again, back to whatever notion he was wrestling with.

Alex did sigh, then. She had wanted to reject the ballet tickets Andre had pressed into their hands as they left his office. The thought of spending four hours in a dark theater pressed against Jon, four hours of being near him but not speaking, four hours of touching without caressing, knowing she would have to smile, clap and act as if nothing had happened between them, when so much lay unspoken, had seemed overwhelming. But Jon had accepted for them, the first genuine smile of the day lighting his face and chasing away much of the weariness.

"It's *Swan Lake*," Jon said now. "Plizetskaya is dancing as the Black Swan."

Alex knew Plizetskaya was almost unparalleled as a prima ballerina, but wished she could have seen the woman dance when her own heart was less burdened.

She didn't know it, but Jon was wishing the same thing. Something was nagging at him, something about Apraskin's being a priest. But he couldn't think. His brain seemed to be chasing itself around, like a dog after its own tail. Thoughts of Alex, thoughts of Roger Copple and pathetic Nancy Abernathy, of his conversation with Ned Sternberg that evening, thoughts of the priest. What was so important about the man being a priest?

And why had Alex sighed.

A sudden swerve caused Alex to slide into him. Their eyes met and Jon felt his heart lurch. He felt he could understand the large brown bears that hibernated above the

Steppes because he felt as though he'd just awoken. Alex's eyes were depthless, her breath as sweet as the spring air, her lips honey to his too-long-starved heart. Like the bears, he was hungry, but it was a hunger only she could assuage.

Had it only been that morning that he'd thought all he would be giving up in pursuing Alex was his loneliness? Now he knew that if he lost her, he would be giving up everything life was supposed to hold for a man and a woman. Everything.

She'd hinted at wrong choices, seemingly rejecting possible new love, new hope because of the past. Didn't she understand that he'd made mistakes, too? That everyone did?

Couldn't she see that part of the reason he wanted her so much, was beginning to think in terms of need, of the future, was precisely because she understood pain so thoroughly, had experienced life, because life touched her so strongly? That her "wrong" choices and her reaction to them made her a stronger, more intensely-caring person?

Her lips parted and he could see that her breathing was shallow, rapid. He read fear in her eyes, and caution. But he read other things, too. Desire, wistfulness, a dawning hope. It took his breath away. If Ivan hadn't been in the car with them, he would have taken her then and there, and damn the consequences.

Her eyelids lowered and her teeth took hold of her lip. Reluctantly, Jon released her. If she wasn't ready for the kind of commitment he wanted from her, he would wait. If she never wanted it...he would try to be content with merely seeing her now and again. He would try not to think of her with other men.

His fist clenched suddenly. Alex locked in another man's embrace was not something he would ever be able to view with any equanimity. Hell, he was already jealous of James Bowden, and James was only a friend of Alex's.

But Jon was certain he had something Bowden lacked...Alex's love. Whether she knew it or not, whether or not she would admit it, she did love him. Whether or not she would ever give in to that love, trusting him—trusting herself—enough to love him, was another matter altogether.

But as the car pulled up to the snow-banked curb outside the Bolshoi Theatre, Alex saw none of the confusion Jon felt. She saw only the light in his gold eyes, saw only his curving smile of pleasure because she was with him. In the dark, as their eyes met, she felt as though his gaze seared her heart, branded her soul.

She looked now at the cream-colored building a scant block outside the Kremlin walls. For the second time, she wished they were not attending the ballet. The ride in the dark car had been difficult enough. Sitting side by side, alone among the crowd, would be even more difficult.

As they waded through the crowd of people holding up ruble notes, offering to purchase spare tickets, willing to pay exorbitant prices for a single evening of ballet, Alex saw the large gentleman from the street—the man who had shot the priest, Apraskin.

She tapped Jon's shoulder and nodded toward the man. Jon took her arm and turned her in another direction. When they reached the doors, she saw him glance over his shoulder, his eyes roaming the crowd. But when he looked back at her, he smiled and shrugged.

Their tickets were taken at one of the many entrances and they joined the long line to check their coats and hats. People of all nationalities surrounded them as they moved through the many-tiered building, looking for their seats, discussing the ballet to come, arguing the merits of ballet versus modern dance, the opera over either.

Alex wanted to wave a magic wand and make them all disappear. Jon's hand beneath her elbow, his breath playing on her temple, his scent, his *presence,* all conspired to make her dizzy. His thumb played idly along her arm, sending sparks of reaction through her, causing her mind to revive its maddening command to tell him about her past.

They followed the door *dijournaya* to a middle row of folding chairs at the center of the Bolshoi's large auditorium and progressed to their seats, facing the people they were passing, Russian-style, murmuring apologies, as they moved down the row, lightly touching the shoulders of each person they stepped across.

No matter how many times Jon had gone to the theater in the Soviet Union, this simple but different custom never failed to throw him. It went against every grain of the American's innate need for space, for privacy. But to turn one's back to other people while being seated was to, in effect, present one's backside to them, an unforgivable insult.

"Poor Jon," Alex said softly. "You look as though you would rather face a firing squad than that particular custom."

Jon chuckled, beginning to relax for the first time that day. This was his Alex. This was not some woman on an alabaster pedestal. He'd allowed his worries to get to him. This was the woman who had shared his bed the night before, shared his dreams. Hell, she *was* his dream.

And this was the moment to tell her so. "Alex . . . ?"

She turned and faced him, a completely unguarded look in her eyes.

It was her very lack of wariness that checked him. For just a few hours—for a lifetime, maybe—he wanted just that look in her eyes: friendly, trusting, unprepared. "Nothing," he said.

She frowned slightly, but a sound to their right caught her attention and he watched as the frown changed to a slight smile. He smiled with her as she drank in the atmosphere in the cavernous room.

"Do you like ballet?" she asked finally, inconsequentially.

"The effort," he said. "That's what I admire about ballet. The years and years the dancers spend beating their bodies into submission."

"Or giving their bodies a chance to know what it is to fly," she said wistfully.

"I wonder if it feels like flying," he said, thinking of the bound feet, the bleeding toes.

"Does it matter?" Alex asked. "Sometimes, isn't it the illusion of something that we really want?"

"Are we talking about dancing or about us, Alex?" Jon asked, seizing the moment.

She jerked as if hit, turning suddenly wary eyes on him.

"I'm not looking at an illusion," he said quietly.

"But you don't know me," she said, her words ragged.

A fear of saying the wrong thing closed his throat, made his heart beat irregularly. Tell me, he urged silently. Just tell me and have done with it.

The lights in the crystal chandeliers flickered and cut. Alex's hand tightened on Jon's arm. He covered it slowly, cursing the misfortune that had caused the ballet to begin on time, cursing the interruption.

Floodlights lit the orchestra pit and the curtained stage. The conductor raised his arm, and the musicians struck the strangely discordant national anthem of the Soviet Union. People rose to their feet and in one voice, devoid of harmony, sang the words. Unlike most national anthems, this one stirred no emotion; it merely was. But when Jon heard it on Alex's lips, he felt the suddenly haunting melody to his core.

As soon as everyone was seated again, the first sweet notes of the prelude to *Swan Lake* sounded and the theater fell silent. The curtains slowly opened, and the alluring ballet began, drawing Alex with it, capturing her as it always did, but this time with a difference. This time, she could feel the pain in the legs of the dancers, this time, as they leapt, they didn't fly. This time she felt each impact of those toughened feet as if they had landed on her heart. For this time, Jon Wyndham sat beside her.

They spoke little during the intermission, his mind too full of questions and her heart too filled with doubt to allow conversation. They sipped at their champagne and nibbled at the rich Beluga caviar that was so readily available in the Soviet Union and so terribly expensive outside it.

This was Jon, Alex told herself. She could tell him. He'd said that the past didn't matter. For the first time in many years, she felt that perhaps that could be true. Maybe, in the telling, it would fade and eventually disappear altogether. Hans would have liked that. Hans would have liked Jon, she thought, turning to look at him.

"Lazarus rises?" he asked with a slight smile. Had he been watching her all that time? she wondered.

"Actually," a small American man said in a nasal voice, "the correct phrase is 'Lazarus, come forth.'"

"What?" Jon asked blankly.

"You did say, 'Lazarus rises,' did you not?" the short man asked, peering at Jon through obviously myopic eyes. He held up a finger. "A common mistake. But quite erroneous. You see," he said, leaning forward as if conferring a great secret, "Christ arrived at Mary and Martha's home after the death of Lazarus. They had already placed him in the tomb and sealed it."

The expression on Jon's face made Alex smile. He looked as though he'd been kicked by a mule. "What did you say?" he asked.

"So, you see," the small man continued, pausing a moment to adjust the narrow black collar around his neck, "Christ went to the burial site—which was, of course, no such thing, it was a cave covered over by a large slab—and called out, 'Lazarus—'"

"'Come forth,'" Jon finished for him. He cried with a loud voice, "'Lazarus, come forth.'"

"Very good!" the little man said, so excited at Jon's awareness of the verse that he patted Jon's arm.

The klaxon signaling the end of intermission sounded, making Jon start and almost spill his remaining champagne. He set the glass aside and took Alex's arm. His face wore the same intent look as it had in the car, as it had in Andre Makarov's office.

Once they were seated, Alex tried getting his attention, but just as in the car, he seemed only half aware that she was there. She could see the look of concentration on his face.

The music for the second act began, and soon Alex forgot Jon's abstraction in the swelling notes, the gliding, lilting innocence of the white swans and the superb evil of Plizetskaya's Black Swan. Caught up in the music, the dancing, the warmth of Jon's body next to hers, Alex drifted with time. The resolution to the second act built, evil battling good, good fluttering, faltering. Herself? She felt as if she were both the White and the Black swan. A wave of hopelessness swept over her.

Suddenly Alex felt Jon jerk on her arm. He leaned close to her ear and, in an excited whisper, he breathed, "*Ivan* is the Russian equivalent of *John,* isn't it?"

Alex nodded, her mind still on the ballet, her heart still caught by the intricate steps of the Black Swan, her mind on the blackest moment of her life.

He said softly, "John, 11:43."

Alex pulled back to look at him, hearing the same words that she'd tried to prise meaning from for days, but still not understanding his excitement.

"John," he whispered again. "You know, John the Evangelist. St. John. Not Ivan. You translated everything else but *Ivan!*"

Alex shook her head. "I'm sorry," she said. "I don't get it." Her eyes drifted to the stage. The Black Swan was swooping down over the single innocent swan in a dance designed to lure the innocent to a darker life, or death.

Jon shook her slightly. "It was a Biblical reference, Alex."

She twisted sideways and met his eyes. They were lit with a sure knowledge, glowing at her in the dark room. Someone in the row behind them shushed them and poked at their chairs for emphasis.

Too full of hope to remain seated for the rest of the ballet, Alex rose with Jon and followed him to the closed doors. The *dijournaya* growled something at them as they departed the dark theater for the brightly lit lobby.

After a few steps, Jon stopped and reached out to grab Alex's shoulders. "The stuff has to be buried in a grave," he said urgent. "It has to be."

"Jon . . ."

"John 11:43. Remember what else that man said? Apraskin? He said, '. . . and he that was dead . . .' Remember?"

"Yes," she said, not at all averse to having him grip her shoulders with such intensity. She was also convinced by the conviction on his face that he was on the right track.

"That's the next verse, see?" When she shook her head, he released her, pacing a full circle around her, his eyes dancing with light. "In John. Chapter Eleven. I don't remember exactly how it goes. Oh, why did I ever dodge Uncle Charles on learning the verses? Anyway, it's something like this. Christ stood before the tomb and had them push away the gravestone. He cried with a loud voice, 'Lazarus, come forth.' Just like that guy said tonight. Then, if I'm right, the next verse reads, 'And he that was dead came forth . . .'"

Alex looked at him wonderingly. "You were close to figuring that out at the circus that night. And again tonight with your comment about—"

"Lazarus rises. Yes." Jon nodded, his eyes fiery with triumph. "Probably my subconscious mind trying to tell me the rest of the verses. I just didn't listen."

"In a grave somewhere . . ." Alex said thoughtfully. "Here in Moscow?" she asked.

"I'd bet on it," Jon said. "Nancy said Roger gave her the ring after going to some dacha, and that Apraskin was going to move everything."

"You think he moved them straight to a grave."

"What better place? He must have guessed by then that he was pretty sick. He must have been terrified. First the authorities are after him for digging up the artifacts, then all the rumors he must have heard start coming true . . . the sickness, the pain. His son is his connection—I think we have to assume that—and his son gets ahold of Roger Copple. They meet, Roger sees the stuff, then Roger dies." Jon stopped pacing. His eyes took on a faraway look.

Alex could see the doctor in Jon trying to make sense of the deaths, trying to come to terms with the fact that Roger had died while under his care. She picked up the train of thought Jon had abandoned. "So, he buries the collection in a grave. But if he knew the artifacts were causing people to be sick, why would he still want to peddle them on the black market?"

Jon came back to the present with an almost noticeable snap. "If he was a fanatic, he might have still believed they should be on display somewhere. If he were greedy—like Copple—he might have wanted the money. We'll probably never know."

"He buried the artifacts, then went looking for his American connection."

"Us," he said. Alex felt a shiver work across her skin at both the concept of the single word, unifying them, joining them, and at the memory of Apraskin dying in front of their eyes.

Jon took hold of her shoulders again. "Everything points to them being nearby."

"Does the embassy have maps of Moscow?" Alex asked. "There must be a hundred cemeteries."

"The embassy has maps of everything."

"How will we know which cemetery?" she asked, then, "And which grave?"

"We've figured out this much of his clue, I bet it'll be easy when we see a map."

"Should we call Ned Sternberg? Or Andre Makarov?"

Jon looked over his shoulder first, then at her, as if he were about to say something. Then he smiled. "Let's look at some maps first," he said.

The doors leading into the auditorium opened all around the lobby, sounding like guns as oak and brass met marble. People poured from the auditorium. The ballet was over.

"Let's go," Jon said, turning Alex toward the cloak-room.

They were soon out in the cold, damp night. It was snowing heavily, the flakes large and wet. Only the red light above the Kremlin tower was visible from the steps of the Bolshoi; the rest of the walled city was obscured by the heavy snow.

Jon grabbed Alex's arm and ran down the steps, calling for a taxi. He held his hand up, extending two fingers, signifying that he would pay double for the ride.

A car skidded to the curb and the back door flipped open. Jon helped Alex inside and stepped after her. He reached for the door to pull it shut, but it didn't budge. He started to get out, but was roughly shoved back inside.

"What the—"

"Sit down!" a man uttered in Russian.

The voice was followed by the silhouette of a man's body, his thick coat filling the doorway of the car.

Out of the darkness created by the man's shadow, a knife blade appeared, glittering in the light, aimed directly at Jon's throat, a knife blade held in a thick, muscled hand with dark hair on the knuckles.

"Be quiet or die," the man growled, holding the knife against Jon's neck, letting them both know how dangerous it would be to disobey.

The stranger stepped into the car and was a stranger no longer; Sasha the Incredible, Sasha Apraskin, still brandished the knife, his meaning clear, his intent deadly. Jon slid farther across the seat, pressing Alex against the other door, half hoping she would open it and escape while he blocked her.

"If you open that door, *dyevushka,*" Sasha growled, "your lover dies."

Jon felt Alex's convulsive movement behind him, but he didn't dare tear his gaze from the deadly blade.

"Drive!" Sasha Apraskin commanded. "Hurry, fool!"

Jon's eyes slid to the driver, hoping for a vain moment that the driver would refuse. But the hope died the instant he took in the driver's features. It was a woman—taxi drivers in the Soviet Union were never women—and her face was taut with the same fear Jon was sure was etching his own features. Her hands gripped the steering wheel, white-knuckled, her eyes on something in the front seat.

"What do you want?" Jon asked, his eyes slowly turning to look at Sasha Apraskin. It took a supreme effort to focus at the man's face and not at the knife in his hand. "What do you want with us?" he repeated. He felt as if the words were coming out in slow motion.

Apraskin laughed. "What do you think we want, Doctor?" The blade wavered as the man's evil laugh filled the car. "We want what every man wants...money enough to live without fear."

"Money?" Jon heard Alex's bemused question.

"Drive! Drive!" Sasha ordered again, coughing hard and punctuating his words with a kick at the front seat.

The car jumped forward, almost hitting a departing theatergoer.

"Fool! Do not attract attention!"

"Sasha..." the woman muttered on a half sob.

The woman was rattled, frightened. Was there a possibility of hope there? Jon wondered. Or was she too afraid of the man wielding the knife to do anything other than obey?

"Shut up! Drive."

"You can't get away with this," Jon murmured. Even to himself the words sounded empty. The man was getting away with it already.

"Shut up. Your time for talking will come later."

"Where are you taking us?" Jon asked, not liking the wild look in Apraskin's eyes. He had the pallor of a man on drugs—or a man who might have touched the death-dealing art.

"I said, *shut up!*" Apraskin snarled, whirling to Jon.

Jon saw the heavy hand raising the knife and ducked to avoid the blade, but it wasn't the blade Sasha Apraskin intended to use. The expert knife thrower brought the broad hilt of the knife directly down on Jon's temple.

Jon felt the blow even as the interior of the car seemed to warm dramatically. The dark seemed to spill down the inside of the car windows like black ink. Dimly, he heard Alex calling his name. Her voice echoed in his mind, a single note of music in a world without melody.

He had to stay awake, alert. There was something he had to do...something he had to find...someone...

He felt his head falling and his body following after. Down and down he fell, spiraling into a world of darkness. He heard the sharp cry of a baby, felt Alex's soft touch on his cheek, thought he heard a man's laugh.

Alex...

Chapter 10

As Jon slumped to her lap, her name on his lips, Alex's heart seemed to stop beating. For a wild, wholly dark moment, she thought he was dead and, in thinking it, felt the most wrenching pain she'd ever known. It was as if every sorrow she'd ever encountered coalesced and became one central anguish, and it tore at her heart and soul.

"No!" she cried out, not at Jon's attacker but at the oppressive fear of losing Jon. Tentatively, terrified of what she might find there, she lightly touched his warm cheek. No blood, no cooling skin. His breath met her fingers, and a shudder worked through her body.

She moaned in relief, wrapping her arms around his shoulders in a fiercely protective gesture, as much to comfort herself as him. She pulled him to her, willing him to revive, willing him to feel her need for him to be all right.

No longer fearful—Jon was alive, what else was there to fear?—she raised her eyes to Jon's attacker. She ignored the glint of the deadly blade, peering through the gloom to see the soul of Sasha Apraskin. His dark eyes gleamed dully in his swarthy face and he no longer exuded the confidence he had at the circus. He looked frightened, desperate. A cough shook his frame. His eyes closed briefly, but opened almost immediately, the knife rising, warning her to keep her silence.

The car was wrenched to the side and for a moment spun, tractionless, on the snowy street. Jon's body slammed across her, and from the front seat came a baby's cry. Alex tried cushioning Jon, all the while maintaining her unwavering gaze on Sasha Apraskin.

"Sasha—" the woman driving the car whimpered.

"Shut up. And hush the child," he answered shortly. Alex saw him press his lips tightly together as another spasm of coughing shook him. Even in the dark of the car, his lips showed white and taut, thin with the pain of his cough.

Holding Jon's body against her in a fiercely protective stance, she felt no sympathy for Sasha Apraskin's obvious pain. She half hoped a spasm would render him helpless, would overtake him completely. Aghast at her thoughts, she looked away, trembling from the force of her emotions, trembling at the memories they roused in her.

The baby ceased its thin wail almost as soon as the car steadied. Their driver had lowered one hand from the wheel and now spoke in broken, half-sobbing phrases to the child.

"Where are you taking us?" Alex whispered, pulling against the door as she did so.

Apraskin merely raised his knife a notch, the silver flash of light on the blade persuading her to comply with his order of silence. She bent over Jon's body, for the moment grateful not to be staring into Sasha's half-mad eyes. As she rechecked Jon's breathing, she wondered if there were any chance they were being followed. Was their tail with them?

If her force of will had anything to do with it, the large man in the fur coat and hat was hot on their trail right now. Following her. Following Jon. Please, God, let someone be following us, she prayed silently.

She repeated the plea in her mind, over and over, a litany against the fear making her legs weak and causing her breath to catch in her throat.

"Where is the collection?" Sasha asked. He asked it almost casually, as if he were asking where she was from.

She shook her head, unwilling to meet his eyes again. But her answer didn't satisfy him. A thick hand grabbed her coat lapel and wrenched her around to face him. The knife blade was a mere inch from her face, silvery in the unlit car, a dark menace, reminding her of the Black Swan. Beautiful and deadly.

"Answer me!"

Alex's thoughts were chaotic. Helpless, she nonetheless tried blocking Jon's body from the knife. She could only stare at the deadly blade. He was mad, she thought. He was going to hurt her.

"I—I don't know," she gasped out.

"Tell me!" Apraskin growled, and waved the knife threateningly. Alex wanted to tell him that he was supposed to assure her that he wouldn't hurt her. *If you do as I say, I won't hurt you.* Wasn't that the phrase? But he offered no assurances, she thought with despair; he told her no pretty lies.

The car skidded again, and the man's grip on her lapel loosened, then dropped altogether as a cough racked Sasha's body.

The intensity of the spasm left him weak, and he leaned back against the seat, spent. The knife rested on his shaking leg, no longer as threatening as it had seemed only minutes before. But, Alex thought with candor, it didn't matter whether or not he could use the knife. She could hardly leap from the swiftly moving car, dragging Jon's inert body with her.

Apraskin had the woman pull over to the side of the road after they had been driving for some time. They had long since left the lights of the city behind and had been traveling for half an hour down winding country lanes, flanked by deep snowdrifts and often slick to the point of loss of control.

At first, Alex assumed they had reached their destination, and she tensed at the thought of the next stage of this bizarre kidnapping. But Apraskin merely tugged off the scarf from around his neck, shoving it at Alex, telling her to wrap it around her eyes.

Loath to touch anything of the man's, not just fearful of contamination but truly repulsed to think of touching anything still warm from his body, Alex cringed, shaking her head. The knife was against her temple in a movement swifter than she could have foreseen, its sharp point underlining his command that she should blindfold herself.

As soon as the nauseating wool scarf was around her eyes, he ordered the woman to resume driving.

The motion of the car combined with the hated scarf blinding her at first numbed Alex to thoughts of anything but freeing herself from the blindfold. Then its significance struck her. He wasn't planning to kill them. He wouldn't bother to hide the location of their destination from them unless he planned to allow them to go free at some point.

They stopped soon enough and when the car engine was shut off, the silence was deafening. All Alex could hear was the wheeze coming from Sasha Apraskin's chest and the heavy breathing of the infant in the front seat.

"Get out," Apraskin said, opening his door. The cold air whooshed into the car, sucking the warmth away, stealing her breath. She reached for the blindfold.

"Leave it on!" he snapped, and she cried out as she felt Jon being dragged from her lap. "Get her," he ordered, apparently to the driver.

Strange hands took Alex's arm and half pulled, half assisted her from the car. "This way," the woman murmured, directing Alex through the deep snow that threatened to trip her. "It's not much farther."

"Jon?" Alex asked quietly.

"Is all right. He's inside already." The words were whispered, filled with the woman's fear.

Alex clung to the woman's arm while branches snagged at her clothing and the snow became so deep it was difficult to walk with any steadiness. She slipped several times and cried out once when a branch snapped her cheek.

She banged her shins against something solid and cried out again. She felt herself seized by stronger hands than those of the woman. She was yanked sideways and knew from his breath that she was facing Sasha. She felt the cold, sharp point of the terrible knife push against the tender spot beneath her chin.

"Do not think we are fools, *dyevushka*. No one will hear your screams here. If you will tell me where the things are now, you and your lover can go free."

She was half dragged through a doorway, the knife cutting into her skin. She was thrust to one side and the abrupt release made her spin. She tripped over something large and fell with a bone-jarring thud. It was Jon she had fallen over.

Even as her hands sought his face, the blindfold was yanked from her eyes, pulling her hair, making her bite back a cry.

The room was lit by a single candle on a dust-covered table. It sent shadows dancing on the walls, skidding across the floor. Alex could see the woman cradling a small child in her arms, her eyes on the man before Alex, one side of her face bruised and swollen. Had Sasha done that to her?

Alex bent over Jon, murmuring his name, touching his cool cheek.

"He lives," her tormentor said, as though the matter were of little importance. "Tell me where the collection is. My father told you. I saw him."

Again Alex was shaken by a wave of hatred for this man.

"Tell him, *dyevushka*," the woman said urgently, her eyes moving to the now-closed door. "You will be free. Sasha will let you go. *He* won't!"

He? There was still more to come? Alex's anger melted as a whole new fear took hold. Jon stirred against her thigh. Suddenly it was not a matter of having to do as her tormentor wanted, it was a matter of choice. She could tell the man what they knew—what they suspected—and hope the woman was right, that Sasha would let them go. Or she could act as though they hadn't uncovered the meaning of the old man's words. Which? Which should she choose, with their very lives at stake?

Sasha Apraskin leaned forward until their faces almost touched. He insinuated the knife between them. "Tell me, or this will be the least of your worries," he said, his voice silky, his eyes rabid. The knife blade dipped toward Jon.

Alex wanted to tell him that he sounded like a bad movie. She wanted to tell him that she knew nothing. She wanted to scream. But she did none of those things. She had to think; she had to make the right choice. After a lifetime of wrong choices, she had to make the right one.

She drew a deep breath, keeping her eyes locked on Sasha Apraskin. She raised a hand slowly, hating the thought of touching him, knowing the need to do so. He would believe her if she touched him as she spoke. *Do it!* her mind raged.

Her skin felt as though it were shrinking as her fingertips fluttered against the rough wool of Sasha's coat. For a heart-stopping moment, her throat closed, blocking her words. Then, gripping his arm, she forced the lie to her lips.

"Jon knows where the things are. Only Jon. I don't know. Can't you see that?"

"She's telling the truth!" the woman cried, and the wail of the baby's voice seemed to emphasize her belief.

Alex watched Sasha Apraskin's face as closely as ever, not taking her hand from his sleeve. Believe me, she willed. She put all her skill into creating a mask of trust for him to read.

His face seemed to crumple as the belief in her lie overtook him. The fire in his eyes flickered, then died. A cough rumbled in his chest; the hand with the knife shook. His eyes slid from hers to the still form beneath them.

"Wake him," he whispered.

"I can't," Alex said, taking the hated arm once again. "He's unconscious!"

Slowly the man's gaze lifted to hers.

"Sasha!" the woman said. "It is too cold here for the baby. He must eat. The man will wake in the morning."

"When *he* comes to take the gold for himself," Sasha answered bitterly.

Who was *he?*

"What can we do?" the woman agonized.

"We can't rouse him," Alex said, adding her weight to the quasi-argument.

Sasha sighed, obviously torn. It wasn't Alex's hand on his sleeve nor the woman's impassioned plea that swayed him, however. The baby resumed its thin wail, ending the high shriek on a choking cough.

"We go," he said abruptly, shaking Alex's hand free. He rose unsteadily. "You will not go anywhere," he said, his eyes on the doorway. "There is nowhere to go from here. You are miles from anywhere. Miles from help." He reached for the candle, then, with a shrug, let it be. "But *he* won't care if your lover lives or dies. See how much he cares?" A cough racked him. "He killed my father. He will kill you. He doesn't care."

A cold blast of wind, accompanied by a swirling dusting of snow, thrust its way through the door as Apraskin opened it. His eyes met Alex's, bleak despair punctuating his words. He pulled the door closed behind them, and the gust of wind doused the candle's flame. The heavy slam made Alex jump. Within seconds, she heard the loud engine turn over and the heavy crunching of the ice-encrusted snow giving way beneath the thick tires.

On unsteady legs, her hands outstretched before her, Alex made her way to the small table and fumbled for the matches their kidnapper had left on the dusty surface. After two abortive attempts, she managed to light the wick. The small flame leaped and danced, a single cheerful note in the dreary, icy-cold prison.

Slowly, as she used the last of her energy to cross the room to Jon's still body, Alex took in the largely empty, dusty cabin. It was little more than a single-room shack, a cold nightmare. She sank to the floor beside him and proceeded to give the lie to the words she'd spoken to Sasha Apraskin.

"Jon?" she murmured, lightly rocking him. "Oh, please, Jon...wake up." She stripped her own scarf from her neck and lifted Jon's head, settling him more comfortably on the folded fabric. The bruise on his head, even in the uncertain light, looked terrible. Would he be all right? Had she saved him only for the moment? And what was coming in the morning?

"Jon..." Her voice caught on a sob. Now that the kidnappers had departed, now that she was alone with Jon, reaction was setting in. "Jon...please...I—I need you."

Jon came to slowly, warm in some places, freezing in others. His cheeks felt wet, and his hands were numb. He tried opening his eyes, but the pain in his head made him close them again. He felt disoriented and was relatively certain he was lying on a floor, though something seemed to be under his head, but he couldn't think why he would be prone, nor could he imagine where he was.

He heard his own name being murmured and felt someone shaking him. Where was Alex?

He tried moving his mouth, but it felt stuffed with a thousand cotton balls.

"Please..."

It was Alex, and she wanted him to do something. He had to save her. The man with the knife...

His memory snapped back. Incredible as it seemed, followed everywhere, under surveillance from all sides, they had been kidnapped. And their kidnapper was Sasha Apraskin, son of the mad old priest who had loosed a collection of deadly art on an unsuspecting world.

"Alex?" he murmured. He tried opening his eyes again.

He was rewarded by a distorted vision of her face; a flickering light caught the tears in her eyes, making them seem huge, drenched with blue, and, incredibly, filled with longing. For him?

"Alex..."

"Lie still," she said, foiling his attempt to rise. "They're gone."

"Gone?" he asked blankly.

"For now," she answered.

"Why—why are they gone? What do you mean, 'for now'?" Even to himself, his words sounded thick. He struggled to rise, balancing on one elbow.

Instead of answering his question, she lightly touched his cheek with her soft, cold hand. He could feel the trembling of her fingers as his skin absorbed her fear. "I thought—" Her voice broke, and she looked away, her eyes blinking rapidly. "When he hit you, for a moment I really thought..."

"I'm all right," he said quickly, cutting through the pain and fear in her voice. Even while his heart exulted in the knowledge that she cared—that perhaps she could now admit that caring—he experienced a stab of embarrassment, of self-recrimination, that he had been lying unconscious on a dirty floor while she dealt with the kidnappers.

He half turned, pushing himself to a sitting position and biting off a groan as his head renewed its frenzied throbbing. "Alex..."

"I'm okay. Now," she mumbled, but her averted gaze and muffled tone told him she was lying.

He pulled her to him, cradling her against his chest, stroking her silky hair, urging her to let go, coaxing her to release her fear and tension at the warmth of his touch.

Stammering, her voice cracking in remembered pain, she gave him a glimpse of the anguish she'd felt at the thought that he'd been killed.

"Ah, Alex, don't..." he murmured, pressing his lips against her temple.

"I thought when my father...died, I knew what it felt like to have the whole world turn black. I couldn't imagine anything being worse than that. Finding him, seeing him that way—" Jon wanted to ask what way, but couldn't. "Oh, God, I was terrified to touch your face...." Her hand lightly traced the bruise on his temple, demonstrating to him just how terrified she had been. "I was so afraid I'd find blood there. Just like before." Brokenly, caught by the past, she told him the sordid story of her father's death.

In a horrifying flash, as if seeing the image through her eyes, Jon realized how Alex's father had died. How the man's suicide had haunted her life. As if he'd been there, he could see the young Alex reaching toward her father's still face, trying to understand why he wouldn't wake. He tightened his embrace, wishing he had been there, wishing he could have wrenched her away from the pitiful sight, wishing he could save her from the memory now.

Was this the something that blocked her from trusting, from believing in herself?

As if the picture of her father's death had been dammed up inside her for years, she began to talk about it, tentatively at first, but then the words began spilling from her in a torrent of pain and confusion.

Jon knew that the peculiar combination of events that night, and perhaps in the past few days, had contrived to unlock this pent-up memory. The fear she'd felt, the horror, the realization that she alone had to handle the situation, all worked together to create a strange time warp as she reenacted a night she had lived years before. He tried telling her so, holding her tightly, as if to draw her inside him, as if by doing so he could cleanse her of the past.

"It was my fault, you see," she said now, her voice low, her hands fluttering in a helpless gesture.

"It couldn't have been," Jon said firmly.

She told him why she had taken the guilt inside. It was a child's reasoning, but left uncorrected, it had festered inside her, distorting her perception of herself. Making her doubt her judgment. She had wanted to attend an expensive private school, and her parents had agreed, though they hadn't really been able to afford it. A bad investment here, an injudicious gamble there, and her father had found himself facing bankruptcy and humiliation. He had opted for the coward's way out, believing the insurance money would provide for them, and committed suicide. But his policy hadn't covered intentional death, and he had left his wife and daughter to the terror of destitution, humiliation and bitter loneliness.

At first, Alex clung to the vision of her guilt, but as Jon argued the case with her, he felt her begin to relax in his arms. Slowly, picking his words with caution, he convinced her of the truth, that it was not her fault, but her father's, that it was *his* judgment that had been at fault, not hers.

She sighed heavily, and Jon cupped her face in his hand, neither stroking nor caressing, just willing her to understand how he hurt for the child she had been, how much he cared for the woman the child had become.

"I wish that were all," she said. "I can see what you're saying, and a part of me believes it. But it wasn't the only time...." She sighed again, raising a hand to her already drying cheek. She said no more, and Jon didn't press her. She'd said enough, been through enough. If there was more to be said, it could be said later, he thought, when they were both warm and the night's terror was over. Slowly, as if wiping away the past with his touch, he lowered his hand and stroked her throat, rubbed the base of her neck, easing the tension, working the tight muscles in her shoulders.

She turned in his arms, bringing her lips to his. Hers was a gentle touch, tentative, questing, as if gauging his understanding, the depth of his perception. He cupped her face with both hands, gently answering her unspoken questions, letting her know he was there for her, it was only for her to ask.

She leaned into him, then, her hands sliding beneath his coat. Her eyes closed, her breathing came rapidly and her touch had an urgency to it, as if only by direct contact could she really be sure he was with her, with her in more than mere body, with her in heart, in soul. Would be with her in the cold light of morning.

He understood that her desperation had been born not only of a desire to eradicate the past, but as a shield against the fear that lay in both of them, fear of the coming day, a fear of the unknown.

The painful throbbing in his head receded as his body responded to her touch, giving her every ounce of affirmation she could ask for. "Alex," he murmured, turning them both so that she lay beside him, her head resting on her own scarf. Her name became both question and answer, her tremulous sigh an acknowledgement of both.

"Love me," she breathed, and Jon had to bite back an oath. She was too raw, too emotionally drained, to love now. If he did as she asked, she would be doubly uncertain later. But if he didn't, the effect would be the same.

"Please..." she asked, her eyes meeting his, hers reflecting an awareness of his dilemma, yet rejecting the reasons for it.

If she hadn't pleaded, if she hadn't looked at him with such need, he might have chosen an alternate path, but she did plead, her eyes glassy with unshed tears and supplication. It was beyond his power to deny her, beyond his power to deny himself. With a ragged groan, he grabbed her to him almost roughly, silencing his doubts, erasing her past, answering her plea with a plea of his own.

Alex knew she'd pulled him to her with her simple words, words as strong as the kisses he was now pressing to her mouth. His hands swept over her body; his lips crushed her mouth. Take the past, she thought, take it away. And with it, the fear, the crushing terror she felt when her mind flitted across the knowledge that their captors would return, intending to maim—or worse.

And so she urged him to her, tugging at his clothing with numb fingers, murmuring encouragement, begging his body to drive the fear and pain from her mind. In his firm touch, at the searing ache of his mouth at her breast, in his heated determination, he chased thought away, all thought but the present, all thought save that of him, her, them together.

Despite the cold, despite the hard floor beneath them, languor stole through her body, making her achingly aware of every stroke of his long fingers, every soft brush of his warm lips.

As their clothing was stripped away, forming both cushion and canopy for their loving, Alex cradled Jon's head, arching to him, as he took first one nipple, then the other into his hot mouth. The chill air in the room struck her as he moved, leaving her, yet not abandoning her, moving lower, trailing his tongue across her stomach, making her squirm, making her moan, making her cling to him as if he were a talisman against fear.

His hands roamed, more demanding now, seeking every curve, lingering here, brushing there. His hot breath played on her now-throbbing body, his fingers skillful, his mouth like fire.

The room was cold no longer, and the night-dark prison felt lit by a thousand candles. Alex tried telling him so, but her words were caught on a sob as her body shuddered, bringing her off the ground, making her cry his name, lost in that spinning universe only he could make her see. But he was with her, calling her name, rising before her, his eyes fiery, his need matching hers.

At last he lowered himself into her, bringing her back, making her begin the journey to that other universe anew. Feeling the rightness of flying together, needing him with her, knowing he needed her, as well, Alex gripped him with her legs, pulling him even deeper inside. She wrapped her arms around his back and pressed her face against his throat.

Faster and faster they moved, their bodies seeming one, their hearts beating to the same rhythm, breath meeting breath, heat meeting heat, fire sparking fire. And then, for a bittersweet moment, a timeless, glorious moment, it seemed to Alex that their very souls joined, fusing, becoming one complete whole, as they spun into that other world, that other plane, that part of themselves reserved for such moments, reserved only for each other.

Chapter 11

A noise outside, perhaps a branch releasing a heavy load of snow or some animal seeking warmth, snagged Alex's attention, drawing her back to the harsh reason why they were in this cold cabin, miles from help, dependent not only on each other, but upon their captors.

She flushed, remembering her abandoned lovemaking, remembering how she'd begged him to comply with her demands, remembering how eagerly she'd responded. She shifted, tentatively, and the warm bands of Jon's arms tightened around her.

"Awake?" he asked softly, his breath moving the hair at the base of her neck, causing her to shiver.

She made some noncommittal sound, half-annoyed that he'd thought her asleep, as if able to totally forget their present predicament. She'd been able—with his help—to ignore it for a time, but forget it?

"Don't worry," he said quietly, not letting her pull away from him. "We'll get out of this."

"How?" she asked, not bothering to hide the sarcastic note in her voice. "If someone had been following us, they would have been here by now. They aren't."

"We need a plan," he said.

Worry over their danger, embarrassment over her flood of tangled emotions and impassioned lovemaking, caused her voice to be sharper than she might have wanted. "A plan? That's all we need? A plan. That's just dandy. Then the Incredible Sasha can bash us both over the head or really use that knife he's so handy with."

To her further annoyance, Jon chuckled. He stopped as she stiffened to move away from him. "Look," he said, his calm voice another source of irritation—couldn't he at least sound a little panicked? "Tell me exactly what you told Apraskin—Sasha the Incredible—and we'll work it out from there."

Alex felt a flash of remorse and fear at the memory. Had she saved Jon for the moment only to put him in greater danger? Ruefully, she admitted, "I told him that you were the only one who knew where the artifacts were."

Jon didn't answer for a moment, and Alex shifted uncomfortably. Finally he pulled her tightly against him, his hand sweeping down to the curve of her waist. "Pretty cool thinking," he said.

Her concern warring against the sensations his hand was sparking in her, she said almost plaintively, "But now you could be in even greater danger."

"Last night, I wasn't expecting anything. Now I am. Or I will be once we're dressed." His hand stopped its slow progression, causing relief and regret to battle in Alex. He patted her hip easily, as if they'd been lifetime partners instead of... Her mind quickly masked the rest of that thought.

Jon sat up awkwardly, spilling the blanket of clothing to the dusty floor. He swore at the chill air attacking his body and tossed Alex her freezing blouse. She caught it, giving him a sour look that he met blandly, a slight grin on his lips.

As he took in the extent of her bad mood, his expression changed.

"Look, Alex, we'll get out of this somehow. If only because after the last couple of hours, I'm not about to let you go so easily."

"Easily!" she all but croaked.

"Sure," he said, dragging his now-dusty jacket over his still-unbuttoned shirt. "If you were in love with someone else—say the ever-pompous James Bowden—now *that* might present a few difficulties. If you hated my guts, that could be sticky. But a couple of thugs—sick ones, at that—that doesn't sound too tough."

Alex could only stare at him, her skirt in her hands. "You were almost *killed* last night," she said, finally, not believing that he would make jokes in the present circumstances. "And that doesn't sound *difficult?*"

"Well, no, not very."

He grinned again, making her itch to say something, *do* something, that would throw him off balance. Couldn't he realize the desperate nature of their predicament? But he spoke again—too good-humoredly for her frame of mind—before she could think of a sufficiently scathing retort. "What's difficult to me, right now, is sitting here watching you half-naked, your hair all mussed, your eyes as blue as—"

"Oh, shut up!" she snapped, turning her back on him and ignoring his chuckle. She pulled her skirt almost viciously over her head and tugged it into place. If he couldn't see the danger, she could. All the jokes in the world weren't going to matter when dawn arrived and Sasha Apraskin and his filthy knife came back. Jon wouldn't be able to joke his way through that particular little interview. For a moment, Alex smiled at the thought of Jon's near-lifeless body at her feet, the engaging grin wiped from his face, his voice saying, "You were right, Alex...."

She gasped aloud, shocked at her thoughts, shaken by a wave of the past, and turned to Jon suddenly, reaching for him, as if to make certain her vision hadn't come true. He caught her hands, the smile gone from his lips, his eyes warm in the faint light from the nearly extinguished candle. "It's okay. We'll pull through this."

"How?" she asked again, but this time without the sarcasm, this time half believing him. Wanting to believe him.

He rose stiffly and pulled her to her feet. "Well, as I see it, we have two choices...." he said, unknowingly echoing her thoughts while he had lain unconscious at her side. "We can tell him what we know—what we think we know—or we can send him on a wild-goose chase."

Remorse over telling Sasha that Jon knew where the artifacts were hidden once again assailed her. She tried to tell him so, but he shook her lightly, then cupped her face with his hands. "You made the right choice, Alex," he said firmly. Deliberately. Accepting no argument. "You saved our hides." To her amazement, he lowered his lips to hers, gently, firmly.

"Now it's *my* turn." He kissed her again, then released her and rubbed his hands together. Whether it was for warmth or because he was relishing the upcoming encounter, she couldn't have said.

But his confidence bolstered her. "What do you want me to do?" she asked.

"Well, for starters, you can bring me that chair," he said, pointing to a rickety but heavy oak stool, the single other piece of furniture besides the table with the now-sputtering candle on it.

They didn't have long to wait. Dawn sent spindly fingers of light through the dusty, frost-covered window panes. They had scarcely had time to go over Jon's strategy before they heard the low rumble of a vehicle making its way over the crusted snow. Jon took his station behind the door while Alex flew to the shadowed lump of their discarded coats on the floor, humped to appear as if Jon still lay there.

"I'm not a very good actress," she hissed as they both heard a car door open, then slam shut.

"Don't I know it," he said cryptically. He blew on his hands, then hefted a slab of the stool he'd broken earlier.

Alex didn't have time to ask him to explain that remark for she could hear the thudding footfalls on the small, snow-covered porch. The door latch lifted and the heavy wooden door swung inward, hiding Jon, throwing the dim light across the room. Instinctively, Alex's right hand gripped the wooden stake Jon had half buried in the mound of coats.

Sasha Apraskin stepped across the threshold and would have paused—directly in line with Jon's upended wooden weapon—but he was shoved violently into the room, making Jon hesitate, tense with uncertainty.

Jon's plan would have been a good one if a sick man, his wife and infant had been their victims. But it wasn't Sasha Apraskin's timid little wife who had pushed him into the room.

Behind Sasha, his imposing figure filling the door frame, his cold demeanor an extension of the icy air outdoors, stood Yury Tursunov, the officer who had threatened to detain Alex at the police station. And Alex could see what Jon could not. Her blood turned to water and froze as the man paused, his dark eyes coldly surveying the room; she could see the dawn light refracting from the dark barrel of a gun.

Her eyes locked with the single dark eye of the automatic, Alex murmured something—a prayer, perhaps. Her hand lifted, whether to warn Jon or to blot out the image of that single eye, she couldn't have said. But out of the corner of her eye, Alex saw Jon check, refraining from bringing the weapon down on Sasha Apraskin's unsuspecting head.

"So, we meet again after all," Tursunov said, stepping across the threshold and pushing the door open wider. "Perhaps now you will tell me—" He broke off, stopping just shy of clearing the door, his dark eyes focused on the pile of clothing the light from the doorway now revealed.

Despite the tightness in her throat, despite her suddenly racing heart, Alex's mind clung to the strategy Jon had outlined, spreading her body over the pile of clothing as if protecting Jon from that suddenly tense gaze.

Sasha Apraskin let loose a snide chuckle that altered swiftly to a rough cough, making all eyes swivel toward him, including Tursunov's. The officer half turned toward the other man, a marked sneer of revulsion on his narrow face.

In the momentary confusion of the moment, the coughing apparently served as the signal Jon had been waiting for. He brought down the slab of wood at the same time as he shoved his full weight against the heavy wooden door.

Alex yanked her weapon free of the coats and whirled.

It seemed as if the world had exploded into action. Sasha crumpled where he'd already been bent over with the force of his coughing. Tursunov crashed against the doorjamb, swearing viciously, but retaining a firm grip on the deadly gun in his hand. Jon's shove had been hard enough to carry him forward with the door, and now he spilled directly in range of Tursunov's gun.

"No!" Alex screamed, leaping to her feet, the wooden stake raised as if it could somehow stop a bullet.

"*Dastatichna!*" Tursunov barked, jerking the gun upward to punctuate his shouted "Enough! Get back!" he ordered Jon, waving the gun.

Jon backed away from the gun, blocking Alex. He still held the wood slab in his hand.

"Drop it," commanded Tursunov, and Jon complied. The resultant clatter made Alex flinch, but served to rouse Sasha from his semi-stupor. He coughed weakly, sending a baleful glare in Jon's direction. "Now get back."

Jon walked backward slowly, still protecting her with his body, Alex realized. The past and future lost all meaning as the danger of the present stabbed at her.

Tursunov stepped into the room and propelled the door closed with his foot. "Get up, fool!" he barked at Sasha, the way an angry man would snap at a stray dog. He kicked at him for emphasis.

Slowly, with labored breathing, Sasha pushed himself to his feet. He rocked unsteadily for a moment, one hand to the back of his head.

"Now, Doctor," Tursunov said, making a dirty word of Jon's title, "tell me where the artifacts are. I know the girl has no proof of their location. My man found nothing in her belongings. This fool here—" he flicked a contemptuous glance at Sasha Apraskin "—says you know where they are."

Alex felt Jon's hesitation to her core. She knew—who better?—the rapid assessment he was making of their chances, of their choices. Somewhat dazedly, she realized he was as uncertain as she had been. She had always just assumed that doubt was her own special purview, her own curse.

Tursunov lifted the gun, aiming it directly at Jon. "Tell me now. I have no compunction about killing you. I've killed more people than you have saved with your medicine."

"Go ahead and shoot," Jon said quietly, his words coming slowly but accurately in Russian, striking terror in Alex's heart. "Shoot me and you'll never be able to get your hands on the art."

"You think I will not do this? You are a fool. Like that Hans Saalard. He, too, believed I would not kill him. He claimed no knowledge of the collection's whereabouts. He wouldn't even tell me who his American contact was."

Alex had to choke back the bile that rose in her throat at his words. *Hans,* she thought with despair. Jon had been right; her first reaction to his death had been right. Hans had been killed because of the art.

Tursunov nodded slowly, a smile coming to his lips. His cold eyes met Alex's, accurately assessing her pain, her despair. The corners of his thin lips rose higher. "But he didn't have to die, did he, *dyevushka?* He could have told me your name."

Because of me...Alex thought with horror. Hans had died because of her.

"He was a fool. Like all of you," Tursunov said. "All I had to do was to alert the customs officials to look for the photographs. And blame that idiot Makarov for bungling the entire affair." He sent another look of disgust at Sasha Apraskin. "So many have underestimated me. This fool here didn't know that I knew about the photographs—that I knew all about the artifacts." His frosty smile crossed his narrow face again.

Alex knew with sick certainty, the senior Apraskin's dying words ringing in her mind, that somehow this man had engineered the entire theft of the collection. "You..." she breathed.

"Exactly. It was me. Those particular items are priceless." He laughed, the sound that of madness. "Not for money. Who cares about money? The collection, each evil piece of it, is my ticket to power. Those artifacts are beautiful, exquisite weapons of power." His face twisted in a mockery of a smile. "Take this token of my appreciation, Mr. Chairman...." He half bowed, miming the handing over of a gift, straightened suddenly and laughed. "And *die*. A slow, painful death."

If Alex hadn't known before, she knew now that Tursunov was insane. He was a power-hungry man who had been consumed by the megalomaniac's need for more and more power. And he'd latched on to the deadly collection as a means of killing his enemies, of erasing those who stood in his way. But how did he think he would avoid the radiation himself?

Seeing his eyes, seeing the madness lurking in them, she knew it didn't matter to him. Nothing so unimportant as becoming poisoned himself would weigh in the equation of power he'd mapped out for himself. And, she thought with fear, he had probably figured out some method whereby he wouldn't come in direct contact with the radiation, anyway.

"So why don't we end this heroic little charade? Tell me where the collection is. My man misunderstood his orders and shot Apraskin. Otherwise, we could simply have followed you to it.'' He sighed; then his cold lips twisted. ''He will make no more such mistakes. Will he, Sasha?''

Alex gathered that the large gentleman was dead, presumably at Sasha's hand.

Tursunov stepped sideways, moving toward Sasha. ''Sasha has made a couple of mistakes, as well.'' He turned to Jon, saying almost conversationally, ''You see, Mr. Apraskin here thought he could get the artifacts for himself and sell them—to you, to anyone. To me.'' He rounded on Sasha. ''What made you believe I wouldn't find out? What made you believe I would allow your worthless life to continue?''

''No!'' Sasha said quickly, his face full of abject fear. ''I would never have—''

''You won't mind if I do not turn my back to you,'' Tursunov said. He turned his eyes back to Jon. ''So, tell me. Where is this collection of the damned?''

Jon merely shook his head and gestured to Alex to keep silent, too. She had to bite her lip to keep from blurting out their scanty knowledge. Couldn't Jon see that Tursunov was perfectly ready to kill them?

In a flash, Alex realized that Jon could see that every bit as clearly as she could. At that moment, she saw him clearly and understood him—understood him completely—for the first time. He was a man whose concern for humanity overrode all other considerations. A doctor, a man of unselfish compassion. A confident, gentle man who understood the frail connection between life and death. A man who had called her spring because he had seen too much of winter.

No, he wouldn't tell this madman where the artifacts were; it would be the same thing as personally unleashing death on an unsuspecting world. He would rather die than do that.

And in understanding him, in knowing him, in finally recognizing him, she felt a wild exultation, a sure knowledge that she loved him. In that moment, with a madman's gun trained on them—perhaps one always thought most clearly when one was close to death?—she accepted the knowledge of her love for him and drew courage from it. She felt steady, cleansed. She felt strong and for a brief moment, wise. She met Tursunov's gaze defiantly. Slowly, with great deliberation, she shook her head.

"So," he said, moving in a broad circle until he stood in the center of the small cabin. Jon also moved, as if he were a dancer following the other man's lead. He held his arms to the sides, gesturing for Alex to remain behind him.

With a smile still on his lips, Tursunov nodded at Alex but said to Sasha, "Get her."

Instinctively, Jon shoved Alex fully behind him. "I wouldn't," he said.

"We'll shoot you, then her," Tursunov said. "Do not think of playing the hero. You would have told her where the collection is by now. You've had all night." He nodded to Sasha again, emphasizing his words by pulling back the barrel of the automatic in his hand with a decisive gesture.

Wary of Jon, Sasha Apraskin edged toward them, his hands out, away from his sides. As he circled closer, Jon circled away, keeping Alex at his back.

While her heart thudded in her throat and her ears rang with the amount of adrenalin coursing through her, Alex was conscious of only one thought: that Jon could be killed trying to stop Sasha. Jon could be killed. *Killed*. It was a thought that couldn't be borne. It was one thing to think of both of them dying, even dying nobly, but it was a different matter to think of Jon dying merely to save her. No matter what the future held for them.... In that split second of self-awareness, she recognized a whole new desperation; she loved him. Now. She loved him wholly. No matter what the future, Jon couldn't die because of her.

She drew in a steadying breath and stepped from behind Jon, her eyes locking with Tursunov's. "Wait!" she said sharply, her voice pitched high in fear, her hands trembling with the force of her emotions.

Jon whirled, his eyes wide with shock and fear, but even as she saw him lunge for her, he was too late. Tursunov's free hand shot out and jerked her to him, twisting her, holding her arm painfully behind her back, the gun pressing against the tender skin beneath her chin. As he propelled her sideways, away from Jon, she stumbled, causing him to wrench her arm upward, making her cry out with the pain. The automatic dug at her chin and she bit her tongue. She could taste the coppery tang of blood. Tears of pain and frustration squeezed from beneath her half-closed eyelids. She stared at Jon bleakly. His eyes were filled with entreaty, with anger. She gazed at him in mute apology, sorry for so much more than merely being taken, too sorry to maintain eye contact.

The thing she regretted most was not having told him that she loved him. She was going to die without being able to tell him that she loved him.

"And now, Doctor, perhaps you will talk more freely. Perhaps you have no desire to live...but would you be so careless with her life?"

Jon ground his teeth together to hold in the string of invectives trying to spill from his mouth. His eyes flicked from Alex's to Tursunov's, his mind a rage of chaotic thoughts. Any higher and her shoulder would be dislocated.... If he rushed the man now, the gun could go off.... If only he hadn't selfishly wanted Alex to remain in the Soviet Union, she would be free of this menace now.... If anything happened to her, he would kill this man.

He'd never wanted to kill anyone before, but he wanted to kill Tursunov now. Looking at Alex, willing himself to be still, forcing himself not to scream with the rage inside him, he tried not to see her pale, tear-streaked face, her closed eyes and the look of self-recrimination on her features. He tried but failed, his mind and body filled with outrage, the lover in him like the wild brown bear of the northern steppes: furious, lumbering, a mindless, raging, destructive force.

Before this was over, he vowed silently, he would make Tursunov pay for every bruise on Alex's body. And he would make him pay with interest.

"Let her go and I'll tell you," Jon said, finally.

Alex's eyes flew open and met his in anguished appeal. He could read the denial in her gaze. He met her wide, frightened eyes steadily, hoping she could read his love, his determination, his hope. For a moment, hers widened and then, in their depths, he saw many things: relief, fear, but most of all, a hot blaze of answering love for him. Even now, even in the face of incredible danger, he could read the love there, and what he read instilled his body with new energy, imbued him with steady confidence.

"You'll tell me anyway, Doctor." Tursunov nodded at Sasha, who stepped forward, giving Jon a wide berth, no longer Sasha the Incredible, but Sasha the menial, Sasha the very sick.

Despite his illness, despite his obvious fear of the other man, Sasha's gaze fastened on Alex's straining blouse, a feral gleam coming into his eyes. It made Jon sick with loathing.

But even as Jon noted Sasha's gaze, so did Tursunov. A cruel smile twisted his lips and stabbed at Jon's heart.

"Let us see how much the lover can stomach before his tongue will work," Tursunov said to Sasha, beckoning the man forward with his head, his thin smile a sneer, his eyes glittering dangerously.

"Stop!" Jon said, but he held still when Tursunov yanked at Alex's arm, causing her to whimper.

"She's beautiful, isn't she, Sasha? Have you ever had an American woman?"

To Jon's horror, Sasha dragged the back of his hand across his lips, his eyes locked on the sight of Alex's heaving breasts.

The look in Sasha Apraskin's eyes made Alex weak with a primeval fear. When Sasha reached for the opening of her blouse, she shrank back against her other captor.

"No," Alex whimpered. "Please . . ."

Dimly she heard Jon's harsh protests as Sasha's hand jerked the soft material aside, tearing it, exposing the tops of her full breasts. As his rough fingers reached for her bare flesh, Alex screamed, thrashing wildly, kicking both forward and back, mindless of the gun, mindless of the danger.

Even as Sasha's hand closed around Alex's breast, Jon lunged across the space between them, a roar on his lips, his fists hammering. He slammed into Sasha's back, one hand battering the lesser man, while the other swung with rage-induced precision at Yury Tursunov's face.

Whatever Tursunov had anticipated, it had not been the suddenly frenzied woman in his arms nor the rage of the seemingly mild-mannered doctor. Jon could read the lack of comprehension—and sudden fear—in the man's eyes as he dropped his hold on Alex and flailed backward, waving the gun wildly at nothing.

Jon lunged toward Tursunov, heedless of the gun, an animal now, conscious of nothing but a desire to eradicate the man from the face of the earth. He grabbed hold of Tursunov's gun wrist and pounded it against the wall, slamming it again and again with enough force that he was certain the hand would break. Tursunov yelled, and the gun slid from his fingers, his other hand frantically clenching Jon's other hand, which was clawing his throat.

Behind them, seemingly all around him, Jon heard the sounds of Alex's struggle with the thinly screaming Sasha. And other sounds.

Sounds of the door, sounds of many feet. And, finally, the sound of a single shot fired from somewhere behind him.

He whirled, his hands still pinning Tursunov to the wall. Someone was pulling a doubled-over Sasha Apraskin from the floor while, incredibly, James Bowden was bending over Alex, gently drawing her to an upright position, while Ned Sternberg stood to one side, his eyes calmly taking in the room.

"I'll take it from here, Doctor," a man's voice said in Russian beside Jon. Dully, willing his rage to subside, dimly conscious of a desire to continue his assault on Tursunov, still aware of the urge to punish the man, to make him pay for hurting Alex, Jon stared into Andre Makarov's eyes.

"It's my job, now," Makarov said quietly, meeting Jon's gaze steadily, as if he understood the battle still raging in Jon's breast.

"Right," Jon said, giving Tursunov a final shove away from him and slowly rising to his feet. "Right," he repeated, reaction beginning to set in. He averted his gaze from Tursunov's semiprone body, disgusted by the thought of what he'd almost done, sorry he hadn't accomplished it.

As if his body were numbed, as though drugged, he moved stiffly to where Alex stood in James Bowden's protective embrace. Still caught up in the animal rage that had prompted his assault on Tursunov, Jon wanted to smash the sympathy from Bowden's face.

"Sorry it took us so long, Jon," Ned said, taking his arm, squeezing it sympathetically. "We lost you."

Jon paused, looking at the older man with faint disdain. That was all he had to say? That he was sorry they were late? He'd been able to be insouciant with Alex because he'd been thoroughly convinced the good guys were on top of things. He'd seen their American tail at the ballet. He'd blithely assumed he had followed them. They'd both damn near been killed, and all Ned could say was that he was sorry they were late?

Jon shook off the older man's hand and turned to Alex. She was facing him, her lips parted, her eyes anything but dull. In them he read a thousand things, saw glimpses of a new life, a new hope.

He reached for her, the hero's reward, the lover's ultimate goal. His heart still pumped with the beast's adrenalin; his head still throbbed from anger. But his thoughts were all for Alex, for the shy acceptance he could read in her gaze, as bemusing to her as it was dazzling to him.

"Alex?" he asked unsteadily, not quite sure what he was asking.

She pulled from beneath James's arm and advanced a step toward him. Her entire body shook. Her breath came and went rapidly, her torn blouse revealing her agitation.

She tentatively held up a hand, lightly stroking his cheek. "You . . ." she said, and tears came to her eyes.

He closed his eyes, as shaken by the depth of his emotion as she was, wanting to drag her into his arms, yet afraid he would never be able to let her go, that he would frighten this precious love away.

On some rational level, a part of him understood that she was every bit as charged up as he was, that her system, her thoughts, her emotions were still in the grip of the adrenalin pumping through her veins, just as it still pumped through his.

James Bowden cleared his throat noisily. "Earth to Alex," he said. "Lighten up, you two. All's well—"

"Shut up," Jon said quietly, not bothering to look at him, the only thought in his head that of taking Alex in his arms and assuring her that the love he saw in her eyes was returned a thousandfold.

To his amazement, James chuckled. Jon turned to him, wondering what on earth the man could be thinking of to make him laugh at a time like this. In his peripheral vision, he saw Alex doing the same thing.

James gestured at the now-handcuffed Tursunov. "Too bad we didn't arm Alex. If she'd had a gun, all your troubles would have been over."

Not understanding the reference, Jon nonetheless understood Alex's gasp as an expression of pain. Seeing her hand rise to her lips, her eyes wide with a horror that had nothing to do with the events of the past few days, awakened the protective urge in Jon once again.

"What the hell is that supposed to mean?" Jon growled, turning his still-burning gaze to James.

"Didn't Alex tell you?" James looked the picture of amazement. "She's pretty handy with a gun. She once tried to shoot her ex-husband."

As if his hand belonged to someone else, as if he had no control over the driving force in his arm, as if he hadn't seen the spasm of pain that crossed Alex's face, Jon's fist shot across the narrow space separating the two men and connected squarely with James Bowden's jaw.

The diplomat stood still for a long, stunned moment before pitching slowly sideways, his blank eyes on Jon, his mouth slack, a trickle of blood already oozing from his split lower lip.

Jon turned, holding his right hand protectively, the flesh throbbing, his head feeling the same way. But Alex wouldn't look at him. Her hand was still to her lips, her fingers pressing into the soft flesh. Her eyes were wide with horror, and Jon, feeling as if he'd been dashed with cold water, again discovered the disordered sensation of having left his rational, human side behind somewhere. He reached for her, lifting the hand that had so recently reduced James Bowden to a sprawling mass on the floor at his feet.

He saw a bloodied scrape on his knuckles and didn't know whether it had come from Tursunov or from Bowden. But the disgust that rose within him came from a lifetime of having nurtured the sick, tended the ailing. Seeing that bloodied hand, he recognized it as a symptom of a disease he had never known lay within him, an incipient, animalistic urge to dominate, an urge for revenge, an urge for destruction. He couldn't touch Alex now, not with his hand still bloody. He pulled it back, lowering it to his side.

Looking at her, seeing her shock, feeling the weight of it press upon his still-dazed mind, he could understand why she wouldn't meet his eyes. Why she couldn't. The animal in him had frightened her as much as it disgusted him.

"Alex," he said, and even to his own ears, his voice sounded choked.

"Don't," she said, and for a brief moment, her eyes met his. In them he read despair, pain, a horror he understood and a sorrow he thought he did. "Don't say anything."

"Alex . . ." he repeated, the word sounding to him like a heron's cry, a mournful wail, marking the end of spring, the need for the long flight north.

"Don't," she said, almost as if he weren't there, as if James weren't sitting at their feet, slowly rubbing his jaw. She shook her head slowly, her eyes meeting Jon's. In hers, he saw the death of hope, the depth of her despair.

Chapter 12

Alex stepped into the chill sunlight, dazzled for a moment by the glittering brilliance, dimly aware of the activity around her, her mind locked on James's words, on Jon's reaction to them, on the past.

Even as she heard Andre Makarov's rapid-fire questioning of Tursunov—How did you know of the collection? What did you plan to do with the artifacts? Why did you do this? Why did you do that? What did you hope to accomplish?—and stood aside to allow some KGB man to lead Sasha Apraskin to a distant vehicle, she shuddered at the memory of Jon's hand retreating, the half-checked gesture, the look of confusion on his already overwrought face.

Her heart constricted with pain, with embarrassment, with abject self-pity. Indelibly imprinted on her mind would be the shocked expression on Jon's face as James had blurted out his distorted version of the truth.

If only... If only she had been the one to tell him. If only James hadn't been there. If only she had told Jon of her dawning love sooner.... She should have told him earlier. If she had told him, he wouldn't have been so shocked. And she should have told him about her past. If she had, he might not have lashed out at James. He would have...what? Looked at her with the same dazed expression, the same lines of disgust etching his face?

Remorse, crippling, searing remorse, swept through her, making her weak, filling her with an aching need to be anywhere on earth but there, her back to the doorway of the small dacha that had been not only their prison, but the scene of their last halcyon moment.

It was in this dacha, this dusty prison, that she had seen the love in his eyes. It had been there that she had felt the tremendous weight of the past slide from her shoulders, if only for a moment. It had been there that she had, in his warm embrace, conquered her fears, forsworn the damage of the multitude of betrayals in her past and had received his love.

She couldn't bear to gaze into those eyes now and see the change, the disgust. Anything would be easier to bear than that. Hans Saalard had understood, had helped her through those dark days, had never condemned her. But Hans had been older; Hans had been the kind of man who would understand anything, any human failing.

Her heart cried out for her to believe that Jon was that same kind of man...but her self-recrimination kept that too-hopeful possibility from her.

She didn't understand James. All her instincts had said that their friendship was strong enough that he could say anything and the caring would remain. But he had said the unforgivable. He'd attacked in a way that showed that he had never really understood her. Never, in all those years. Only someone who didn't understand could have joked about such a dark day in her life, such a black moment.

She wondered if it had been deliberate on his part. She didn't love him; had he decided she could no longer have even his friendship? She thought fleetingly of the many visits, the lunches filled with laughter, the wry humor he displayed to all too few people. Was he trying to put a final period to their many years of friendship? A tinge of sorrow underscored the anger she now felt toward him.

The many years of barbs, the strange moods she'd ignored after the flash of his brilliant smile... They seemed suddenly important now, as though each one had been another straw on the proverbial camel's back, until this day, this last remark...and it had been one thing too many, a back-breaking load.

But he'd done worse than destroy their longtime friendship. He'd stolen the moment from her and Jon; he'd tipped her hand, not letting her savor that brief time when triumph and determination had colored Jon's eyes and love had been untainted by doubts and uncertainties.

And after James's comments, when she'd seen Jon's face change, the disgusted twist of his lips, she'd known the reason and felt the anguish. She understood it, even accepted the death of his love for her. She mourned it, but she accepted it. It was, after all, her due.

We are what we are because of the choices we have made. Jon had said that. For the first time, she had begun to believe it, begun to feel that perhaps her judgment wasn't sour, that she could not only trust others, but trust herself. But now? Did Jon believe it now? Now that he knew?

She shook her head, trying to make her thoughts fall into order. From the anguished chaos she drew one comfort: he didn't know everything. She clung to that slender reed of hope. She hadn't told him. He had only James's cruel words to go on. And they had been misleading. Cruel and inaccurate. Unfortunately, there had been enough truth in them to let Jon see what kind of a person she really was. Really could be. It showed the kind of anger she was capable of, the kind of poor judgment she could exercise.

Gripping her hands tightly together, wringing them as if she could rub away the past, rub away James's words, as if she could rid herself of the desire to erase the despairing look on Jon's face, she sobbed an incoherent plea.

"Are you all right?" Ned Sternberg asked beside her. He draped her coat around her shoulders.

She looked at him dumbly. She would never be all right again. Ned met her eyes for a long moment, then looked over his shoulder at someone behind them. Alex turned. Jon was talking with Makarov now, apparently recounting their experiences, his voice dull, his eyes, those warm and gentle eyes, lifeless. He wasn't looking at her, and Alex knew with an instinct born of her love for him that he couldn't.

Because of the past, because of what she'd done.

Oh, Jon . . . The loss of his smile, the loss of the warm glow in his burnished eyes, tore at her with the ferocity of a blizzard.

The loss settled in her with the same racking anguish that was brought on by the memory of the horror she'd felt all those years before, when she'd stood with a gun trained on Tony's black heart.

Though she'd lived with that image, with the pain of it, with the ultimate humiliation all these years, she had never really allowed the full memory to surface. Now, as if seeing it through Jon's eyes, through Hans's or even James's vision, she pictured herself with blazing eyes, tears streaming down her cheeks, both hands tightly clutching the gun.

Always before, she had told herself, not in expiation—she would never be able to forgive herself that moment of murderous intent—but in rationalization, that it was love of Tony that had brought her to that moment.

But standing here now, the cold of the morning slapping at her face, the dull expression on Jon's face tormenting her mind, she knew that love hadn't been the motivation behind her deadly action. It had been a wild, searing anger at being betrayed, being embarrassed, a rage against this proof that her judgment was faulty, that she'd chosen so unwisely that her husband was actually married to someone else.

And Hans . . . dear Hans . . . had stopped her.

"I'm sorrier than I can say that you had to go through this," Ned said, drawing her coat tighter, forcing her to meet his eyes.

Alex stared at him, much as Jon had done earlier.

"We lost you on a turn. We never would have found you if Apraskin and his wife hadn't gone back home. Thank God they were stupid." He smiled, but the smile slipped when she continued to stare at him.

It was as if he were speaking a language she didn't know. He was saying words, but they had no meaning.

Why did the past always have the power to hurt her? Why did the past have to intrude now? Why now, after she'd cried so much of it free the night before, rocking in Jon's arms, lulled by his lips gently pressed against her temple? Ned was talking, but saying nothing. Only the flat look in Jon's eyes, the despair she felt in her soul, only those had meaning.

"The woman, Tanya, couldn't talk fast enough. She told us where they'd taken you," Ned was saying. "She was terrified that the baby had primary radiation sickness—the doctor at the hospital says no, he doesn't. But Apraskin does. So does his wife. They must have come in direct contact with the stuff. But the baby is sick enough—probably just from contact with his mother."

Alex shook her head, not in sympathy, but in confusion. Nothing mattered anymore. Nothing.

"Luckily for you two, the doctor—not Jon, but a specialist in Wiesbaden—says that in order to get really sick, you have to come into direct contact with something that has been contaminated. You have to actually touch it, and for a fairly long period—longer than a couple of seconds."

Was he saying this to comfort her? What did she care about radiation poisoning now? Now, when her whole life was poisoned? When she'd poisoned it herself years before?

"Sasha Apraskin has it, doesn't he?" she asked.

Ned blinked, realizing that she hadn't been listening to his words. He shrugged. "Yes. You'll have to be checked, of course, but I doubt you have anything to worry about."

At that, Alex's lips twisted into a sour smile. She glanced up at the sky. How could the day be so bright when her soul felt so dark, so lost?

"It was Makarov's boys who actually saw you being snatched. We were right there, but we never saw a thing," he said, shaking his head ruefully. "Luckily for you two, Makarov likes you well enough that he tipped me off."

Suddenly Alex felt she could tolerate no more of this, no more dimly understood conversation, no more awkward sympathy, no more halfhearted attempts to cheer her from a depression too deep to be accessible. She just wanted to get in one of the cars and leave. Leave the dacha, leave Moscow...leave Jon. She wanted to run as fast and as far as she possibly could.

"Can we go now?" she asked, turning her eyes to Ned's. Lord knew what he saw there, but he agreed quickly, a nervous hand raking through his silver hair.

"I'll take you myself. I feel rather like a third wheel, anyway." He led her down the few steps and assisted her across the snowy expanse leading to the country lane beyond the dacha. "Makarov has been keeping tabs on Tursunov ever since that day they detained you. It seems Tursunov knew entirely too much."

"Hans Saalard," Alex said.

"How did you get that?" Ned asked, opening a car door. "That's what tipped Makarov off."

"Andre Makarov knew he'd been killed. He let it slip that day—yesterday...?" She trailed off, stunned for a moment by the passage of time. It seemed she had known Jon all her life. He *was* her life. Yet they'd had so little time. So little time.

"He let it slip...?" Ned prompted.

"That Hans had been killed? Deliberately. No accident. Andre must have figured out that it was Tursunov who did it. Maybe from something Tursunov said." Her voice sounded as weary as she felt. *Jon*...

"That's what he said. He also said something about the two of you needing to exchange the toast of friendship." He closed the door. The dull thud echoed hollowly in Alex's heart. It was as if a door had closed to her future, a door that had, for a brief, glimmering moment, stood wide open, beckoning, urging her toward a bright promise.

Involuntarily, as if seeking that promise, she turned her head and looked back at the dacha. Jon was outside now, his coat loosely draped around his shoulders, his hands in his pockets, his eyes on the car, on *her.* James Bowden stood to his left, nursing his jaw, talking rapidly. Jon seemed to be ignoring him, his face grim, his eyes, even from this distance, bleak.

Ned opened the door and slid behind the steering wheel. "Ready?" he asked, turning the key in the ignition.

"Yes," she lied, dragging her gaze from Jon and turning it toward the snow-covered road. She felt as if she'd left the part of her that was vitally alive, the part that could think, love, laugh, the part of her that made her wholly a woman, she'd left that part behind, in the dacha.

Ned glanced in her direction, then eased the car into a U-turn and headed for the city. "It'll be all right," he said after they'd driven for a while. He said it awkwardly, a gruff note in his voice.

"No," Alex said. "No, it won't." She turned her head away from his curious gaze, hot tears spilling down her cheeks. No. It would never be all right again.

A week crept by, each minute without Alex an hour, each hour a year. When Margaret had died, he'd found himself stumbling across her loss a thousand times a day, in a hundred little ways. He would be engrossed in a novel, hear a noise and look up, expecting to have her walk into the room. He would read an article that triggered a memory of some conversation they might have had and he'd find his hand out, his mouth half-open to call her name. He would take down two coffee cups from the cupboard in the morning, instead of just one.

He felt that way now, yet even more so. For in the end, he hadn't really loved Margaret. And she'd know it all along. That had been the damning message in the journals he'd found.

He and Alex hadn't had enough time to develop the intimate knowledge of each other that lovers had. Yet he saw her in every dark-haired woman; every pair of blue eyes he looked into begged an unfavorable comparison with Alex's. A distant laugh at a cocktail party would bring him around, his body tense, his eyes searching vainly for Alex.

In the week that had gone by since that dark night and too-bright morning at the dacha, he'd relived, rethought, replayed every second of their time together. He no longer believed Alex had pulled away from him in disgust at his violent behavior. That had been only a feeling extension of his own shock at what he was capable of thinking, capable of doing. No, she'd pulled away for entirely different reasons.

And it was thinking of those reasons that made Jon's heart tighten in fear, made sleep elusive and morning a hell.

By the time he had arrived back at his apartment, she'd already removed her things and installed herself in the guest quarters in the old embassy building. She wouldn't answer his knock at the door nor respond to his repeated phone calls.

He never should have let her drive away with Ned Sternberg, never should have let her leave. But he'd seen the confusion on her face, the stunned horror dulling her beautiful eyes. And, sick at what he'd just done, he'd thought her horror was a mirror of his actions.

And he'd let her leave.

What had he said to Alex about choices—there were no good or bad ones? He'd been a fool. There were always good or bad choices. Thinking about them one way or another didn't make them that way; they really could be right or wrong. Had that moment been the very worst moment, the very worst choice he could have made?

Jon stared out the window at the heavy spring snow swirling around the buildings and trees, coating everything with that velvet white lace endemic to spring snows. His mind saw the beauty while his heart rejected it. As it had been rejecting everything, every thought but those of Alex since the day at the dacha.

Why wouldn't she talk to him? Was the chasm between them so broad, so deep, that she couldn't see beyond it?

He'd felt it then, the distance, seeing it in her averted gaze as Ned Sternberg had eased the car into the country lane and left the dacha behind, the wheels churning up a spray of ice and snow.

James had blubbered his apology-cum-explanation, his words scarcely impinging on Jon's consciousness, but that hadn't been the reason why he hadn't flagged down Ned's car, hadn't stopped her from leaving.

He hadn't stopped her because he'd still been reeling with self-condemnation over his actions. He hadn't stopped her because he loved her too much to halt that instinctive flight.

"You could always take up boxing," James had said, rubbing his jaw. "If doctoring ever palls, I mean."

Jon had simply looked at him. The anger in him was gone now, the beast once more in hibernation. It left him curiously drained, strangely reluctant to relinquish its fiery hold on him.

And as he heard the crunch of the car's tires on the snow, had seen her sorrowful face, he'd felt reason once again entering his mind. Why *had* she left? Surely it hadn't been James's asinine comment that had propelled her to look at him with such dismay? Who knew what the man had even been talking about? Was the weight of the past that oppressive? Had he misunderstood the look of love in her eyes?

"I've never taunted her about that night," James had said. "Not once, not in all this time." He had pulled back from Jon as if anticipating another blow. "I guess the look in her eyes made me see red. And I just couldn't help myself."

"What look?" Jon had asked.

James looked surprised. "That hail-the-conquering-hero look. I'd never seen her look at anyone that way before."

The admission and the regret on James's face made Jon feel oddly in sympathy with the man. He'd realized that

James was half in love with Alex, probably had been for years. He hadn't thought the man was capable of deep emotion. He eyed James then, as if seeing him for the first time.

"See, I've known Alex for quite a while. I knew Tony."

"Tony?"

"Her ex-husband. We went through the same Foreign Service class. I was best man at their wedding. I think I fell for Alex then. She had class."

Jon had said nothing to that; there was nothing to say. She did have class. She had style; she had grace.

"But she had so much more than that." James paused, remembering. "Unlike Marja. They were as different as night and day. Marja was all giggles, babies and rosy cheeks."

"Her husband had an affair?"

James had shaken his head, his eyes again meeting Jon's with that wary look. "Marja was Tony's other wife."

Jon had stared at James, not really comprehending. "His other wife? He remarried?"

James had grimaced, then winced as the expression hurt his swollen jaw. "No." He squirmed. "Tony was a bigamist. Married to both of them. I've never quite forgiven myself for not telling Alex sooner."

"You told her?"

"No. No, and I should have." He shook his head. "She found out the hard way."

Unaware of the questions springing to Jon's mind, James continued. "Tony was stationed in Norway then. Alex had her business in the States. So he didn't have too much fear about either one finding out. But one day, Alex took it into her head to pop over to Norway and surprise him."

"And she found him," Jon said, almost as if plucking the image from James's mind. He ached for the younger Alex, already having been through so much, betrayed by her father in his cruel suicide, betrayed by her mother into believing it was her fault, then betrayed by her husband.

And now betrayed by the foolish words of one man and another's never-completed gesture. God only knew how she'd interpreted his lowered hand. The fact that he hadn't followed her out of the dacha.

He gazed at James, not bothering to hide the disgust he felt. He waited for the other man to elaborate, to explain his earlier remark, half wishing the animal in him would roar again.

"It was some Norwegian holiday. Tony had invited me over—I was stationed in Germany then. We were all staying with Marja's uncle—Hans Saalard."

"Hans..."

"Yeah. Hans Saalard."

"What happened?" Jon asked, hating talking to James about Alex, but needing to hear, needing to know everything about her, needing to know the whole story that James had referred to earlier. Maybe something would give him some clue as to how to get through to her, to make her see that she wasn't alone in this self-disgust, that everyone suffered from it at some time during their lives. That she couldn't throw their love away because of something in her past. And if what James said offered no clue, he would at least have the memory of her, at least know the story of her life.

"When she found out what was going on, she sort of lost it. She wasn't the calm, cool Alex we all know now."

Jon stared at James. Did the man really think of her that way? She was a far cry from calm and cool. She was fire and passion and deep wells of pain. The other was a mask, a thin one at best. One he'd seen through that first evening. One she'd shed completely in his arms, in his bed, in the dark cold of the dacha the night before and again that morning.

"Anyhow, she went into Hans Saalard's study—and how she knew where to look, I'll never know."

Jon felt his stomach tighten. She'd gone in to look for a gun. He didn't enlighten James as to why she had looked in the study; she had known to look for a gun in the study because her father had kept—and used—a gun in his.

"... And she came back out with a gun. She pointed it at Tony, just as cool as you please. She had tears streaming down her cheeks, but her eyes were right on Tony's heart."

For an aching, heart-rending moment, Jon could see Alex with the gun in her hand, aimed at her husband. He could see the fire in her eyes, the trembling of her hand, the anguish in her fine features. And his soul darkened at the thought of the husband who had so cruelly used her, so betrayed her trust.

She had doubted her own judgment—taking the blame, accepting the guilt after this man had hurt her so badly. Didn't she understand that it hadn't been her fault, that the man who had betrayed her deserved the guilt?

Almost randomly, Jon wondered if Alex had loved Tony? She'd been hurt by him, but had she truly loved him?

"Did she shoot him?" he asked, almost as if it didn't matter. And to him, it didn't. Not that way.

James shook his head, an almost rueful expression on his face. "No. Marja was having hysterics, and Tony about had a heart attack. But Uncle Hans talked Alex out of it. Kicked Tony out. I don't quite know how it came about after that, but she and Hans—and the family—always stayed close."

Jon could have told him, but didn't. If the man couldn't see why Alex had loved Hans Saalard, then he didn't deserve to know.

Remembering now, thinking about that too-bright morning when the whole world had gone crazy and how the look in Alex's eyes had torn his heart apart, he wondered how he would survive the day ahead, and the months and years after that.

If only she would talk to him, give him five minutes of time, he would make her see that walking away from their love, walking away from him, was to run away from life itself. That in denying him, she was condemning them both to a life of loneliness. For he was as much the man for her as she was the woman for him. He knew that with a certainty that brooked no arguments.

He watched a Soviet Zil pull to the curb in front of the embassy and he turned from the window, a faint hope stirring in his heart.

Today they would have to see each other. They would have to ride in the same car and stand near each other to witness the recovery of the collection.

With Sasha and Tanya Apraskin in protective custody in the hospital, both fearing for their lives, authorities on both sides had assumed they would find the artifacts swiftly and easily.

But it had been Alex who figured out where the collection was hidden. Ned had told Jon that the two of them had gone to Andre Makarov's office in "one of the damnedest examples of modern détente" to try to pin down the possible location of the grave where the collection might be buried.

Maps of Moscow had been spread out on Andre's desk; they had been poring over them and then Alex had started to chuckle. But, Ned had told Jon, her eyes looked as though she were going to start crying any second. She had pointed out the Lazarevskoye Cemetery, a poor man's cemetery, used predominantly by Gypsies, on the outskirts of Moscow.

Ned has asked why she thought it was that particular cemetery, and Alex had muttered something about Lazarus. And then she had recounted Jon's explanation for the collection being in a grave in the first place.

"I think—and so does Makarov—that she was right. Said it translates to Lazarus's Cemetery. But for the life of me, I can't figure out why she chuckled, or why she was crying when we finally got back to the car. Is there something wrong between you two? You have a fight or something?"

Jon hadn't given the older man an answer. He had none to give. An entire life, the dark past, had to be stricken from her heart. And how could he hope to do that?

He'd seen her, but only from a distance, from the distance she kept between them. But he hadn't been allowed to talk with her privately. She avoided his gaze, making him seethe with frustration. During the debriefing session, she'd ignored him pointedly, making him long to shake her, making him grit his teeth in order to keep from demanding that she talk with him.

But the time for letting her work it out alone was over. The time for hanging back was done. James Bowden had told him this morning that a joint Soviet-American delegation had been tapped to attend a "certain funeral" in Lazarevskoye Cemetery. Jon was on the team, as were Alex, James and Ned. Then, said James, shortly after the ceremony, Alex was due to leave for the States.

"Not if I can help it," Jon said grimly now, slamming the door of his clinic and marching down the hall to the waiting limousine.

Alex stiffened at the unaccustomed knock at her door. Her heart thudded, and her fingers flexed in a quick, involuntary reaction. *Jon?*

She both wanted it to be him and yet, perversely, prayed that it wasn't. She'd felt his silent entreaty in the debriefing room, felt his eyes on her profile. She'd felt as if he were hammering at her, demanding that she look at him, demanding that she talk with him.

How could she? Now that he knew? How could she bear to see the disgusted expression in his eyes?

It was easier this way, she thought. She would just leave, slip away as easily as she had arrived. Never see him again. Never look into his brown eyes, never again know his velvet touch.

The thought of leaving was torture, but the thought of meeting his eyes, of telling him the entire story of her past was agony.

The questions in his eyes had unnerved her. She couldn't stay in the same room with him without wanting him to take her into his arms and hold her. She couldn't sit next to him without wanting to scream out against the weight of the past, the judgment he must have made about it.

She wrenched the door open, setting her face to an expression of impassive coolness. She frowned as she saw James Bowden.

"The limo's here," he said.

"Fine," she said, preparing to close the door.

"Wait, Alex!" he said, his arm blocking the door. "I—I want to apologize."

Alex said nothing. She had studiously avoided any contact with James up until this moment. She felt that he had killed their friendship with his comment at the dacha.

"All I seem to do with you anymore is apologize to you," he said. His grin shone in the dark hallway. Alex didn't smile back, and his grin slipped.

"Alex . . . ?"

"What?"

"Forgive me?"

She sighed wearily. "James, we've known each other a long time. But this time, I don't think I can forgive you."

"Come on, Alex. You know how sorry I am. If you want, you can take a leaf from Jon's book." He turned slightly, thrusting his still-bruised jaw in her direction. "Hit me," he said.

"I believe it was the other way around," she said. "You hit me."

He stepped back, his grin noticeably absent. "I was jealous, Alex."

"That's what you said that night at your cocktail party. Give me another one, James."

"No, I mean it. Hell, you'd have to be blind not to see that you're crazy about him. And he is crazy about you, too."

"Well, you've done a good job of driving a wedge between us, James. Satisfied?" Once again, she started to push the door closed, but he shoved it open. She knew a pang of fear.

"No. No, I'm not satisfied!" he snapped, pushing his way into her small living room. "Do you think I'm proud of what I did? Do you think I feel good about it?" He turned around, bringing his face within inches of hers. "I've spent half my adult life trying to make you see that despite being friends with Tony, I'm not like him. I thought that if I played good-buddy James, you'd eventually give in and learn to love again. Learn to love me!"

Alex could only stare at him, aghast.

"Then you come here and it's like watching the Italian thunderbolt! You were half in love with Jon before he even told you his name! Of course I'm jealous. Of course I wanted to drive a wedge between you!"

He reached for the door then, oblivious to her. But he whirled suddenly, making her shrink back against the wall, shocked at the fury in his eyes.

"But it's not *me* who's driving that wedge now, Alex. It's *you*. Don't kid yourself about that. It's *you*. The man's almost sick with love for you. Do you think he's the kind of guy who goes around taking punches at people just because he doesn't like their faces? Hell, he's as decent as they come.

"*You*, Alex . . . *you're* using the past as an excuse to run away. You're running away because you're just plain scared of loving. You always have been. You were scared with Tony. You insisted on keeping your career. You were scared every time some guy made a pass at you. And now? Now you're running away again, Alex." He turned from her then, a defeated sag to his shoulders. Without turning back to her, he said in a dull tone, "And if that isn't apology enough, too bad."

He pulled the door closed behind him.

Alex stared at the door in shock, her mind in chaos, her thoughts chasing after his words, trying to dodge the truth in them, trying to sort through them to find an escape.

But her heart wouldn't let her; her Russian soul demanded the painful truth. James had been right. James . . . poor James had been speaking from his heart for once. Speaking the stark, torturous admission of a love she had never given him credit for. He hadn't merely apolo-

gized, he had given her the greatest gift his love could offer:
the unvarnished truth.

What on earth could she do now?

Now that there was nowhere else to run?

Chapter 13

It was an unlikely group that assembled inside the coffin chamber at Lazarevskoye Cemetery. Rows of huge drawers, looking like a modern American morgue, ran the length of the large, marble-floored room. Each bore a number; each housed a dead person. All except one.

The joint Soviet-American delegation was stiffly standing at the far entrance, huddling awkwardly together, all eyes on the expanse of closed metal doors lining the room. Some crossed their fingers, American-style, while others hooked the forefinger over the thumb, Russian-style.

It was a tense exhumation, officials from both the Soviet Union and the United States serving as a strange, completely unique funeral party.

Ned Sternberg, his demeanor kingly, his alert eyes darting everywhere, stood beside a subdued James Bowden, whose eyes looked anywhere but at Jon or Alex. In the cold glare of the room, his bruised jaw showed clearly. André Makarov stood to one side, dapper, sharp, the new insignia on his gray fur hat indicating a change in status.

And, of course, Jon. *Jon.* Alex felt his presence keenly, felt his eyes on her. Standing beside him, avoiding his gaze, knowing she was leaving, knowing she would never see him again, she drank in his scent, tried to memorize his occasionally averted face as if it were to be all that would comfort her on the long and lonely nights to come. And she pondered the question of what to do, what to say, how to stretch across the distance and put things right.

She felt the truth of James's words as she looked at Jon. He'd suffered sleepless nights; it was evident in the dark circles beneath his eyes, in the new lines around his drawn lips. His fine mouth, his usually generous mouth, was pulled inward with determination . . . or disdain?

Which?

Jon had once said—a thousand nights ago? A thousand lovely thoughts ago?—that trust involved action. It wasn't enough merely to have trust; one had to act upon it. It required action. But what could she do?

She looked at the assembled crowd as if they might tell her, might help her, might show her a way to break through the past and into the future.

Away from the official delegation stood the rest of the small crowd, a group comprised of men sporting protective clothing, white, lead-lined, resembling space suits.

Because of Tursunov, she thought. All because of Tursunov and his power-maddened urge for supremacy.

She wished her own troubles were as easy to resolve. Tursunov had wanted the deadly objects in order to control the world as he knew it—a frightening place, from what Andre had told her after long, grueling hours of interrogating the man. He had, according to Makarov, seen the Chernobyl incident as something he could use, power he could wield in the face of the declining interest in the secret activities of a declining KGB. He had bided his time and after reading about the continued objections of one misguided curator-priest, he had acted.

But what of her? The dark weight of the past sat heavily, urging her to run . . . but James's words stopped her. Jon's avowal that trust required action held her in check. What could she do? What could she say?

How could she erase the past with a mere wave of her hand? With a mere wish?

She chafed at the crowd around her, urged this strange funeral to reach its conclusion. But it moved to its own cadence, this bizarre finale to one man's twisted contrivances. The coffin was easy enough to locate; the men in the space suits used Geiger counters, which clicked and hummed busily and all but screamed when the drawer in the center of one long wall was approached.

Ned Sternberg had been skeptical, at the meeting in Makarov's office, of the notion of a coffin holding the contaminated artifacts. But in the cold Soviet Union, where the ground was frozen for half the year, it had been a logical hiding place. A somewhat chilling reality: Soviet burials couldn't take place until late spring.

The ceremony was swift, with Makarov doing the honors.

"Through the joint efforts of two great countries, a grave danger has been averted," he said. He nodded at Jon and Alex. Alex again felt the cold-dark air of that empty dacha, smelled the dust from the floor mingling with the scent of Jon's body. She couldn't look at him now, in his dark, official suit, sporting his official persona. His obvious disdain.

Makarov's voice carried easily. "We will now retrieve these deadly artifacts and again bury them in the ruins of Chernobyl." He glanced at Alex briefly, sudden humor flashing in his eyes. "This time, God willing, they will stay there. Mr. Tursunov no longer holds any position in this government, and be assured that no one else has any desire to obtain the . . . dubious . . . treasures left behind."

In an embarrassed, quick presentation, he handed Ned Sternberg an envelope. "A small token of our appreciation for your involvement in helping us to discover the whereabouts of this collection," Andre said.

Without bothering to open the envelope, Ned turned and handed it to Alex, saying to Andre, "It was really due to the efforts of this young woman that the artifacts were located. It was she who was placed in the greatest danger. I feel it's only fitting that she receive the—er, token."

Andre nodded, his smile broadening. "I, too, find that acceptable," he said. He gestured for Alex to look inside the envelope.

She did so and with difficulty, held in a gasp. It was enough money to send every one of Hans Saalard's many children to their university of choice. And the money she'd brought to the Soviet Union to purchase the collection would be sent with it.

Slowly, feeling the first smile she'd worn in days cross her face, she announced her thanks and described what the money would be used for. With the American half of the delegation having been embarrassed at the offer in the first place, and the Soviets' love of children, everyone was pleased at the way the money would be spent.

Alex slid the envelope into her bag. She would wire the money to Hans Saalard's widow. Hans's family would never have to face, as Alex had, the crippling fear of poverty. And Alex felt as if a small measure of the debt she owed Hans was finally being paid.

Watching the team of space-suited men rig up a portable laboratory and transparent defensive screens in the center of the room, Alex had the notion they were all attending the funeral of the people who had died for this collection. Roger Copple, the senior Apraskin, possibly Sasha... and Hans... The artifacts had killed him as surely as they had killed the others and had made the remainder ill, possibly to the death.

The artifacts that had brought her into Jon Wyndham's life.

With the protective covering in place the protectively-clothed men pulled the coffin from its metal tomb and quickly sealed off the narrow opening in their transparent pocket. One of them swiftly released the coffin's fastening, and two others pushed the heavy lid to an upright position. As one, the delegation shrank back, as if the contents of the coffin could spill from the protective bubble into the room with them.

But all released sighs of relief when one of the team held up a gold chalice. Jon and Alex had been right. *Jon had been right,* Alex reminded herself. It had been his discovery. It had been the memories from his youth that had pointed the way to the artifacts. His past working for the good of all. She couldn't say the same about hers.

Whatever had sparked it, she thought resolutely, whatever trouble had ensued over it, the deadly collection had been found at last. But found only as Jon's love had died.

Watching the men remove another artifact, carefully marking it on a list, Alex felt a perverse desire to urge them to smash the treasure to bits. It was beautiful, but deadly. It had caused so much pain, so much anguish. It had inspired greed and even murder. It seemed a symbol of evil, a representation of man's inhumanity to man.

Alex shifted, cold now, unutterably saddened by the thought of so much destruction, so much harm caused by these simple, inanimate treasures. She stiffened, feeling Jon's gaze resting on her.

What could she say or do now? She felt defenseless, vulnerable. And so very afraid of meeting Jon's eyes. James had been right, but he had also been wrong. Maybe she *had* been running away all those years, but he was discounting the role her judgment, good or bad, had played.

And she couldn't subject Jon to her inability to make the right choices in life. She couldn't.

That wasn't running from Jon. Was it? No. She stiffened. It wasn't running; it was protecting him. Protecting him from her.

He'd already suffered one marriage with someone who had exercised every variety of bad judgment. It wasn't fair to subject him to another.

Her throat closed, holding back an involuntary sob. No matter that at the moment she felt a tearing, searing pain.

No matter that letting him go wasn't what she herself wanted.

Finally... finally, she had met someone she could love completely, easily, wanting to run to him rather than from him. Finally. And the crushing irony was that it wasn't fair to him to do so. Not with her history of bad choices, impulsive decisions.

With a look, with a touch, he could still the fear that had lived so long within her. But with a look, with a touch, she could, at anytime, hurt him. And that was something she couldn't bear. Wouldn't do.

Her back stiffened with resolve. He had said that trust involved action. Well, she would take action. With a final lingering look in Jon's direction, a look he didn't even see because his eyes were on the men inside the protective bubble, she slipped from the small group and out into the dull afternoon.

Walking swiftly through the deep, spring snow, one hand held up to flag a taxi, the other holding in the threatening sobs, Alex tried to ignore the pain in her heart. Never again would she touch his face; never again would she feel his honeyed eyes roaming her body, inflaming her skin, warming her heart.

If she didn't hurry, didn't run now, she would never leave. She would run to his arms and stay there.

Hot tears spilled from her eyes as a taxi pulled over and she slid into the back seat.

"The American Embassy, please... then the airport."

Jon turned when he heard the outer door closing with a distant thud. *Alex.*

Slowly, so as not to attract attention, he edged through the crowd and toward the door. When he reached it, he glanced back. Only James Bowden had noticed his departure and he nodded, a half smile on his lips, a rueful look on his face. He held up a thumb in the classic good-luck gesture.

Jon tipped his head in the diplomat's direction, then opened the heavy outside door.

She had moved quickly, Jon thought; she was already at the street, reaching for a taxi's green door.

"Alex!" he called, and the sound seemed to come straight from his heart. "Wait!"

But if she heard him, she gave no indication of it. She slid into the taxi and gestured. The taxi was off in a spray of black snow, rapidly disappearing into the careening traffic.

For a moment, Jon's mind seemed to have deserted him. All he could think was that he was too late. Too late. Too late. But his feet were already pumping, forging a path through the deep snow, his hand out, fingers extended, offering to pay double for a taxi.

One skidded to the curb, its snow-packed tires sliding on a patch of ice. The back door flipped open. With a memory of the last taxi ride he'd taken, Jon quickly checked driver's identification for authenticity.

"The American Embassy," he said, handing the wide-eyed driver a fifty-ruble note. "And more if you can get there in ten minutes."

The sudden motion of the car slammed Jon against the seat as the driver flipped the brake release and the car shot forward, the tires screaming in protest on the blackened ice.

Another taxi, its exhaust clouding the air, waited in front of the embassy. Jon flung open the door of his taxi, not bothering to close it behind him as he sprinted for the door, sliding dangerously here, skidding against the guard booth there, fumbling in his pocket for his identification card.

He flashed it at the guard, all but shooting through the security enclosure, the double sets of glass enclosure, and around the back to the elevator leading to the guest quarters.

He paced the small elevator restlessly, a caged, determined animal. He pushed the button a dozen times, as if reminding it would make it move faster. He pressed against the thin crack in the elevator door, ready to burst into the hallway the second the groaning device halted.

He didn't know what he was going to do. Didn't know what he was going to say. But he was not letting her go.

It was that simple.

And that complicated.

Alex closed the last suitcase, her fingers pressing the latch down while her lips sealed a despairing moan inside. She swept her gaze around the room. She'd left nothing behind.

Not a trace.

In a few moments, she would be gone. The art would be buried in Chernobyl, and everyone's lives would return to normal.

All except hers.

A sob of despair escaped her, and she wrenched her suitcases from the low stand, swinging them toward the door.

Even as she reached for the door, it slammed open, shoving the suitcases into the corner, making her jump and back away.

Jon stood in the doorway, his shoulders squared, his chest rising and falling rapidly, his mouth set in a straight line. His entire body was a threat, his eyes blazing.

She looked away, uncertain of his reasons for being there, knowing that his presence could undermine her determination to leave.

Seeing him there, seeing the real man, not some image she'd conjured up to console herself on lonely nights, seeing *Jon,* she again heard James's accusing words.

She felt the weight of them, and the ache in her heart twisted, showing her how much her hard-won determination was worth: she was doing it again. She was running away from love.

No matter how nobly she disguised her motives, she was still running.

And how could she run from this man? This man, whose warm gaze lit a fire in her soul? This man, whose firm touch drove her to the very edge of sanity and then showed her a new world? This man, who had thrown over his most cherished beliefs to protect her, to fight for her...to prove the depths of his love for her?

She raised a hand, intending to ward him off but involuntarily reaching for his arm. He gazed down at her, his tired face closed, his eyes neutral, no longer burning.

Dear God, had she waited too long? Was it too late?

She wanted to cry out. She wanted to run.

But she did neither, willing her body to stay where it was, forcing herself to accept the truth in James's final apology. She drew a deep breath. She didn't know where she was going, but she wasn't going to run. No matter what the future held, even if it was too late, even if he had changed his mind or decided he couldn't love her...even then, she wouldn't run. She would face her problems. Defy the past. Defy her own fears and mistakes.

She had to stay where she was and confront the present, confront the future.

"Jon...?"

Something flickered in his eyes, and a pulse jumped along his jaw while his throat muscle worked.

In a split second, as if divine knowledge were laid open to her in that brief encounter with Jon's shuttered gaze, Alex could see her own future clearly. A future without Jon would be a future spent growing gray, bitter and lonely, spending longer and longer hours in her gallery, an aunt to her friends' children, never having children of her own, never again experiencing the feelings Jon had inspired in her, never giving the tremendous amount of love she had to give.

With a shiver and a rush of warmth, she felt the last of her inner defenses crumbling, leaving her feeling shaken, oddly bereft, exposed.

But she wouldn't run. She didn't know how to explain the past, but she wasn't going to run. She was going to *act* on the trust she felt.

Jon stared down at her, willing his heart to slow down, commanding his hands to say at his sides. Incredibly, miraculously, he read her struggle with her self-protective instincts, seeing how far she'd come in the vulnerability clearly imprinted on her features, the shocking lack of defenses in her eyes. The miraculous vulnerability.

"Jon . . . ?" she asked finally, her voice hoarse with unspoken need, breaking with sheer, raw fear.

He had to say the right thing; it had never been more important than now. This was *Alex*. And he wasn't going to let her slip away from him.

"I can't let you go," he said. His voice was ragged. He heard it. He felt it. At the staggering spasm of relief that crossed her face, he had to check the impulse to drag her into his arms and hold her there forever. There was still too much to say, still too much ground to cover. He wanted her. All of her. But he didn't want the specter of the past ever to raise its ugly head again.

"I won't let you go, Alex. Not now. We have to talk, but I won't let you go." And after they talked, after they had buried the past as effectively as Makarov was burying the artifacts, then what came next would be her choice. It *had* to be her choice, he told himself, despite the urge to choose for her. But he couldn't; he didn't dare.

Alex met his eyes squarely, never having had to summon such courage to meet someone's eyes before. "I—I was going to. . ." She trailed off at the sudden fire in his eyes, the flush staining his cheeks. Was he angry?

Jon flicked a glance at her upended suitcase. "You would have gone without saying goodbye?" he asked. His tone sounded dead; his lips were drawn.

As she had done earlier, Alex saw the future unfold, saw it clearly in Jon's blazing gaze. She saw that behind the fire, behind the anger, he was harboring a fear every bit as great and as deep as hers. He was afraid of a future without her. In that future he, too, had gone gray, his features softened by time, new lines etched around his mouth, not lines of laughter, but lines of weariness, marking a man who had spent too many hours alone, who had spent too many nights alone.

And every weary, heavily-scored line on his face, that face of the future, every sorrowful line had her name beneath it.

She blinked and the world was rearranged, showing her not the Jon of the possible future, but her Jon, the man who had loved her with such tenderness, who had placed his life in jeopardy to preserve hers, who had told her she was like spring. The man who loved mankind with a fierce protectiveness that left her aching with longing to do the same, to be shown how. The man who could read her soul and see it as something beautiful, not something dark and clouded, the man whose laughter was forever locked in the deepest recesses of her heart.

Something in her eyes, something in her stance, must have told him some of what she was feeling, for he suddenly gripped her shoulders, almost as if *he* needed steadying.

"I love you, Alex. Nothing you say or do is going to change that. Do you understand? Nothing. Not your past, not anything someone says. Nothing." He shook her, as if emphasizing his point. "Nothing can change that love, Alex."

His eyes roamed her face, her exposed throat, the length of her, as if daring her to deny his words. As if daring her to deny his love of her.

"I thought," he continued, his voice harsh, "that after Margaret died, I was just fine living alone. That it didn't bother me. And it didn't, until now. But now, after you've been there, after *you,* the apartment seems like some empty cavern. It feels dead. I find myself looking for you, wanting to call out to you, needing you, Alex."

She realized dimly that he wasn't merely saying the words, he was practically shouting them. Her mind offered a thousand objections. But it was her heart that listened.

"Jon..." she said, needing him to understand, needing him to *know.* "I tried to *shoot* my hus—"

He interrupted her with a shake, saying, "I know that, Alex. James told me. I *know.* Alex, darling, I *know* what it feels like. I was *there!* Not with you all those years ago, not then, but last week. I was right there with you. I *know* what it feels like to—to want to kill. It's like betraying every belief you've ever held dear.... I *know*."

His hands, his eyes, the rigid line of his body, all told her how much he knew. How very well he understood. How far he'd traveled in that dark morning at the dacha, how far he was willing to travel for her.

"Oh, Jon..." The words didn't seem to come from her lips but from her very soul.

"But, Alex...you *didn't* do it. Don't you see?" He shook his head, his face a study in pain, his eyes haunted with memory, with understanding. "You *didn't* shoot him. No matter how much you wanted to at that moment. No matter how much the blood in your veins urged you to pull that damn trigger...you didn't do it." His hands softened, lowered, stroking her arms, taking her hands.

"Alex...please let me believe I'm saying the right things, the right words.... It wouldn't have mattered if a thousand Hans Saalards had been there to stop you. The truth is, the very *hard* truth is, that you stopped yourself. *You,* Alex. *You.* You stopped it."

He saw that she half believed his words and he pressed on, his life, his love, his very existence hinging on her belief.

"We're not people who live life passively, Alex. We've both tried that. We know how empty it is. We don't merely trudge through. We're people for whom every nuance of life holds passion. Depth. Intensity. You know that. You feel it every day. I can feel it in your kiss. In your touch. But we're also people who agonize over every wrong turn, every misbegotten choice."

He pulled her hands to his chest, drawing her now-unresisting body to him. He met her luminous blue eyes with all the force of will he had in him.

Raggedly, he said, "We're not given too many second chances, Alex. Not really. If we were, everybody would be wandering around with happy grins on their faces. Second chances, real chances, real *love*—they don't come along very often." He stopped, dragging his gaze from hers to stare at the high, curved ceiling, as if seeking help. He looked back at her, in his eyes a plea that stole her breath, a promise that made her knees weak with longing.

"I didn't know I was running..." Alex said, the pounding of her heart muffling the words. "I didn't know, Jon. I—I'm so afraid."

"Don't be afraid, Alex! There's absolutely nothing to be afraid of. Not of me. Not of yourself."

"I've spent my entire life running from...oh, everything." She waved her hand in a helpless gesture. He caught her hand and pulled it to his chest in a quick, possessive action.

"I won't let you run from me, Alex. Margaret ran from me, and I let her go. I won't let *you* leave." He sighed heavily. "I can't. You see...I love you."

Alex felt the strength of his words, saw his face set in painful anticipation. Her fingers unconsciously sought the rapid pounding of his heart.

"I've made so many wrong choices..." she said.

"Don't make the wrong choice now, Alex."

"But what if I let you down?" she asked.

"You couldn't," he answered simply, stating it as an irrefutable fact. "Not ever. I love you, Alex," he said again, quietly. "And you love me. You know that. Don't deny it. Don't run now, Alex."

When she didn't say anything, his face shifted, sorrow sweeping across his features. "Don't make me beg, Alex. Please."

Tears filled her eyes. She moved a hesitant, staggering step nearer, pressing against him. His hands released hers only to encircle her back and pull her tighter.

"Stay with me, Alex. Always. Stay." His voice shook with the force of his emotions; his hand on her hair trembled. His lips whispered against her temple. "Please don't go away. Please..."

Tears swimming in her eyes, her love for him stronger than any force of nature, stronger than the fiercest hurricane, stronger than the most ferocious wind, she gasped, awed by the depth of his love for her, awed by the sheer glory of it. And she knew, in that beloved embrace, that there would be no more hiding, no more running away.

A wrong choice? There was no choice at all. She loved him. And if he wanted her, if he needed her, she could no more turn her back on that love than she could end her life.

She *loved* him. More and better than she had ever loved anyone. Ever. She shifted in his arms, and he released her abruptly, standing back from her, his expression ravaged, his eyes fevered. She slowly lifted her hands to his pained face, feeling the merest hint of moisture on his cheeks, memorizing his face, memorizing this moment in time.

In his anguished eyes she could see that it wasn't enough to merely love. Just as he had said about trust, love, also, was a responsibility. Love was a commitment of all one's dreams, a sharing of every hope, every fear, every touch.

Softly, with trembling fingers, she smoothed away the lines of that bleak alternate future, letting him know the depth of her love.

"You called me spring," she said slowly, her voice shaking with the intensity of her feelings.

"Yes," he said raggedly, with shocking honesty.

"Do you know what blue ice is?"

"No."

"It's the first ice to melt in the spring. It trickles blue, reflecting the sky. It's the first hope of the new season."

"What are you saying, Alex?"

"You are . . . blue ice. You are that hope, Jon."

He crushed her to his body, his hands pulling her tightly against him, his breath coming raggedly in her ear. Fiercely, demandingly, his lips pressed against her collarbone, the hollow of her throat, her lips.

"You made the right choice, Alex . . ." he murmured before his lips once again covered hers. "Dear God, you made the right choice."

* * * * *

SILHOUETTE·INTIMATE·MOMENTS®

FEBRUARY FROLICS!

This February, we've got a special treat in store for you: four terrific books written by four brand-new authors! From sunny California to North Dakota's frozen plains, they'll whisk you away to a world of romance and adventure.

Look for

L.A. HEAT (IM #369) by Rebecca Daniels
AN OFFICER AND A GENTLEMAN (IM #370) by Rachel Lee
HUNTER'S WAY (IM #371) by Justine Davis
DANGEROUS BARGAIN (IM #372) by Kathryn Stewart

They're all part of February Frolics, coming to you from Silhouette Intimate Moments—where life is exciting and dreams do come true.

FF-1

 Silhouette Books®

Take 4 bestselling love stories FREE

Plus get a FREE surprise gift!

Silhouette Special Edition®

proudly presents
the long-awaited "prequel" volume of

★ **LOVE AND GLORY** ★

by
LINDSAY McKENNA

Dawn of Valor

In the summer of '89, Silhouette Special Edition premiered three
novels celebrating America's men and women in uniform: LOVE
AND GLORY, by bestselling author Lindsay McKenna. Featured
were the proud Trayherns, a military family as bold and patriotic
as the American flag—three siblings valiantly battling the threat
of dishonor, determined to triumph . . . in love and glory.

Now, discover the roots of the Trayhern brand of courage, as
parents Chase and Rachel relive their earliest heartstopping
experiences of survival and indomitable love, in

Dawn of Valor, Silhouette Special Edition #649.

This February, experience the thrill of LOVE AND GLORY—from
the very beginning!

DV-1

Silhouette Books®

SILHOUETTE·INTIMATE·MOMENTS®

PAULA DETMER RIGGS
Forgotten Dream

AMNESIA!

Mat Cruz had come back to Santa Ysabel Pueblo to be healed. A car bomb had left him a widower with two young children—and no memory of the first twenty-six years of his life.

Susanna Spencer remembered Mat all too well. He had broken her heart once, and now she swore he would never do so again. He might be staying right next door, but that didn't mean she had to be neighborly—no matter how much she longed to relive the past.

Silhouette Books®